WINE &

CHILDREN

Sara Dahmen

To John

Chapter 1

The winery smelled red. It was as though the color permeated the walls of the tasting room, soaking it with a salty, fermented heaviness that bled into the fibers of the wood and hung limp and solid over her lungs as she walked in.

It was an old space, hung with rough beams as thick as her waist and stained with thousands of spilled drops and dusty feet. Hers were just one more pair that edged along the faded taped out queue lines, but thankfully today was not very busy. She didn't think she could handle a busy winery. In fact, if she was smart at all, she'd have just bought the customary labeled bottle at the door – or two – and taken them to her car to drink alone and in solitude.

Would she get in trouble if she were drinking in her car, but not actually driving?

She could even sleep in her car, she rationalized, eyeing up the perky bottles paired up along the edge of the counter at the far end of the room. Then she could drink both tubs of wine without having to drive or even look for a place to spend the night.

"Red or white or we have a lovely light rose?"

"Red," she said, without considering or getting particular. Red fit her mood and also was so strongly fumigated in the rom that anything else felt sacrilegious. The young man behind the tasting counter ducked dutifully out of sight to select a red, but came back with three.

"Here are my favorite blends," he chirped, as bright and sincere as those damned bottles winking and twinkling at her from the checkout.

"I don't care, really," she said, her voice sounding as numb as she felt. Apparently she ought to care, as she watched the man – *Darren*, his nametag said – wrinkle his nose and shoot his eyebrows well past the top curves of his dark rimmed glasses. Well, it was true, she reasoned. She really didn't care. Perhaps eventually, after some days in Napa and the surrounding areas, she might become a connoisseur, or even a bit of a wine snob, but right now she just wanted to smother herself with the blank inebriation of booze.

"Well, um." Obviously Darren was valiantly trying to make her experience special, even in the face of her frank declaration of flippancy. "This...is my favorite?"

He poured her a small sample, and she tried to do the customary swirl and sniff, but decided, half-sniff, that today she was allowed to do anything she wanted. Today she could stop following every rule and expectation. Giving her head a small shake, she set down the glass, untested and without a sip, and then promptly left the winery, ignoring the beckoning bottles and stacks of glittering glass and heading directly out to her rarely used car.

Checking behind her — that's just what she'd need, running over a child! — she peeled out of the gravel drive and shook off the sliver of guilt that niggled at her. She should have at least tipped that young man for his trouble.

No. Today was about her. Today was a day to try and heal, and whatever it took, she'd do it.

As she drove across the winding highway, she tried to breathe, relax and once again give a long, litany of tired, worn excuses on why she was driving through wine country alone. Sometimes, if she had enough to drink, she could explain everything as Peter's fault.

She could shed herself in some sort of martyred glow and pump herself full of positivity. But really, who was she kidding? She was the one who had failed him, the one who had stopped working, the one who – frankly – had never worked properly. If anyone was to blame for the loneliness today, it was herself.

Under her feet, her foot petals seemed to jump, and she wondered, for the umpteenth time, if she should take it into the shop.

Shaking the heavy gloom, she sternly repeated the mantra. *Today was a day to heal.* A day to be open to change, the unusual, and carefree. And damn it, she'd do it.

*C*hapter 2

He swung by the far field before heading in for the rest of afternoon before it crept down the mountainsides. The morning was bright, clear, with a bell blue sky and colorful flowers still bouncing and skipping in the breeze. It was not quite the end of summer, but near enough. His heart felt full. Days like this made life feel perfect. With his jeep taking the brunt of the dry earth, the smell of grass in the air, and the occasional twitter of a bird, there was not much left to making him happy. Besides, he had a very nice white wine sitting in the fridge back home, and both kids were still in camp for another two days. He missed them, but the silence was golden.

The pasture was thick with grass; he'd let the horses out in these few acres tomorrow. He had already checked the vines, and had made an appointment to hail out to O'Brien's the following day to look at buying some of the Grenache that would be coming due soon. He had some ideas on a wine he wanted to try his hand at making, even thought the prospect of becoming a garagiste was a little daunting.

He made to swing back toward the ranch, but slowed the jeep as he went, doubling back.

He wasn't seeing things. A car had parked nearby, on a siding of his property along the road. It wasn't a well traveled road; any car would seem out of place if it wasn't his.

Spinning the tires, he moved back out towards the fence line; someone was leaning there, looking out towards the mountains, but they turned when the jeep noise became obvious.

It was a woman, someone he didn't know, he didn't think. She had a shiny, fresh scrubbed look, and he could tell she wasn't a local just by the clothes she wore.

"Can I help you?" he asked, leaning out through the open side of the jeep.

She shook her head mutely at first, then gestured towards the scenery. "I was just taking a break from the drive to see the view. It's so pretty."

He could appreciate the sentiment. It was why he'd bought this ranch in the first place - the view. The pasture was a second reason, because he'd wanted to try his hand at converting some of the acreage and making some wine, but the view had captivated him at first.

"It is," he agreed. A shadow passed over her face at the pause in their brief conversation, and she turned her back to him again and stared out over the land. Her shoulders were hunched and her arms crossed over her belly as if she was cold, or ill; he only noticed because it was a balmy day.

"I'm not trespassing, am I?" she asked, her back still turned away. "I figured as long as I stayed on the road side of the fence it wasn't breaking any rules..."

"Ah...nope. You're still legal."

He paused, waiting for her to rejoin, but she seemed set to ignore him, her body curled up toward itself as though she wanted to squeeze the blood out of her gut.

As he stared at her profile, the tantalizing blip of a memory slipped silently into his mind and he tilted his head.

"Haven't we met before?"

That jogged her to attention, and she looked at him straight, weighing and measuring his face. Finally she judged. "No, I don't think so."

"Yes," he pressed, taking in the lightness of her hair. "It was in LA – but a while back. A...gallery show, maybe?"

Now she straightened, giving him deeper scrutiny. "Perhaps?"

He thought back. He hadn't gone to many such events, but he felt she looked vaguely familiar. It bugged him. "Don't ask me the name of the gallery. But I bought a painting there."

"There's a chance," she amended. "I go to quite a few gallery showings."

Sam snapped his fingers and it made her jump. He gave her a half-smile. "Sorry. No – I was there because my buddy was trying to impress a new girlfriend, show her that he had friends with culture."

"I'm sure I wasn't the girlfriend." She was wry, but listening.

"No – you were her boss, though. An...Amanda?"

She finally gave a glimmer of grin, and she let out her breath. "Yes. I do have an Amanda who works for me."

"That's it then. I knew we'd met."

"Is it unkind of me to say I don't really remember?"

"It was maybe two years ago."

"That explains it. Small world," she intoned, and then the moment was lost. She turned back to the view, obviously disinclined to share the brief euphoria of meeting an acquaintance on a back road in the middle of California.

"Are you sure you're alright?" he pressed, feeling as though he couldn't just leave her alone on his land now that he'd engaged her in a chat.

Her head went down, and came up, the pale blonde of it catching the late morning light. She gave a brief glance over her shoulder, but didn't quite connect with his eyes.

"I'll be fine."

The response wasn't what he was expecting to hear; most people would give a blasé wave and hearty reassurance. It was if she was willing herself to be okay.

"If you're waiting for a sunset, you've got a while to wait," he said, swinging his jeep keys.

"I've got to get an Uber," she finally admitted. "My damn car decided today was a perfect day to finally break down."

He thought of the wine at home, and the offer slipped out almost simultaneously. "Look - it's a hot day. I've got some white chilling and it's too delicious not to share it. Care to pop over for a glass? It can take at least twenty minutes or more for the closest Uber – it's not exactly metropolitan around here."

Now she turned again to look at him fully, with a look both incredulous and flattered. "Why? You don't know me."

He gave a little shrug. "I know you...sort of. We've met before, even if you don't completely remember it. And you'll want to call the garage for a tow, and I'd feel bad leaving you here to roast while you waited for that too. Besides, you seem like you could use a pick-me-up."

She laughed a bit at that, a small sound that made him smile in return. Her laughter grew silent quickly, and she sighed.

"How far is your place?"

He jutted his chin forward and north. "First driveway on your left up the road. Can't miss it - it's a low concrete house, only thing you'll see. Come see which painting I bought – you'll probably recognize it."

She seemed to spend another minute considering, enough time for him to really think about his suggestion. He hoped she would be a bit more engaging conversation as all this, that his random offer of kindness wouldn't be repaid in an ugly way.

Finally she nodded. "Alright. Today's my day to do whatever I want. Thank you...Mr...?" She met his eyes and he shifted back the gears of the jeep again.

"Sam Gaffney."

"Sam. I'm Charlie."

He nodded at her, and pulled his vehicle ahead as he saw her move to get her purse out of hers. He suddenly wondered if she actually did need an Uber, or if she would get into her car and drive away, disappearing over the edge of the road and into her own choice of oblivion. Well, no matter now. She got in beside him, silent. He drove the jeep back through the pasture, around the fencing, and past the old barn and sheds kept from an earlier time. Sam loved those buildings - the cracked wood, exposed soft stone and plaster, faded roofs and the creaking floors and the eccentricities that came with old spaces. They were the essence of wine country living, unlike the modern behemoth of a house that had been built before he had bought the property.

As he drove next to the entry, he heard the familiar crunch of tires on gravel, and smelled the swirl of sediment that twirled around the jeep whenever he drove up the long lane. He'd always wanted to plant trees along both sides of the drive, to tone down the dust and make it feel more like a private vineyard. He loved sharing a good wine with others, and didn't like drinking alone if he could help it, but this was a bit unprecedented, even for his extroverted nature. She'd just seemed so...sad.

When she got out, he was able to really get a look at her. She was tanned, so he didn't think she was a tourist, and the pale blonde hair wasn't a dye. He couldn't figure her for an area of SoCal, but her athletic clothing seemed very LA.

She met him on the porch, a wide, spacious L-shape that swerved around the house to overlook a dip in the land around back, so from the kitchen, the whole wall opened up with sliding doors to a heck of a view. When he pushed open the heavy oak of the entry, he felt the familiar whoosh of cooler air. Everything inside was grey and black and steel and concrete and glass, even though he'd slowly been infringing his own style on the place, from the double wooden foyer doors to the organic wooden light fixtures. He was starting to really like the place, and it was a good space to raise young kids as there wasn't much they could wear and ruin.

"So then...Charlie," he tried her name, and wondered what it stood for. She swung from looking up at the large piece of art on the sidewall to him. He liked that painting particularly - it was a lovely huge one of a vintage vineyard, with warm light and ruddy color. It added good style against the hard concrete of the walls. And now he waited for her reaction too.

"This is the one, isn't it?" There was relief in her voice, as if she needed confirmation that he had been telling the truth — that they had indeed met at the gallery opening once upon a time.

"Yup."

It was dim in the house, but the midday light spilled halfway through the wall of glass next to the dining area. It was a great concept for the living space, he'd always thought. Perfect for entertaining, though he didn't do it as much in his own house as he'd thought he might. The long kitchen and island tapered to the eating space, which was right next to the sliding door windows. He went to open immediately, instinctively feeling that having a stranger in the house required escape hatches, though for him or her he wasn't sure. The kitchen overlooked the great room, where black leather couches, an entertainment wall, and soft rugs created a large place for his kids to sprawl out with their friends or video games when they were over. The ceiling was vaulted, stretching into shadow, giving the feel of a cave everywhere.

"It's very nice," she said, still looking around, and then her eyes fell on his and she smiled, though it did not quite reach her eyes. Yes, Sam decided. She was sad.

He shook off the feeling of pity; who knew her story? Going to the large steel wine cooler built into the cabinet, he pulled out the white he'd been thinking about all morning. It was a new one, a sauvignon blanc that was supposed to be a little less acidic than usual. He was interested to see if it retained the crispness he expected from a blanc.

"Do you like whites?" he asked, uncorking it deftly. She moved to stand across from him by the island, her fingers playing over the pocked surface of the cement counter.

"Yes, though I'm not much of a wine aficionado. I have my favorites and things I prefer to pass."

"What don't you like?" He could talk wine for ages.

"Rose. Chardonnay. Anything too sweet, really. Dessert wines are definitely not my thing."

"All reds are ok, then?"

She nodded her head, and watched him pour a tiny bit into one of the glasses and swirl.

"I used to really like Pinot Noir, but I've moved away from it, and really am enjoying Chilean reds and Bordeaux when I can get my hands on it. Reds from France are great."

He handed her the glass and she copied his swirl, then held it to her nose. She had old freckles across it, her tan deep enough to almost hide them.

"Try it," he suggested, and she paused, glanced at him, and then took the swallow. When she'd finished, she gave a little smile.

19

"Very nice. I like it this cold too, almost adds to the flavor."

He agreed, then poured them both a full glass. He motioned her to the terrace, and she followed silently, her eyes still taking in the height of the ceiling, the glass of the table, and the wide wicker of the patio chairs.

"Have a seat," he said, and then took one himself with a sigh. She followed slowly, sinking with a grace into the cushions, sipping a bit as her eyes raked over the valley. There was at least six feet of air in between them, and he could feel that she'd take more if the seating allowed it.

"Is all of it yours?"

Her voice had mellowed a bit though, as if she'd decided to relax. Sam followed her gaze, taking in the pastures, the vineyards, the hills.

"I've got about fifty acres - not quite as far as the eye can see from here, but a good way of it. Kinda trying my hand at a bunch of ventures while I enjoy my investments."

He'd made a good bundle before the economy tanked, and was living decently from a good stock portfolio and reinvestments. He also had money in land, which he rented, and in a few up starts in the area that had promising business plans. It was enough, and allowed him to enjoy his midlife years without scrabbling off to a desk job any more.

"That must be nice," she said, her tone not demanding any further detailing from him.

"It is, though I still need to get two kids through college," he remarked casually, his head turning once more to them. He did miss them, and was looking forward to a few weeks of happy chatter in the house before they went back to stay with their mother.

"Two?" her eyes met his. "How old?"

"Twelve and eight. Both boys." Sam adored his sons, and was glad they enjoyed coming out to the ranch, where they could let loose a bit and get dirty. They had a few friends in the area, so they were never completely bored and dependent on him to entertain.

"They're at camp, back in two days," he explained. "House feels quiet without them around - I generally get them lots in the summer."

"You're divorced, then?" Her question was an apology, as if she didn't think she should pry.

"Yup. A good six years now." Sam had had a rather amicable divorce, especially after hearing how some of his friends' went down. Of course, he and Amy had their moments, but that was hardly surprising.

"That's a long time," she rejoined, a finality to her voice that made Sam want to pry but was afraid he would actually make her more reserved.

"I guess. Time flies with kids around."

His off-handed comment seemed to make her quiver, and he watched as she carefully set down her glass on the low table. The action was deliberate and slow, fluid only until she released the delicate swoop of the stem and then her hands shook before she turned them over and pressed them hard under her thighs.

"Don't your children have school soon?" she asked, the conversation continuing but only like this, with a painful forced thread tying them together. Sam was debating if he regretted inviting her in. His jury was still out, but he was teetering toward keeping things to a single glass and then showing her out.

"Soon enough," he said. "I'll enjoy the last dog-days of summer with them here before it goes back to every other weekend."

"So she got the kids in the divorce?"

"Once they started school, yes. Makes it easier for them, obviously, to stay in one place more steady, but that's why I get them over the summer more. It's really manageable if we talk about it."

Sam wondered why his children's schedules mattered so much. Was this her idea of small talk? It wasn't what he'd expected, but then again, he hadn't really had any expectations. He'd just known he should offer her something – anything – and sharing a bottle of white was the first thing he'd thought of.

Charlie's eyes had clouded over, and she looked back over the land, drinking a large sip of the wine, as if she wanted to get tipsy. He couldn't place her age, though he figured she was a bit younger than his forty-five years. There were lines around her eyes even when she didn't smile, but perhaps it meant that she used to smile quite a bit. It made him wonder.

"What about you?" he asked, but knew there was no ring on her finger.

She looked into her wineglass. "It'll be one year divorced for me today, actually."

So that explained things a bit. Sam felt himself sympathize. It was a rough time, for certain, especially if the separation wasn't desired on both sides.

"Tough," he commented. "I'm a stranger, and can be completely on your side if you want to talk about it." The offer, like the one for wine, came unprecedented and unthought.

She was quiet for a moment, then give a little shake to her head. "I'd rather not, though it's nice to know you'd take my side." A small attempt at a smile lightened her features for a moment before she lapsed into silence again.

"I'm so sorry I'm not good company," her apology came out, catching her voice. "Truly, I usually enjoy people – it's even part of my job. I—it's just. A year is hard."

"It is," he agreed, knowing that the only reason his own divorce didn't hit him so tightly was because the boys had tempered it. They kept he and Amy communicating, even when they didn't want to, even when they would have cut each other out of their lives, they were forced into harmonious discussions about bed wetting and parent-teacher conferences. Children did more than met the eye, Sam thought.

Charlie washed down the white with a tremendous gulp of the vintage. It seemed too soon to ask her to leave at this point. Holding up his empty glass, he cocked his head at her. "Another pour?"

She looked at the bit left in hers and swallowed it quickly, her eyes closing as it dripped down her throat. "Sure, if you don't mind."

She followed him into the kitchen. "Do you often ask random people to come into your home for wine? I mean, even though you remembered me from the past, we are as good as strangers. This a common practice for you?"

Sam gave a little chuckle, his voice carrying through the space. "Nope. Not ever. Must be your lucky day."

"Well that's something," she said, and she gave a laugh with his, a true one, and he suddenly saw that her reveal made her shoulders straighter, and as she looked him in the eyes with her dark brown ones, and he thought she was actually very pretty.

"You're not going to get too sloppy on me, are you?" he heard himself ask, watching her lean over the counter and take another deep drink from her fresh glass.

She started and jerked up, the pale liquid slipping over the corner of the glass. She looked guilty and ashamed, and suddenly closed her eyes.

"No, no. Nothing like that. I...um. I thought I could wash it all away today by drinking wine at different tastings, but it felt so incredibly lonely to do that that I couldn't take even a single full tour. But I do enjoy wine and I just...I'm not being very eloquent. I wish I could just clear my head."

"Well..." He jumped into the quiet that followed her comment. "You should probably call for a tow before it gets too late in the day. There's an auto place about ten miles south of here. I don't know the number though."

"Yes, of course." She went to her purse and pulled out her phone, walking away discretely. "Is it Trident Auto Body?"

"I think so," he nodded, watching her from the side of his eye, and forcing himself not to completely eavesdrop on her conversation.

"Yes. An address?" Charlie turned to look at him, and Sam rattled off his number, which she relayed carefully. "Ah—how long? Tonight?"

He heard the panic in her voice. "It's OK!" he mouthed at her, and she shook her head. He didn't know what she was saying 'no' to, but continued waiting, fully engaged now.

"Really? It might take that long? I—well, look, maybe tomorrow morning would be better. Can we schedule that? I'll Uber until then."

Sam chuckled under his breath. She obviously had no idea that Ubers were scarce around here. But that came from LA living, he figured.

She turned around as she hung up, looking a little bewildered. "They said the earliest they could get here today would be 'around five' which feels like forever."

He gave a half-committed gesture, his mind swirling. "You can stick around for a bit, if you want."

She stared off in the gloom of the house for a minute. "I told them that they could meet me tomorrow morning. So I'll an Uber now."

"Look, why don't you hang around for a bit? You wanted to clear your head. I've got chores but, feel free to hang out..." Sam felt the offer was required, and didn't know how he felt about what he wanted for her answer.

"Well...I was wondering if I might hike a bit nearby – that was going to be my plan if my car hadn't decided to die. Do you know of any trails?"

Well, she certainly didn't seem to mind the wine, then, he thought, and was surprised at the dismay that settled over his chest. Perhaps she thought *he* was poor company that she wanted to head out and away! And here he'd been wondering if he should ask her to leave. Well, there weren't many official trails in the area, at least that he could rattle off first hand. He wasn't much for the active lifestyle. But he could offer what he did know.

"I'm not sure of hiking in the area, but you could go on my land, wherever you please. Is forty or fifty acres enough for you?"

He rose and went to a nook off the kitchen for a pad of paper and started sketching out recognizable boundaries for her. She took their wine glasses, leaving his at his elbow and washing out hers before gulping water down.

"It's plenty. I may double up some. I just can't go a day without doing something athletic. It's an addiction, I guess."

He labeled some of the trees she'd come across, explaining as he went. "Follow the line of the vineyard until the oak, and then turn left, otherwise you leave my land. Eventually you'll end up in the pasture where we met earlier, and you can find the house from there."

She peered around his shoulder and arm; it was the closest she'd ever been to him all day, and Sam felt himself get a bit tingly. It could be the wine and a woman's presence in his otherwise mostly male environment. Or it could be because she was pretty and fit and relatively interesting. He wanted to know more about her. They had more in common than either of them probably realized, and the idea of her leaving already made him more eager to keep her around.

"Thanks for this," she said, taking the paper and studying it. "I can just head out from here?"

"Go around through the porch here to the front of the house and start from there," he offered, and she nodded. She was already dressed in her activewear, and without another glance at him, she took off. She was intense, bent and quiet, as if corralling her nature and emotions into the act of walking. He followed her out, and watched her retreating back until she wasn't visible over the lower crest of the hill. It wasn't until she was gone that he realized that he didn't have a way to reach her if she got into a spot of trouble. Well, at least she'd be on his land and he could eventually find her.

He went back inside, but didn't touch the wine again. It wasn't as much fun to drink alone, especially now that he'd had chitchat with someone. Sam missed people more often than he cared to admit, even though usually his kids took up enough of his time.

Checking the clock, he went back outside, thinking to check on the couple of horses and such before dinner. Maybe Charlie would be back by then and he could scrounge up something to cook. She seemed like someone adept in the kitchen, though whatever gave him that notion was hard to place – maybe he was thinking wishful. They might have a lot to discuss over the making of food.

With that surprisingly happy idea, Sam moved out into the warm sunshine.

$\mathscr{C}$hapter 3

Charlie felt the sweat trickle down her spine and into her shirt. It felt good to move out here in the mountains, even with the thinner air making it a tougher walk. She'd normally go for a run, but she didn't know the area well, and the wine was coursing through her blood.

With the buzz of cicadas and twitter of the birds overhead, she counted back the months since her divorce was final. Peter had been so bluntly factual about the whole thing that she sometimes felt guilty having any emotion about the ordeal. He was right, after all. Why stay together when a fundamental part of their lives couldn't be reconciled? She couldn't give him what he wanted, and he couldn't bend to her desires. It was fair and normal, and they were like many couples who find, after some time, that they cannot get along because of a single, gigantic, unobtainable rift.

If she didn't think about the divorce, she could be herself – vivacious and generally likable. She found it naturally easy to close a sale with panache and grace alone. She knew her impression on Sam was a poor one. He probably thought she was some pity-filled thing, and kudos to him for putting up with her and trying to give her some cheer. It wasn't his fault she wasn't in the mood to be happy today.

Still, it had made for a far better day than she'd hoped. Aimlessly driving through wine country, she stopped when she felt like it, and was going to stay at bed and breakfasts as she found them. It was meant to be a mind clearing activity, but all it did was make her feel the loneliness more acutely. She could cover it up with work, client dinners and meeting friends for drinks, but the long and short of it was that she came home to an empty apartment now. It wasn't what she had expected for the rest of her life.

Charlie loved Peter. She'd loved him hugely, widely, passionately. He was wonderful to her - they'd had laughs and jokes, special holidays and lusty bedroom romps. She didn't expect to find anything like that again, and the realization of that ate at her. What could she possibly do with her life that could be so fulfilling as being the lover, soulmate and helpmate of a man one lived and breathed?

No matter. She'd learned to keep busy enough. Charlie redoubled her focus on the surroundings and pulled her weight into the hiking, doubling back whenever she felt herself veering too close to the house compound. Should she leave the land without saying good-bye? Instinctively she knew he was waiting on her. The thought was a little exciting, and even a little titillating. That was something unexpected, and certainly in line with her hopes and expectations of the day: to do whatever it took to make it a good day.

Sam was interesting. What an offer, to have a strange woman come into your house for wine! She still couldn't believe she'd taken him up on it, though it felt as though it wasn't completely outrageous. He obviously remembered her from the recesses of his mind, even though she didn't. Of course she wouldn't. Two years ago she'd been in the beginning convulsions of Peter's heart-wrenching choices, and seeing her divorce on the horizon. But he must have met her. He knew Amanda, and he had a painting she half-recognized from one particular gallery show. How serendipitous.

Still, it was a daring, dashing decision that would normally have included her choosing to bypass his house after agreeing to come in. But then, there was his wide expansive words, the way he was so clearly a homebody who liked to talk, an endearing combination that she found a bit comforting. He would make a very good friend, and she needed those.

$\mathscr{C}$hapter 4

Pouring them the rest of the bottle, Sam glanced at the clock. It was nearing noon. "Did you want something to eat?"

"I think I've imposed enough on your hospitality," she demurred, but he insisted, feeling that he should redouble his efforts to entertain her.

"I'll either eat alone when you leave or you can join me. Do you like salad and cheese?"

"Sure. Let me help," Unexpectedly, she took the bag of fresh lettuce from his hand where he stood by the open fridge. "Do you have a salad spinner?"

"Good God. There isn't a woman in this house, so no, I do not," he laughed, and saw her look up at it.

"You have a nice laugh," she complimented, and he felt himself flush a little at the attention. She had a gentle spunk to her way of speaking, and he could tell she was simply being sincere. At the island, she ran the cold water and started cracking the lettuce leaves. He brought her bowls, and then got out the cheese, berries and other condiments to make a light lunch. He'd taken to eating healthier since buying this place. Maybe he was subconsciously trying to cleanse out the LA living in whatever ways he could.

They carried the food to the table, where a light breeze was playing through the open wall. He brought a pitcher of ice water over, as well as a fresh bottle of white. She looked up at him, eyebrows raised.

He shrugged. "Well, we're not drinking alone. Makes it feel more festive. And it's a celebration."

"It is?"

"Sure. You're celebrating a year of freedom." He was trying to create a positive vibe about it. He knew the heartache of breakup, especially from a marriage; that which came with ideas of infinity from conception onward. It was hard to spin it in a good way no matter how hard someone tried, though, and he could tell she was still hurting.

"Freedom." She gave a laugh, and then took the bottle, gazing at the label. The cold glass left a small round mark against her belly, where she rested it. He noticed the flatness of her stomach – perhaps a mark of no children, especially if she was nearing forty and kept in shape. He thought of his own ex-wife, and her softer skin. There was a beauty in that, he'd always thought. The quiet rivulets of stretched flesh that celebrated life. Then again, some women never had marked skin after having children. Sam shook himself inside. He needed to stop assuming, and jumped back into the conversation.

"Well, what else would you call it?"

She set the bottle down and picked up the opener, wrenching the cork out violently. "Forced isolation."

Her anger surprised him. From the moment he'd met her, Sam had thought she was a sad sort of woman, and inherently he'd wanted to cheer her up a bit. Suddenly he saw she could be passionate, vibrant, capable of hard feelings. It made him wonder, and even hope, that they could get beyond whatever was eating her and talk like real people.

"Isolation. Until today. Now you've got another friend in me," he said, hoping it didn't sound too silly.

She smiled a little as she poured the glasses, and then filled the tumblers with the water.

"I know. No, Sam," she handed him the wine, and tipped her own glass into his briefly. "I really am a fun person to be around, and do I have friends and staff that seem to love me. Like I said, it's just a bad day. You've made it enormously better."

He sipped the wine. It was one from France, a Cheverny style white from Clos du Tue-Bœuf, and he enjoyed the brisk, melon of the vintage. There was a mineral taste which lent to the large amount of sauvignon blanc in the press, but it was rich for a white, and he let it wind down his throat. She was staring at the table, running her finger along the glass, and then glancing up around his space, her eyes a bit unfocused.

"You like some of the earthier elements, don't you?" Her question was unexpected, and he put his wine down quickly.

"Um. Yes. I'm trying to soften the place up a bit. Can you tell?"

She looked at the painting in the foyer, visible through the open kitchen. "You picked that out on purpose, didn't you? At the gallery opening where we apparently first met?"

"Yes."

"And the rough wood mantle over the fire, under the TV?"

He nodded, impressed. She glanced at the table again, and wiped at the glass top. "You should replace this piece with a reclaimed wood trestle or something. It would help with the kitchen space."

Sam sat down at the table, the cold metal of the chair biting into the backs of his legs. He hated the pieces but they had come with the house and he hadn't figured what he wanted yet. Now that she'd mentioned the idea of the trestle, it made perfect sense.

"Love it. I'm going to do it."

"Good. You'll be glad." She joined him at the table, and started to serve both of them a salad, as if she was used to managing for two. He let her, enjoying the company in the early afternoon.

"How did you figure that so quickly?"

Her eyes were on the food, but she answered easily, fluidly and without preamble. "It's my business. The interior design. I never seem to be able to shut it off."

"Why aren't you working today? Thought you'd escape?" It was a Thursday - a day that Sam remembered was always busy if one was still tangled in the professional rat race.

"I'm taking a sabbatical. It's been a long time coming," she admitted, stabbing her salad. "I started working overmuch as things fell apart between Peter and me, but I was burning out. I handed off all my clients to my staff, and have been taking my time traveling north out of LA, seeing the little towns, trying to give myself a breather."

"How's it coming?" He added berries to the salad and a slice of cheese. It went perfectly with the wine.

"Not so good. Not until the wine," she lifted her glass in thanks, as if she was including him in the list, and he toasted her back. "Anyway, enough about me. So you've got kids."

He didn't know how much she would care, and she certainly wasn't opening up about her own family life. If she had children, where were they staying while she ambled around wine country? Had the father gotten the custody? But then again, Sam loved his boys and took any chance to rave a bit. He couldn't force Charlie to talk anyway.

"Conner's twelve and going to be starting eighth grade next month. He loves his video games, and I think girls might start to be a problem pretty soon. Thank God he can't drive yet."

She gave a hearty laugh at his vehemence. "Is his voice changing too?"

"How did you know? It's hilarious!" He laughed with her, thinking fondly of the up and down cadence of Conner's tone. "But of course I can't make a single mention of it. His younger brother notices, but is too much of a gentle soul to say anything. My sweet little Cole is the artist. He's not turning goth on me, but he's quiet and introverted. Nothing like me."

"No," she laughed again at him, and he liked the spark that came into her face, the crinkle of her eyes. "You are anything but introverted, Sam."

"Probably why I got out of business. I couldn't stand the cold fake face play everyone did," he mused aloud. It was a theory he'd long told himself ever since leaving the fast paced financial quarters.

"Good for you, to recognize your own needs," she said warmly, and drank the wine. He wondered how

41

well her tolerance went; they were nearly a bottle in, and while his own blood could handle it, he wondered about her, driving back to wherever she was staying.

"What does Charlie stand for?" he asked, watching her strong, bunched arm muscles flow under the tanned skin. There were sunspots on her shoulders, and blue veins on her hands. Her nails were unpainted, something he wasn't quite used to seeing on a woman in California.

"Charlotte. It's such an old fashioned name," she wrinkled her nose. "I was a tomboy from the start - I grew up north of San Francisco, near Sausalito before it started to get a bit rundown in the 90's - and I have a brother. Nothing girly about me."

She turned back to the salad. Sam joined her, but he had to disagree. She was not unfeminine.

They didn't speak as they finished their meal, and when done, she immediately stood and started to clear the table, as if sitting still was irritating. He saw her wine glass empty, and made to pour more, but she stopped him from the island, where she was rinsing their bowls.

"Hold off, Sam, if you don't mind."

He paused, his hands filling with the wet moisture coming off the cold bottle. Their eyes met across the slab of concrete even as her hands continually moved, cleaning out the salad bowls.

"Feeling the buzz?" he asked, deflation bubbling up inside. He'd almost been hoping she'd stick around for a while. The company was actually becoming welcome. She could get an Uber whenever she wanted – there was no rush for her to leave.

"No – at least, I don't think so. I um. Well, I hate to be in such a mood. The only way I can think of getting rid of it is to head out into nature again."

He tried not to gape at her, but his comment blurted out without a protective thought to shield its baldness. "Do you always exercise so much?" The incredulousness in his voice was tempered to his personal reaction. Sam wondered if he was able to be so naturally open with her because they actually didn't have a prior relationship to guard their words.

"Oh – no!" She paused to chuckle briefly. "I just…today's *my* day. I want to do whatever my gut wants to do, and it wants me to be active. If I can just shake the gloom, I promise I'd be much more entertaining."

"Go for a jog on the property," Sam offered, wishing he didn't have more barn chores or he'd recommend another walk and, hell, he'd join her if it meant he could pry a little bit into her life. "And then just see how you feel afterwards."

Charlie methodically filled the dishwasher and then wiped down the counter, almost as if cleanliness was a nervous tick. Did that mean she did have children? Sam judged the notion, standing off uselessly to the side as she took over his kitchen. She was certainly efficient around dishes. As he stared at her quick movements, she finished and turned to face him. Sam was unaware of how close they were standing, and felt the first burn of attraction sear into his stomach. Christ, man! He felt exasperated with his body. The women was clearly not interested in men at this juncture in her life, and was smarting hard from a bad divorce. The last thing he should do was try to jump her, regardless of how quickly he was finding her fascinating.

"Look, I'll go for a run," she decided. "If you're still around when I get back, I'll make sure I say good-by at least. And really – thank you for the lunch."

Her words sounded so final and formally distant, so his initial reaction to take her hand or offer a loose hug was strangled from the start. Instead, he nodded mutely and watched her pick her way off the porch again and down into the yard, disappearing into the wide flat leaves of the winery rows.

Chapter 5

It was getting later in the afternoon. It would soon be
dark enough that he started to think about her not
having a flashlight, and that she might get lost if she
didn't come back within the next hour or so. There
were a few critters that might get in her way —
everything from poisonous spiders to coyotes, but
mainly he was just worried. He didn't want anyone
getting tangled outside in the hills, and especially not
on his own land. He thought about the skort she'd
been wearing, and the lightweight runner's shirt. She
didn't look like she would keel over walking and
jogging around, but still. It'd been three hours.

As he peered outside once again, he saw her detach
from the gloom and make for the dim light inside the
house. Her smile was white against her skin.

"Waiting around for me? So sorry!"

"No - not that. Just hoping you didn't get lost or sprain an ankle on me," he said casually, as she took the steps up toward him. There was a spring to her walk that had not been there before. He was sure he'd read countless times that exercise could make a number of emotional maladies go away; it seemed Charlie was a case in point.

"I'm fine. And I'll get out of your hair and off your property!" she said tartly, smiling directly at him. It didn't matter that her face was shiny with leftover sweat or that her skin was damp with early dew. She was downright pretty, he thought suddenly, and he almost wanted to reach out and touch her arm, simply to feel her.

"Well, it's a bit late to start anything now…" He thought of the food he'd imagined them making together, startled to realize he expected her to stay on with him, as if she'd nothing else to do but hang out and talk. "But want to share a delivery pizza?"

She stopped moving past the kitchen, and spun on a heel. Her movements were quick now, spritely, and determinedly cheerful. "Aren't you wanting me out of your space?"

He shook his head. "I'm glad for the company, especially with the boys gone yet. Stay for pizza. Please."

She paused. He watched her weigh, consider, and shrug off whatever questions piled into her mind at his continued insistence of her time. Charlie shook her head at him once, a bemused smile tacked onto the end of her mouth before nodding the affirmative. She turned again and went to the fridge for the pitcher of ice water, as if she knew where everything was. Watching her, he realized she at least knew his fridge and his glassware cabinet, having seen where he kept things earlier. Her casualness was unexpected and yet a bit calming. He realized he had stopped feeling like an uptight host.

"What do you like on it?" He was referring to the pizza, picking up his cell phone from the sideboard as he asked.

"Anything."

"Even anchovies?" he had to ask, and she smiled over the rim of the water glass.

"You know, I've never had it on pizza, but there's always a first time. I recall they are pretty salty."

He grinned. "Just checking. We'll do a basic works and call it good."

Once he'd rung for delivery, he went over to the TV and flipped it on, putting some restful rock and roll on for background noise. Charlie was wiping her face with a napkin, and he suddenly thought to offer the guest washroom. It'd been a while since he'd had more than a casual wine tasting at the house, and he felt rusty in being hospitable beyond offering alcohol.

"Do you have your things with you in your car?" he asked. "I could go and grab them out of your car and bring them in and you could take a shower, freshen up, if you like."

She started to protest. "I've done enough on your kindness, Sam."

"Oh - the pizza will take half an hour. Pretend you remember me from the gallery opening and we're old friends. I'll go now – do you have your keys? How long will it take you to shower?"

"Well…maybe fifteen minutes?" He tried not to shoot her a skeptical glance. Even though it'd been years since he'd shared living space with a woman, he knew better than to expect it to really be a fifteen-minute shower and change. But he was certainly not going to call her out today.

"Just enough time for a red to breathe. Go," he instructed. She stared at him, and then wordlessly dug out her keys and tossed them at him. He went out to the Jeep, and found her car, gleaming pale and ghostly in the deep dusk. Her suitcase was sitting like a wide black log in the back, and he grabbed it and shot home. When he walked back into the house, she was leaning against the counter, her thumbs flying on her phone, but she took the bag with a smile.

"Thanks." Then without another word, she disappeared out the front door for her suitcase, a medium sized piece of luggage she wheeled easily into the foyer after a few moments.

After showing her the bathroom, he went to the cellar, where he kept a huge variety of California wine. Reds and whites and roses, all stretched out in handsome wood-stacked rows. He recalled she didn't like anything too sweet, so he pulled out a deep cabernet and blew off the dust.

Leaning against the cool cement basement wall, he heard the pipes running overhead and the tick of the water heater in the corner. She was different after her hike, as if she'd cast off her shadows. He wondered if this burst of sunnier personality was her true self, or if it was now a show to appreciate his hospitality. Sam didn't mind either way. It wasn't as though her behavior matter to him beyond the evening. Besides, everyone had their moments, down days and bad memories. He liked the company, liked entertaining.

Charlie was a nice distraction, and she was allowed to be moody on the anniversary of her divorce.

By the time he came back into the great room, he realized the shower had already stopped. So she *was* fast. He uncorked the red and inhaled the bouquet it wafted up immediately. Yum.

She came out of the bathroom hauling her suitcase, and propped it against the wall in the foyer, along with her purse.

"I'll get the pizza, Sam. It's the least I can do," she announced, meeting him at the kitchen island. She was wearing jeans against the night air that flowed through, and a pale pink tank that made her skin glow. Her hair was already drying, hitting her shoulders softly; before it'd been pulled back so he couldn't see what it looked like. He saw she wasn't wearing cosmetics, but a gold necklace was strung around her collarbones. She struck him as utterly human for a moment – flawed, careful and unique. And he thought, even though small lines tugged at the corners of her eyes and her cheekbones were starting to raise out of the flesh of her cheeks, that she was by far one of the most attractive women he'd met in a while.

"I won't argue over it," he said, tearing his eyes away from the thin outline of her bra under the shirt. Since when had he become interested in looking a woman over? It was probably all the wine and the good conversation.

"Good. Thanks."

She leaned over to smell the bottle. "A cabernet. Good choice with pizza."

"And it's cooled off. That's what I like as the nights creep into September around here. A red wine suits. Soon it'll be time for a fire in the evenings." He thought about this with relish. He loved being home, loved relaxing and reading and playing board games with the boys when they were around. It was really great, and he knew he was lucky to have this type of flexibility in his forties. Of course, there was the odd investment meeting, the coffee shop brainstorms with the guys working the start-ups, and some days his financial adviser would stop by. But all in all, he was glad he'd spent his midlife crisis time taking a step back instead of diving into something crazy.

Charlie was looking at him with a little smile. "You're a homebody, for all your extroverted tendencies, aren't you? I thought as much."

"True," he agreed with her analysis. "It's probably why I like to entertain instead of going out. I don't even throw parties here near enough."

"You have a great space for it." She looked up at the high ceiling again. "It's such a mix of California austerity and wine country. You could do with more wood and textiles though."

"Maybe I should hire you." It was half a joke, but as he said it, he realized it would be fun. He could tell she wouldn't be the type of decorator to force a piece or a project. And they got along.

"Maybe. When I go back to working I'll let you know," she said absently, still looking around the walls, which were mostly bare. He hadn't found any art yet for most places. It was a process.

The pizza arrived, and she went to get it, grabbing her purse as she went. Sam flicked on the lights out on the patio with a fast jab of a forefinger. They could eat outside yet: it wasn't too cold. He took the red wine and the glasses out, and then grabbed the pizza from her as she came back to the kitchen with it.

"Plates are second from the left above the counter sink," he instructed over his shoulder, and watched her search for them. She had to stand on tiptoes to get them out; he realized she was barefoot. Her toenails were painted a brilliant orange - something unexpected. Maybe there was a bit of fire and spice under the calm. Sam wished she would talk more about herself. What woman was so quiet about her life? He felt like she knew half of his life's history after their gabbing all day, but he couldn't even figure out why she was divorced. Maybe it was something awful, he wondered. Maybe she'd cheated, or maybe there were money issues that were irreconcilable.

"Well, Sam. Other than drinking wine and knowing your grapes, what are your other hobbies?" she asked pleasantly, as she joined him. He opened the pizza box and thought. Obviously she was still willing to deflect conversation to his life. Well, he could go along with it as long as she wasn't bored. If this is what it took to keep her mind occupied as she'd wished, he could play along. He shrugged at first to her question. Other than his boys, his horses and his wine, he didn't have much to keep him busy. But then he reflected.

"Reading, I guess. Old bookstore searches type of thing. And I can appreciate art. And I do like the kitchen. I just don't often get to do the gourmet thing with just me; the boys are into it if they're around, but it's usually busy when they are here so I don't get to try my hand at it as much as I'd like."

"You're a renaissance man," she smiled, taking a slice of pizza.

"I suppose you could call it that. Do you recognize that tendency in yourself?"

She wiped her mouth. "I do, a bit. I'm all for reading and cooking or baking. I'm not into the wine and horses though - I'm more for the arts, the theater, or even travel. But I can appreciate the wine for sure." She took a drink from the glass in front of her, tasting it carefully.

"Wow. It's pretty oaky."

"Do you like it?"

"It's really delicious. Slides down warm and ends with dry spice. Thank you - good selection."

"I'm glad you can appreciate it," he said, glad he'd taken care to choose, as she obviously had some talent for recognizing vintages. "Even though you're not from wine country."

"No." She sighed, taking a second slice of pizza onto her plate. "And my company is based out of LA so I'm stuck there. Well, I was until last week when I decided to get out. Speaking of - any good bed and breakfasts around here? I haven't checked into any yet."

He glanced at the clock. "It's getting a bit late to just pop into one unannounced. And you'll find vacancies harder to come by as we get into fall. I know there's a Holiday Inn a few miles back from where you were coming."

"I saw it," she nodded. "That'll do."

They were quiet, munching into the pieces of pizza. Then her prodding began again.

"So you have the two boys and an ex-wife...?"

"Who's remarried," he added, wiping his own mouth. "Happily, I should say. Good for her."

"Alright," she glossed over it. "And you work...?"

"A bit." He dove into a rudimentary explanation of his assets, investments and past exploits in investment banking, hedge funds and international schemes. Whenever he listed it all out, it always sounded like a lot, even coming from his forty plus years. They'd been busy ones. He was glad he could sit back and take a minimal role in the care of his estate and finances now. He was lucky in that way and he knew it, reveling in the freedom he had every day.

She stopped eating, and reclined into the wicker seat, arms crossed across her stomach, but her eyes were warm and a smile on her face. She seemed to understand much of what he was talking about, and even had valid, conceptual comments or questions about the investments and the start-ups he was overseeing. Eventually they found themselves strategizing.

"Don't you have a contract with them?" she finally asked, when he outlined one of the issues with a group of young men planning to do a unique type of computer server. They had promising ideas and a good business plan, but they were a bit less adept at keeping in touch with their investors.

"I do."

"Then why not enforce it?"

"Because I don't want to make them cranky so soon in the game. Suddenly they might…find a way to cut me out, and all." Sam wished he could be more forthright with some of the small businesses he was working with on their ventures. It didn't do to have them running amuck with funds, but he didn't want them to get stupid from pressure either. Charlie shook her head.

"You're not in the friend's business, Sam. You're in business. You have a right to expect certain things from people you're investing in. It's only fair. Can you pull your money if they don't comply?"

"I'd have to check the paperwork, but I think so."

"I'm sure you don't want to," she amended, rubbing her arms. "But there's no reason you can't make them understand they have an obligation to you. I mean...I don't have the personal connection I'm sure you feel to the project, but just looking in unbiased..."

She trailed off, and he got up from their tableaux. In the dim of the porch light, he'd seen her goose bumps, and went silently to the wardrobe in the foyer to pull out one of his flannels. He handed it to her, and she wordlessly pulled it on; the shoulders and sleeves dwarfed her shape.

"Thank you. Anyway...it's just my two cents, and I can't say I'd do the same, but it's fair of you to expect and explain that. And maybe they have no idea, if they're young and it's their first venture. You could guide them."

He hadn't seen it that way. Be a mentor. There was merit in her ideas. He decided she was more level headed than the brilliant orange of her toenails suggested, and poured them both another round of the red.

"I'm afraid I'm drinking all your wine," she commented, raising the glass up to the lights.

"You aren't even making a dent, I promise," he chuckled, thinking of his extensive cellar.

"Still...you've been ridiculously generous."

"Think of it as providing me with entertainment for the day otherwise spent in solitude." He clinked his wine glass with hers, and let his eyes travel over her. She looked comfortable, the one leg crossed over the other and swinging freely. There wasn't a hint of the sadness that she'd had when they first met earlier in the day, and she looked cozy in his coat. It was definitely nice not being alone.

"I will drink to that!" she rejoined him, and took a sip. The darkness out in the yard was profound, except for a few low voltage lights near the doorway of the barn and garage. He loved the privacy in this respect. Nothing could compare to the quiet and restful vibe of the country.

"So...your ex?"

"What about her?" Sam didn't often dwell on Amy. They'd moved on, parted ways, and she was happy.

"You get along?"

"Sure. Kids make you, really."

She was quiet, reflective. "Glad you're not married anymore?"

Sam shrugged and shifted in his seat, swirling the wine. It looked almost black in the shadows. "Sort of. I don't think I'd be happy if I was still with her. We had so little in common. So if my choice is her or being alone, I'd always choose what I have now."

"You don't miss being married?" There was a wistfulness to her voice, as if she did. And suddenly he realized she really did miss it. He had happily adjusted after the initial shock and sorrow of dissolving a marriage. As long as the boys were ok and content, he could deal and he had. Amy had liked fashion, fast cars, and wine, and the wine had drawn them together at first. They'd shared a passion and many a romantic stroll in a vineyard. But she wanted to stay in LA, and he wanted country living. And when it came down to it, they couldn't exist in the same space without somehow getting on each other's nerves. There had been no peace after the first flush of love wore off.

He said as much to her, and she seemed to reflect, swirling her wine thoughtfully.

"I suppose that is the danger of quick love. Though from experience, even longer love can wear thin. It's unnerving."

"It's reality," he shrugged, not really caring.

"This has been a far better day that I could have ever expected, Sam," she said finally. "You have been...simply wonderful. But I think it's time I get that Uber." She pulled her phone from her back pocket and starting jabbing at it absently. "What's your address again?"

He grinned and told her, then added. "You're quite welcome for the day. It's been fun meeting you."

She stood and picked up the empty plates and glasses and he followed her lead with the rest of it. Without any prompting, she opened the dishwasher and started to load it deftly. She wore the domesticity easily and it suited her. He stashed the trash in the bin, and went to wipe off the table outside before closing up the glass doors.

"I hope you can manage one more dull day before your kids come home," she said, wiping down the counter with water.

"Oh, there's always something to do," he said, watching her bare arms stretch out of the plaid jacket as she took it off and handed it back to him. He folded it over one of the chairs at the kitchen island and followed her to the foyer. Popping on the interior and exterior lights, he smiled a bit, thinking over how great the day had flowed by. He certainly hadn't expected it either, and it had been good to have someone to talk to, or share silence and a bottle of wine. He really should do more entertaining.

"Well. I'll see about the Holiday Inn or whatever else I find." She straightened from her luggage. "Thank you again."

Outside, the telltale crunch of gravel announced a car, and her phone pinged to confirm it. She glanced at it, then up at him.

She held out her hand at first, as if uncertain, but he felt himself propelled forward. They'd shared too much wine and he'd offered too many personal stories for a handshake. He bypassed her hand for a hug with an awkward beginning. But he held her appropriately, and she put her arms about his shoulders in a friendly embrace. After the initial customary seconds, he found himself intentionally holding onto her for a few extra moments. It'd been a while since he'd hugged a woman, and it felt heady.

"It was great to meet you too, Charlie," he said, finally releasing her. When he found her eyes again, he saw she was smiling warmly at him.

"Take care. And thanks!" With the final note of appreciation, she pulled open one side of the great wooden doors and moved out to the waiting car. He followed to the threshold and watched her load up the small bag and herself quickly and the lights of the car burst around with the rev of the engine as the driver spun around.

As he raised his hand in a silent wave good-bye while she pulled out of the driveway, he realized he hoped to see her again. And then he suddenly remembered he had absolutely no way to contact her.

$\mathscr{C}$hapter 6

The owners of the bed and breakfast she'd ended up finding were wonderful about taking her to her stranded car the next morning, bright and early, and even waiting while the tow truck and mechanic showed up.

Popping the hood, the young man brushed his fingers over the pipes and valves of her engine, his greasy fingers slipping in and out of the bewildering mix of metal. "Oh. You said it just stopped running?"

"Yes – the gas pedals have felt odd for a while," she explained. "And then it all just stopped."

The mechanic shrugged, then moved back to his truck. "We'll check it over. Should take at least the morning. Do you want our loaner car?"

She took him up on the offer, and since she didn't have here a wine hangover from the day before, she spent the rest of the morning rummaging around two local wineries, tasting and trying different varieties, and replaying yesterday's activities. After the weight of the divorce anniversary lifted, and a happy day with Sam, Charlie felt as though she could try her hand at tastings again. But she spent much of her time leaning over the stained countertops, thinking about Sam and absently twirling an empty glass.

It had been really a very special type of day, one filled with unexpected happy surprises, so different from what she'd dreaded. Maybe she put too much weight into the date anyway. Maybe she should be more carefree about being a divorcee. Sam carried the label so easily, she envied his affability and calmness. But then again, his split sounded so effortless, as if he and his ex had had a civil discussion about parting ways.

Charlie sighed, putting down another wine stopper. They all started to look the same after a while. And it wasn't that much fun to sample wines alone. She wanted some one to chat about flavor, color, bouquet or aftertaste. It all only exacerbated her loneliness. Would she ever get comfortable in the solitude? She felt she had to – she had to strive for that comfort. It seemed as though everyone she knew was willing her to do it, assuming that it was the natural progression after a divorce. But she couldn't. She loved being married. She adored belonging to something bigger than just herself.

She'd found that bed and breakfast a bit closer than the Holiday Inn last night, Googling in the backseat of the Uber - only a handful of miles from Sam's ranch. He must not explore much if he didn't know about it. Or, typical man, didn't pay attention to what he drove past most days. It felt tantalizing to be so close to him.

As the afternoon waned, she found herself thinking about him almost constantly. Maybe she should drop off a thank you - a wine or something to replenish what she'd drank. Glancing around the winery where she had ended up this day, she saw a wall of unique wines, labeled as specialty or hard to find. Charlie walked up to the bottle as they glimmered and beckoned. She had no idea what was good or not; in truth she was a relative novice to wines compared to most people in the area. One of the young men behind the counter came and stood next to her. Why did every salesman have to look about twenty-six and bearded?

"Anything you want in particular?" He was pleasant, his voice surprisingly low and he fixed her with a earnest stare behind dark glasses.

"Are all these local wines?"

"Most - usually rarer or old vintages. A few from France." His fingers trailed along the tips of the bottles, leaving a streaky trail in the dust.

"What have you got from France?"

"A few very nice Bordeaux. A couple from the Chateaux."

"This is a gift," she explained, taking a bottle from the bottom, and wiping off the gritty layer of time that had accumulated. "I'm not sure exactly what he likes."

"Oh. Well, try this from France – one of the Châteauneuf-du-papes, a Clos d L'Oratoire des Papes. It's really great in terms of spice and licorice if I remember right. Last one in stock."

The clerk crouched on his knees and pulled out a bottle even lower than she'd found and blew on the glass. It had an ornate label, and looked very nice, even though she had no idea what it might taste like.

"The man I'm buying it for is very well-versed in wines from around the world. You say this one is special?"

He shrugged and rubbed a hand on his meticulously groomed stubble. "The demand for it has lessened over the years slowly, so it's more obscure, which, as you know, makes it seem more special."

She didn't know, but nodded.

"I am pretty sure there's a lot of berry in it too — strawberry and cherry. Hey — Anthony!" He hailed another clerk from the back room. "Do you remember much about the L'Oratoire?"

A surprisingly grizzled man ambled from around the corner of the counter. The grey eyes behind the small glasses seemed to light with passion as he spotted the bottle in their hands, and Charlie felt apprehensive. She didn't really think she needed a full lesson on vintages, but then again, perhaps if she saw Sam when she dropped it off, she'd have something new to tell him. Resolving not to glaze over, she smiled with encouragement at the two men, and Anthony took the wine lovingly, cradling it in his square hands.

"Yes, of course. You cannot go wrong with a Château," he remarked, looking at her openly. "But you want to know the vintage first, yes?" His quaint speech was rounded with a half-hidden French inflection.

Charlie nodded mutely, and he continued. "This one, yes, this one is very nice. Some blackcurrant. It is very deep red, like a ruby." He looked at her again and then stared back a the label, as if looking at the markings would unveil all of the wine's secrets or trigger his memory.

"Some spice, of course, anise and cola and the licorice too." He grinned suddenly. "It is a…*sexy* wine. Warm, melted with the ganache, so some chocolate too, with the berries. You will like it."

Charlie didn't think wines could be called 'sexy' but she could see that the reverence with which all its properties were recited weren't simply fabricated. Anthony seemed to take his role very seriously.

"Okay. I'll take it."

She followed both men to the counter and tried not to gag at the price tag. It was nearly one hundred dollars. But. Sam had sheltered her on a bad day, given her several glasses of wine, two meals and trails to hike. It was the least she could do.

The sun wasn't as hot as she left the winery, and she calculated the distance from the winery up the road to his ranch. She'd made the call to stay local for the day, visiting wineries and tasting rooms that she could walk to from the bed and breakfast. She let the thought tantalize her as she meandered back to the B&B.

It would be a good run, if she could bind the wine properly in her lightweight bag. Charlie took a towel from her room to wrap around it and she stashed it tightly into the nylon. Strapping on the backpack, she did her usual stretch and then took off. There was freedom in this, at least. She could wear her running outfits all day and go for a quick couple miles whenever the light, the notion or the trails found her.

She figured it would be an easy four miles to his ranch, and even with giving herself an extra minute or two a mile she made it in good time. Who knew if he was out and about? If he was gone; she'd leave a note with the bottle on the porch and call it good. As she ran, she thought of him. Apparently that's all she was going to think about today. Sam.

He was unlike Peter. Peter had been tall, lean, a tad lanky and a bit bookish and ever so determined. His unfiltered honesty was one of the things she'd liked about him, and generally she was the one that had brought the fire and excitement to the relationship. They'd been a good balance, or so she'd thought.

Sam was broader, older, with grey in the temples of his darker receding hair, a ruddy complexion and a deep chuckle. He seemed livelier than Peter, more easygoing and less careful. He was certainly more relaxed about life. Charlie was hopeful they could somehow stay in touch and remain friends. Maybe he'd invite her out when he would have a party and she'd start to meet a whole new circle of people. She needed that.

As she rounded the corner to the pasture where she'd met him, she smiled and wiped the sweat from her face. Yes, yesterday had good memories, even though she'd been in a sour mood. It had definitely been unusual. Taking a strange man up on his random offer for wine! But he'd been so obviously kind, and it'd worked out in the end.

When she drew up to the house, she slowed to a jog and then walked up to the large double doors. She didn't see the jeep, and figured he was indeed gone. It was odd, but she felt a bit let down. She had really been looking forward to connecting with him again.

Well, nothing to it. She unbound the wine, and set it in the long shadows starting to creep over the land. There were clouds today, and the sun looked like it might make a proper California sunset in a few hours. Pulling out her wallet, she slipped out a business card - the only paper she'd brought - and a pen, dashing off a line: *Thank you for yesterday. It was wonderful. Charlie*

As she slipped the card under the bottle, the gravel crunched and his jeep came ricocheting around the bend. The windows were all down, and the back was piled high with a few wooden crates. Sam barely had it in park before jumping out and approaching her. She straightened and shaded her eyes. In the dust of the jeep and the mellow warm light, he looked debonair, and she felt herself give in to his smile, matching it.

"You're back!" He spoke with happiness, almost relief.

"I am," she gestured to her feet and came off the porch to meet him. "I had to drop off a thanks. The least I could do."

He glanced at the bottle, but came back to her face instantly, his eyes searching her and then taking in the empty driveway.

"What the hell. Did you walk here?"

"Took a run," she shrugged and smiled again. "I love to go for a few miles."

"All the way from the Holiday Inn?"

"Didn't stay there - found a bed and breakfast that would take me in, even after nine in the evening. It's quaint and just enough."

Sam shook his head, and reached the short space between them to touch her arm absently, as if he needed to assure himself she'd returned. "Well I'll be. Good to know there's one close by."

"Yes. Good to know," she echoed.

"Did you get your car fixed?"

She shook her head, "Not yet. They said they'd have it ready by the end of the morning, but obviously that's not happening. I might need to beg for a ride back to my loaner car."

His head came up. "Stay for supper?"

It was another invitation unlooked for, and it made her draw up inside. He was so welcoming, unassuming, and open. And she wanted to join him. The moment he asked, she knew she'd have to say yes, because a dinner alone somewhere else would pale by comparison. Somewhere inside of her, she craved the time with him.

"I will," she nodded and smiled at him. "Maybe cooking tonight, though? I don't think I can do pizza after a four miler."

"Suits me. I'd love it." He moved back to his vehicle. "But first I have to unload these."

"I'll help."

"You just get the doors." He threw her the keys to unlock the front door and went to the back of the jeep. She opened them up, and held it open while he passed her with the first case. His shoulders were bunched through the white of his shirt, and she was inherently impressed with his strength. Following him into the cool concrete of the foyer, he directed her to the cellar door and light switches. When they got to the basement and the wine stretched out in front of her, she gaped.

"Oh my God. I've never seen anything like this in someone's home!"

"It's not unusual around here," he shrugged, but Charlie could tell he was pleased with the compliment.

She stared around them while Sam cleared a space for the new crates. The wine bottles gleamed like jewels – deep ruby and pale rose and the dancing yellows of all the whites. It was a glorious, marvelous space that spoke to her of vintage cellars and old crotchety men asking for a particular year or grape.

They took four more trips, and then when they came up, Sam went to get the bottle of wine she'd left him. He walked back in the house, studying her card, while she moved decisively around the kitchen. It was a bit strange to be so familiar in someone's home, but Sam was so casual it would be odd to stand on formalities with him. She gazed in the fridge, and took out a white package.

"What's this?"

He peered over her shoulder. "Um. Steak?"

"You should probably heat up the grill then."

He smiled and her and grinned. "Yes ma'am. Anything else I can do for you?" His tease made her more comfortable; apparently he liked that she wasn't shy.

"Tell me where your spices or marinades are. We don't have time to make our own. It's what...almost four thirty..." she glanced at the clock.

"On the island, second drawer from the right of the dishwasher." He stopped moving and took a hard look at her. "I'm glad you came back."

Charlie paused too and looked up at him. She reached out and squeezed his shoulder. "Me too. Yesterday was very nice. Made me want to repeat it." His body was meaty, broad and warm, but she released him almost immediately. It felt odd to touch him, but not so much so that she wouldn't want to try it again.

He gave a little nod, and then headed out to open the patio doors and drag off the grill cover.
She pulled out salad, vegetables and small potatoes. Innately knowing he wouldn't mind her poking around, she found tin foil, salt and pepper and oil. Slicing the potatoes *anna* and dashing out some spice with oil and butter, she brought out the potatoes to Sam, where he was revving up the gasoline and opening up the steaks.

"Do you want vegetables grilled or steamed?" she asked, thinking ahead to what she might do with the zucchini, squash and carrots. She already knew what she'd do with the mushrooms.

"Oh. Grilled?" he looked at her, eyebrows raised. He had a sliding, surprised look, as though he wasn't quite used to making a full meal. But even though she had only met him yesterday, Charlie could tell he was enjoying himself and the anticipation of a meal all cooked and primped.

"Coming right up, then." She slid the potatoes next to him and moved back to the kitchen. She'd already found the cutting board and the smooth knives. It was quick work to make two more tin foil boats filled with fresh vegetables, oiled, buttered and spiced a bit differently than the potatoes. Salad would be easy.

By the time she brought the next round out, he had the grill on hot, and was ready and waiting.

"Will I have at least fifteen minutes to make the ragout?"

"The *what*?" He swung around, looking pleased.

"The mushrooms for on top of the steaks. You have any open red?"

"From yesterday's bottle – the one we didn't finish." As he tossed the comment to her across the patio, she realized she liked the sound of it. They'd already created a little history. She missed that – the sharing of memories, the making of and recalling them together. Her friends all had significant others and were always talking about recent experiences together, and the past year she'd had to keep quiet most of the time, so much so that she'd stopped going to many group gatherings. She'd not had much to add to the conversation.

"Alright."

"And open that red you brought for tonight - I bet it will go great with steak," he reminded her. She turned on her heel.

"I bought that for you - to have at your leisure."

Sam gave her another little smile, and the tangible thread between them stretched obscure but comfortable. She could feel him, understand him, but he was still an enigma. What did a small smile like that mean? "Well, it's my leisure. Open it and let it breathe."

She did as he asked while pouring out the rest of yesterday's red with the mushrooms, rosemary and garlic. It would take a bit for the mix to heat and reduce so she found the wine glasses and poured out a serving for each of them. Another search through cabinets found the necessary steak knives, napkins and plates. She had the water glasses filled and the salad made by the time the mushroom ragout was nearly finished. Charlie had a hand in the kitchen, and she knew her timing. Sam came in with steaming steaks and tin foil packages, took a look at the table and gave a little shake of his head.

"I hope you don't mind I took the liberty to get it all set up," she said from the stovetop, where she was turning over the mushrooms.

He set the hot plates down at the center of the table and then went over to watch her. She was suddenly very aware of his proximity, even though he wasn't anywhere near to infringing on her personal space.

"I don't mind at all. And that smells divine," he commented. "So that's a ragout?"

"Goes great on top of the steak."

Peter'd loved her cooking, but he had had his preferences and much of what had been in their pantry was strictly monitored. It was nice to cook for someone again, and with someone who would appreciate the tastes, and perhaps not count the calories against the morning's workout. Sam took up their wine glasses and gave her one.

"To us!"

"Us?" she clinked her glass with him and took a sip. So *that* was an expensive wine! She didn't think she'd have figured it. The overall response to her tongue wasn't an insanely different taste from other reds she'd had, but it was nice to try it and she knew her palate wasn't refined enough to understand nuances. Sam smacked his lips appreciatively and checked out the bottle closely before setting it down and looking back at her. His eyes were warm.

"Sure. To us. To our new friendship!" He touched his glass with hers again before moving to get a bowl for the ragout and a serving spoon.

They sat next to each other, facing out so they could see the land spread out ahead of them. The views, especially with the day's sunset, were sublime.

"Wow!" Sam had taken a bite of the steak with the mushrooms and was obviously enjoying it immensely. "This is delicious!"

She felt herself blush a little. "Glad you like it. Old family recipe."

"It's great. Perfect, all together," his fork gesticulated around the table of food. "It's a feast."

"And it was quick," she amended, giving in to a little pride of still knowing how to manage a meal and make it hot and ready all at once. It was so much more fun to plan and cook for more than one person. It'd taken a while to learn to cook for two, and she'd always planned on having children so she could make little feasts every night. When time had passed, and the children never came, she'd resigned herself to learning to prep for two, and then down to just herself again. The whole food endeavor had been balm to her soul.

"Just what I need to do with the boys around." It was as if Sam was reading her mind, but she knew he wasn't; he was tucking in happily. "Fast, healthy and good to eat. They'd eat this. Well, Cole would. Conner's in a pizza phase, though maybe that has gone at camp."

"Which camp are they at?"

"One with the local YMCA. It's just a two week thing, and then I get them for another two weeks until they head back to LA for school and their mom's."

"How often do you get to see them?"

"Just every other weekend during the school year."

"Wow. That gives you a lot of time to fill." She thought of him, alone during the week with nothing but land, vines and horses. He was an investor, of course, and she was sure he had friends and some social life to keep him active, but she wondered what he was doing halfway retired in his forties. At least, she thought he was only in his forties. Maybe he was much older.

"Oh, it fills. It's crazy how much work the vineyard takes, and the animals too. And then usually a trip to LA once a week for a day of meetings...sometimes twice. The calendar can get busy."

"You don't have time to plan any parties then," she smiled at him, taking another sip of the wine. It was starting to grow on her; she could see how the tannins made it more mellow.

"No, but I should. I need to return the favor of being invited to all the neighbor's multiple events."

"You'd be good at entertaining here, and the room is perfect," she glanced back into the huge great room. The vaulted ceiling disappeared into darkness as the evening waned. Very much an austere California style.

"I will. You'll have to come."

"You have my email now; let me know when."

Sam put down his fork and folded his fingers together over the empty plate. "That was amazing."

She had a few bites left herself, and ate them quickly. "It was. Nothing beats home cooked food."

"And the preparation was half the fun," Sam's response was almost suggestive, and she met his eyes, hoping whatever little flush she felt inside was nothing visible. Was he flirting with her?

"You're right," she had to agree. He smiled widely, his appreciation – for her or the food? – transparent.

"Well," she sipped the wine, ignoring the crackling that danced between them. "There wasn't time to make a dessert. If you drive me back to town, I'll buy you an ice cream."

"What a deal," he joked, but she could tell he thought it was a good idea.

"After the wine is gone, that is," she amended.

"Can't leave it to waste," he said, and refilled their glasses. "It's really sublime, Charlie."

It *was* great, and certainly stronger than the one she recalled from yesterday - or maybe it was the long run before drinking today. Either way, she felt a bit hotter than she should. It could be the wine, or it could be the attention from Sam.

"Glad you like it," she finally said, and then tried to steer the conversation to safer ground. "Will you be able to enjoy so many vintages when your kids are home?"

"Sure. Just not as much fun, as they can't share and enjoy it like we do."

There was a soft pause as they both minced small tastes of the grapes, stalling the inevitable but the conversation waned then too.

"Listen, Charlie," Sam leaned forward over the leftover food, and she felt herself get nervous. His enthusiastic earnestness was flattering but yet more than she was used to, and certainly still along the lines of unexpected. "Yesterday was just...great. I know it wasn't a happy day for you, but I am glad you came back. I spent most of the night last night worrying that I had no way to see you again."

So her impression on him wasn't so terrible as all that. He rushed on, as if determined to speak, as if he was trying very hard to communicate.

"Stay in touch, if you can. I mean...I don't have a lot of people I talk with regularly, but this has been a great two days, or...nearly."

Without thinking, she covered his hand with hers - the small fine hairs on the back of his palm were pale brown. Slipping her fingers around the sturdy width of his, Charlie felt the stab of connection that she had been thinking about all day.

"I'll stay in touch. This has been such an easy thing, spending time here, with you, in the kitchen. Makes me want to never go back to reality and Clear Studios."

He gave a smile and squeezed her fingers. "I know how you feel. Thankfully I get to stay here."

"Lucky you."

Her phone trilled, unsettling them both, and she took the call after checking the ID. It was the auto shop, finally calling. Her car would be ready in the morning – there was no time to pick it up anymore today. She shrugged as she explained this to Sam, feeling as though it was meant to be – to give her just a few more minutes with him.

The mood was broken, so she stood to clear the table. He followed her lead, asking about the wine, and she gave as good an explanation as she could without having the right vocabulary.

"They said it was full of currants, plums, raspberries...lots of berries," she remembered. "And...spice. Not sure what kind. Licorice."

He grinned at her, and she stopped herself from repeating the rest of it – that the wine was *sexy*.

"It's a frank wine," he added, and she had no idea what that meant. "Some floral, too, maybe acacia. And camphor. They didn't mention any camphor?"

"Isn't that like...a medical thing?" Charlie wasn't sure if Sam was teasing, but he was nodding.

"Sort of. Menthol too – that can be in wines, and this one has it. Very fine tannins. Silky."

Good heavens, they were heading into that sexy territory.

"It's a great wine for the vineyard," he finished.

Sam certainly loved his wines, and she could tell he'd be fun to work with decorating his space. Maybe he'd be a business opportunity after all. If she thought about it truthfully, she would have to admit that she wanted to see him more. It was a personal admission that came strangely, sneakily. For so many months - years, really - Charlie felt as though she was a failed woman. She believed she deserved to be alone.

Peter's failure to love her through thick and thin had dashed a lot of personal self worth. Most spare moments were spent dwelling on how unworthy she was, and it had consumed her. Doing these things here with Sam made her find her center more so than she had in the past year, so that she actually felt as though she might be able to warm to another person again. It just so happened he was a kind, gentle sort: open, unassuming, and rather good-looking.

"Do you know any ice cream parlors?" she finally asked, as they finished the kitchen clean up.

"Nope. Kids are too old for that sort of thing. We'll have to Google it."

"Thank God for iPhones. I'll research while you drive," she offered.

She hadn't brought anything but her sack, now empty save for a nearly finished small water bottle, the towel and her wallet. Sam grabbed a set of keys and they exited the house to the dusty jeep. The night was chilly against the warm afternoon, and he started the car, took a look at her and got out.

"You'll need more on than that. Hold tight."

He disappeared into the house again to pop back out with the same flannel she'd worn the night before.

Charlie was grateful for his thoughtfulness. As she slipped on the light coat, and smelled him on it, she realized she wasn't looking forward to taking her leave of the area to continue to explore. Would it be forward of her to stay around in the hopes he'd have time to hang out in the coming weeks? But then - no, she remembered - his kids would be back tomorrow and he'd be too busy for her anyway.

Well, nothing to it. She knew where he lived and he had her card with phone and email now. This would be good-bye. As he pulled out of the driveway, Charlie was surprised to feel herself clench, as a burning ache built in the low part of her chest, right under her diaphragm. Was she *that* upset about the prospect of leaving? It didn't matter – she could drive up another time. Perhaps they could schedule a coffee or a drink when he was in the city. They were adults, and they'd both been married before. Part of her wanted to stay connected to him, to dissemble, to connect. She certainly had a connection with him, and she was quite sure he felt the same. But what did one do with that? How did that become anything more than a flirtation, especially with all of their baggage?

$\mathscr{C}$hapter 7

Sam felt the chilly air around his shirt. The odd mix of crisp air and damp apples shifted around them as he drove toward town. Next to him, Charlie was looking up ice cream parlors on her phone. The pale gleam of her screen caught her face, creating a green-white luminescence to her long cheekbones and the fine thin cut of her lips.

"There's one on Main...oh, wait, it just closed. Damnit." She continued to fiddle. "And there's a family restaurant that does sundaes, it looks like, on their menu."

Sam shook his head. "No fun."

She kept looking, and as she did and the roar of the engine consumed their airspace, Sam glanced over at her again. She'd been completely happy today, the sadness from the day before a memory. He wanted to hang out, make more food with her, talk wine and explore shops for artwork. There was a soothing calmness to her personality, with a bit of fire and spunk to keep the conversation going. As they came into town, she sighed.

"There's really nothing else. You may as well turn around and just take me back to my bed and breakfast."

He pulled into the large parking lot at the supermarket. Putting the jeep in park, he placed his hands on the wheel and formulated his words carefully.

"What are your plans?"

She turned in the seat to look at him squarely, her face blank. "What do you mean?"

"I mean, where from here? You said you were traveling up and down wine country to get away from work. Where to next? For how long?"

Her expression flickered and twisted into a puzzled thoughtfulness. "I guess I don't know. I thought I'd figure it out tomorrow when my car is – hopefully - ready. Why?"

He pressed his mouth together and then decided to play with the feelings he had tight in his chest. "Stay."

"You want me to hang around for another day or two?" her voice was incredulous, but a smile played around her lips, as if she was trying to hold back happiness. It made him hopeful. Maybe he wasn't too much off his rocker on thinking this could work. Like the previous prepositions that had popped out of him, this one filled him with a strange excitement, not unlike the first flushes of a new attraction and desire. He would feel pretty low if she declined, but would understand. It wasn't exactly a common request from a relative stranger. Their thin tie from a single, brief meeting years prior was hardly enough to make them anything more than acquaintances.

"More than that. Stay with me. Hang with my kids - I want you to meet them. Help me find a piece of art or two." He held in his breath without meaning to. It wasn't as nerve wracking as asking a woman to marry him for instance, but it was still assuming quite a bit about her expectations and her personality. Perhaps she'd be offended, thinking him lewd and too suggestive. He didn't mean to have her around for more than friendship, and started to reel through his brain on how to best explain what he wanted, but even he didn't have a fully clear picture.

"Stay with you," she repeated, still staring at his face. He took his hands from the death grip he had on the wheel, forcing himself to feel calmer, still hopeful. At least she hadn't flat out refused. Maybe his heart could stop racing a bit. Sam knew he wanted to get to know her better, that he had felt from the start she was interesting. He was certain they'd have laughs, they'd have things to talk about. Hell, maybe she could convince him to take up hiking. He just didn't want to have to say good-bye yet.

"Please, Charlie. It's been too much fun to end."

"It's a strange offer."

"Maybe," he agreed. "But it's not like we're complete strangers – we haven't been, if you count our first little meet in LA."

"I don't remember it," she reminded, but her eyes had a trace of humor in them.

"Well, it's cheaper than staying in bed in breakfasts. You have to admit it'd be fun."

"You'll get sick of me," she warned. "You have to promise to tell me to leave if you want me gone tomorrow."

"I won't."

"Well, then I'm not coming. You'd have to be honest about this. It's a huge offer, you know."

Damn, he wasn't as good at communicating as he liked to think he was. "No, I mean I won't want you gone tomorrow." His breathing was coming easier. She was laying out the terms. She'd stay!

She smiled a bit wider at his comment. "And you have to let me help out. Pay for groceries and food, and wine. And help with the land...and clean."

"I've a cleaning lady twice a week for that," he jumped in.

"That explains it," she quipped, then turned serious again. "I'll stay, Sam. Let's give it a week?"

"A week, and then renegotiate," he wanted it open-ended. He was in a good place in life, and knew what he wanted. Right now he wanted to hang with her. He felt a relief ripple and then flood him. It hadn't hit him how much it would mean to have her keep on. His relief was followed with a moment of panicked apprehension. Sam didn't do much by the way of overnight guests. He'd never really needed to play long-term host. What if he disappointed her, and ruined her vacation? Well, he was up for a little challenge. "Definitely we'll renegotiate."

She shook her head at his forceful comment, and he started the jeep back up, doubling back. In the evening light, the street lights raced by them in blurs, crickets singing and droning in a zipping half-sound under the engine.

As they pulled out, she unexpectedly put her hand in his. It was a tentative, careful move, as if she was calculating how it could be done so that it was not overt. It was friendly, but at the same time was an acknowledgement of the romance that tickled their senses. Sam knew he was attracted to her and it was hard not to grasp her fingers in response. He didn't want to come off hungry for her - it would scare her. And he still didn't know half of her past. Had her ex-husband beat her? Abused her? What if any type of masculine overtures would send her scurrying back to LA? Well, she'd said she'd spend some time with him. He could tiptoe on ice for a few weeks if need be.

"Thank you, Sam. I don't know what else to say. I find myself finally happy about this whole little sabbatical now."

"Wine country isn't meant to be explored alone," he amended. "You gave yourself a tall order to enjoy this. Lucky for me."

She laughed a bit at that, lightly. She was nervous, he could tell, and he wished he could figure out how to put her at ease. Well, it was odd and unorthodox, what they'd agreed to try. They'd only known each other two days, but there was a casual comfort from the start - from the moment she'd helped make lunch and put away dishes, as if she was a part of the household. People had jumped into the sack together after less time, and Sam was too careful to even let his mind stray to the bedroom this early.

Charlie directed him to the B&B, a quaint, refurbished cottage tucked behind a lot of trees and only noticeable by a small sign at the street. She was resourceful to have found it. Or maybe she was just better at Google than he was. Sam drove them up the crunching gravel, and it echoed against the broad trees around them, closing them briefly into a black cocoon of late summer. There was a dim light at the patio door, waiting for any guests who meandered in after dusk dropped. A rain barrel jauntily played silent sentinel.

"Need help?"

"No; it should be quick."

She hopped out and walked briskly in, the thin screen door whisking along the warped wooden floorboards. He watched her go; she still wore his oversized flannel and it highlighted her tanned legs, making them look long and strong. She was still in her running gear, he realized.

Ten minutes ticked by. Long enough for Sam to start wondering if she was having second thoughts. Should he go in after her? They didn't have enough history for him to make a case: if she changed her mind, it was entirely her prerogative to simply ignore him. Sam's muscles tightened and he put a handle on the door, realizing he was perfectly willing to go and beg one last time, but there was a slam that rang across the short yard and then she was rolling her suitcase out.

"All settled up with management. Let's go!"

He did jump out and took the bag from her to haul it in back of the loaner car. It was a gentleman's gesture that came suddenly, naturally. As if taking care of her was second nature. And as he climbed back in, he realized that was a part of this. Since he'd met Charlie, he had wanted to make things right for her, from taking away her sadness to opening a door for her. Even though she didn't expect the chivalry or the help, he wanted to, as if he had just remembered what it was like to take care of someone again. Well, someone who appreciated his attention and noticed his actions. It felt good to be helpful. And it was nice to have a companion that wasn't a pre-pubescent teen or middle schooler.

She started her engine and followed him back to the road. He had even more time in the silent drive back to contemplate why he'd blurted out such a huge offer. Did he really think there was something worthwhile between them? He could have just had her stay at a nearby B&B again for a few days to see some sights together. But that hadn't seemed enough. Their time together – their connection – had to be more than that, even though it was going to disrupt the method and cadence of his carefully curated peace and quiet.

When they arrived at his house, he got out and helped her again, taking the strap in a hand. They walked in the foyer; he'd left on a few lights so it was dim and shadowy everywhere. The glass and metal shone even in murk.

"This way to the guest room." He led her down the hall, past the washroom she'd used yesterday and to the room that was beyond the two spaces that his kids used. It was clean and spare, a full sized mattress on a simple frame, an empty bureau and a few leftover decorations from the previous owners that Sam had never gotten around to replacing. He turned on the lamp on the side table, and smiled at her. She was looking out the large window, where the land was black outside now.

"Must have a great view in the morning."

"Yeah. Pull the curtains - it's pretty bright early."

"I will. Sam," she moved to him but stopped short of touching him. "I'm so happy to be able to stay with you a few more days. I've felt more alive now that I have in years."

"Well, I'll take all the credit," he put lightly, worried about the seriousness in her tone, as if she was regretting staying on.

She shook her head. "No. You have to understand I've felt less a woman for a long time. You don't care about that - you don't care about my...my... You just want to know...me. It's been more healing than anything else. Thank you for that."

"Well, that's impressive of me to do all that in forty-eight hours. It's what any friend might do," he put gently, his heart hurting a bit for her and the obscure pain she was explaining so baldly. Without being able to stop, he reached out and pulled her into a hug. Who was he fooling? There was a part of him that wanted, eventually, to be more than a friend to her. But it was too soon to ask that of her, he thought.

He knew what she was going through - and someday, out of the blue, everything would be alright for her, and she'd be able to be really touched by another person again. Not yet.

She hugged him back, and then pulled out, looking rueful. "We never did get that ice cream."

"You owe me," he said. "And I got something better. I got a houseguest." He felt the excitement welt again in his nerves, tingling in his hands.

She laughed, and agreed. "Well, it's barely nine. What time do you turn in?"

"Not for another two hours or so, give or take. Another glass of wine?"

"It seems the best idea, now that I'm officially staying here in the middle of wine country," she nodded and followed him out back to the kitchen. He flicked on some lights and went to the red they hadn't finished with supper.

"Start with this - let's not let it go to waste. It's so good!"

"What makes it so?" she wondered, watching him pour two new goblets.

"It's the spice, really. Can't you taste it? There's an ampleness to it too, and all the licorice means it goes down very silky and long, but is fresh for a red."

"I um…I can taste the…cherry?" Her eyebrows went up as they both took another taste.

"Yes, that," he nodded, encouraging her to feel as though she could comment. "What else?"

"I do taste the spice, I guess," she said, inhaling. "And it smells…fruity."

"It's all the berry."

Sam loved wine. He thought it was one of the most interesting topics in the world, and it was art, food, booze and beauty all wound up together in one bottle. He couldn't wait until his own vineyard ripened in a few weeks and he could start working on the next phase again.

"These old French wines and vineyards to have something going – age, time, a name for themselves. But around here, we're doing our own thing. It started in France, of course, but it's picked up here. It's so…*American*." He grinned at her. "Have you heard of the garagiste movement?"

"Um. No." She actually chuckled, and traced the lip of the wineglass with her thumb. Her eyes met his, and she asked. "Tell me?" She seemed serious enough, so Sam dove in, hoping to include her in his passion and hobby.

"It's a French word, of course," he amended. "Means 'garage wine' essentially."

"As in…a bunch of people are making wine in their garages?"

"Sort of…but not really. It's kind of controversial," he admitted. "It started as a protest against long, drawn out aging of Bordeaux, and became quicker, faster, and more…commercial, I guess."

"But you aren't selling wine. You call yourself one of these…garage guys?"

He held in a wide grin at her resistance to replicate the word. "Not entirely, but I believe in their overall philosophy."

"Which is…?"

"You want me to bore you?" he was only half-kidding. It was a little refreshing to talk to someone who wasn't so deep into the wine business that every discussion ended up a note comparison or a competition.

Charlie smiled at him. "I'll let you know if I'm bored."

"Alright, don't say I didn't warn you," he teased, and then dove in, brushing over the garagiste movement that hit France in the mid-90's pressing the traditional vintners and wineries to compete differently in certain circles. The new, artisanal makers sometimes had outrageous prices for their newly minted status, and the European market was steadily declining in terms of interest.

"But not here in America," he added. "It's only been here for a handful of years – if you get further north of year, you'll hit bedrock for the garagistes. Paso Robles is where it all began - there's even a festival sometime in the fall."

"Why the high prices? I thought only the old, European wineries could ask so much," she inadvertently gestured to the French label they were drinking, and he wondered how much it had cost her.

"Well...that's one of the criticisms," he tilted his head. "All the high prices and limited bottles per batch is more of a collector's game, if you're into that.

Some of us are mainly into it because the notion of designing a wine is exciting."

"So…you *are* something of an artist," she accused, a hand going to her hip. The smile quivered on her lips, and he grinned at her sauce.

"I think it's better explained as a cult following. Like *Rocky Horror*."

"Is this just a hidden gem of California?"

He was impressed with her questions. Were they actually having a conversation about this? Sam didn't know many people outside of his wine pals who cared, at least enough to make in-depth conversation.

"Well, there's at least 2,500 or more garagiste wineries in the states. I'm not sure how many are in California, but the mid-state weather is really perfect for the grapes. Plus, I consider it something a little old school, something that I might make into a family hobby with the boys."

"Making booze is now a family tradition?" Charlie took another sip, and then gave a small poke at his glass. "Sort of like the illegal stills back in Prohibition?"

"Oh, you know it's not illegal," he chuckled. "But it's a lot of husband-wife labels, or families, or a woman or two. Very democratic. Except where the grapes themselves are concerned. Most make red wines."

He explained it all in further detail, and she leaned on the cold concrete counter watching him, her eyes taking in his hands and his gestures and his excitement. Sam knew he sounded obsessed, but it was such a creative process for him, and so different from finance and distilled, formulated portfolio meetings that it was a release for him to do the whole thing from vine to bottle to aging. He hoped he wasn't mind-numbingly single minded, and she had more questions as he went, so at least she was paying attention. Sam wasn't under any illusions that Charlie was as fascinated with the vintner process as he was, and he knew that it took more than wine to keep a relationship from falling apart. But it was nice to see her listen, and genuinely seem to care a little bit.

"Wait, so what you got today, those crates, those were not final bottles of wine?" she finally stopped his story. He'd picked up the grenache at O'Brien's, and he was going to mix it with an aging sangiovese.

"How do you know it will taste OK?" she asked, and Sam twisted up his mouth, trying to explain the designing concept.

"Well...it's like...painting? Except, with flavor. Like...baking and adding different spices. I don't know," he threw his hands up a little. He was losing some of his natural eloquence with the wine. "It's...a merlot can soften tannins. Pinot is watery, so if you want it to be more exciting you add cabernet or syrah."

"Can we try some?"

"What?" he paused, looking at her hands tracing the wine bottle. They were broad palmed and slender-fingered. The ring finger still had a faint line, where years of wearing a wedding band still whispered a memory along the rib of her knuckle. Sam twisted the small signet ring on his own pinky, lost in thought for a moment as he watched her caress the lines of the glass.

"The new grenache. How do you know it's good enough to mix?"

"Well," he sputtered, the entire train of his passionate story on winemaking coming to a peppered halt. No one had ever asked him quite such pointed questions on the process. Anyone around the area doing what he did knew all the terminology and didn't have so much curiosity about each wine as they did the mixing and chemistry. "Er...O'Brien has good stuff, never had trouble..." He trailed off when he met her eyes and realized she was just teasing. She didn't know enough to truly care deeply, and she must trust that he knew it was good stock.

"I thought...maybe, since this bottle is done, would you just want to taste it?" Sam stared. Charlie actually wanted to be part of the experiment? She continued. "I mean, you've spent the last five minutes raving about this Grenache. What if it sucks? What if you realize it doesn't have the...ah...notes? that you want in your next batch? I vote we try it."

Excitement blossomed in his head. This was what he was hoping for by her staying with him. Another adult, another person to connect with on all these things. The boys would never give a damn. He grinned at her.

"Sure," he splayed his own hands on the counter, inches from hers. "Let's go try it, just in case."

She followed him down into the cellar, still wearing his flannel. In the dimness, he opened one of the boxes and pulled out one of the bottles. He couldn't wait to do this - maybe Charlie would join him in creating this newest concoction. Sam had dreamed for years that he would open his own small label, something every vintner wanted to do as they played with different grape combinations and aging practices in their make-shift studios.

"So...how do you organize this?" She was running her fingertips along some of the bottles. The oils from her hands picked up the dust on the first handful of wines and then slowly sloughed enough dust to allow her to just transfer grime from one glass body to the other. The trail she made through the row tapered, a squiggly snail's meander from one end to the other.

"Country, region, winery, type of grape," he listed, following her. She stopped at a particularly dusty part.

"And these? They've been here a long time."

She'd picked a section of wine that he had not opened in years. They were from a trip to Italy with Amy, and opening up one of those would just make him spend the whole bottle thinking about how great it had been. Wine had been the connecting point with his ex. She liked the expensive types. At first, he'd thought it was because she had a particularly sophisticated palate, but as their marriage plundered on, he realized it was usually just to say she'd had a three hundred dollar bottle no matter that it was actually an excellent vintage or not. But they'd gone around the world to a few well-known places to try, taste and buy early in their marriage, and they were the bright times. Still, if he thought of those treks or drank any of those wines, he would get lonely and he knew it.

"Do they need to age?" Charlie asked him, her question benign and her eyes already wandering to the next rows.

"Yeah. Age," he echoed, touching one of them. He made a motion with his hand. "Shall we?"

She nodded and followed him back up, and he pried open the bottle.

"So, where are you from, originally?"

"Phoenix," he said, getting new glasses out. Wouldn't do to contaminate the flavors if they were going to do this trial properly.

"Oh nice. Why the change?"

"Work. The jobs were all in LA when I was looking, so there I went. The difference is LA just goes forever. At least in Arizona there's the feel that the desert is close, the mountains a quick jaunt away...I always felt closed in those twenty-some years working in the city." And he had never loved his work. It was necessary to pay bills and have a certain standard of living. Now there were kids and all the trimmings of divorce too to pay for, which is why he kept his hands in some finance instead of just pouring his resources into the wine and hobby horses.

"Well, you've distanced yourself well," she said, twirling the ruby and garnet liquid.

They spent the next two hours talking about the evils of big city living, and he felt himself sink happily into the leather couch, watching her lean leg bounce over the other. She was lively, interesting, and he finally saw the flush of wine on her neck as the night waned. Happiness mingled with contentment as he realized that this was going to be his life for several days, this illusion of compatibility and possibility.

Her eyes sparkled as they joked about stereotypical types, and she leaned into him when they argued about how to best handle the homeless situation. She was passionate, articulate, and he was now decidedly thrilled she'd stay a week. It would be good for the boys to have someone around to get them active. Anything in that category would be better than what he did. And he was doing this for a selfish reason too. Sam liked Charlie. She'd grown on him quickly.

When the grenache was gone, she stood and took her glass to the sink.

"What time are Conner and Cole arriving?" Deftly she washed out all of the used glasses and popped them into the dishwasher.

"Bus drops them off at noon or so, if I remember," he said, watching as she took off the flannel and hung it back up. He was acutely aware of her body, suddenly, as if by exposing her arms and shoulders she was almost naked. He knew part of it was the wine. Still – Sam thought she was a bit of a knockout. It didn't matter that they didn't have much history, or that he'd yet to give her any more than a platonic hug. There was a spark of something deeper that welded them together through their conversation and their preferences.

Yet, the first flushes of excitement can wear thin, and Sam was also acutely aware of that. Sourness could creep into a relationship quickly, innocuously, without one or the other aware of the fact that the ties had already died.

But that didn't make Sam any less attracted to the lines of Charlie's arms right now.

To distract himself from staring stupidly, he bent and filled the dishwasher with soap and turned it on. The blurry whir swished into the sudden silence.

Starting it up, he straightened and looked at her. She was standing in the middle of the space, where the kitchen melted into the living space and the seating began. The tall ceiling made her look oddly short.

"Well. Time for bed."

She smiled at him, and they walked side by side down the long hall. The energy that drifted between them at times suddenly leapt and twisted, curling around his gut and pulling at his breath. Still, he kept his hands down, suspended and ineffectively empty. His bedroom was at the end, and she paused next to her door.

"Sam." Her hand was on his arm and gave him pause. He couldn't help it; when she touched him, there was heat. He looked at her; her face was near, and he saw the faded freckles even in the soft light pouring out of the spare bedroom lamp.

"I'm nervous...but happy to be here. It's been another great night."

She gave his arm a squeeze and released him. He wished he could pull her into a hug, kiss her forehead. Anything. But even with the wine-washed evening, he knew she was too fragile for any overtures, that if he reminded her of their mutually recognized attraction that he'd make her so uncomfortable she wouldn't stay. And Sam wanted her to stay. He wanted to see what would happen, and he felt in control enough of his life that he felt confident he could handle it. She started to move into her own space and he gave her a small smile.

"Good night, Charlie," he said, and walked to his room alone.

Chapter 8

She woke at her usual hour; her body clock rarely let her sleep past seven, even with a late night and wine. She pulled off her pajamas, yanked the covers up to make the bed and got back into running gear. She had to go early to clear her head one more time, and she knew the pastures enough after the previous jaunts that she could get a couple miles in, hopefully before Sam woke.

Picking up her things, she opened the closet door and put her suitcase inside so the room was tidy. She wondered what time he would wake up. Peter would always wake early too – driven, particular Peter. They'd get their exercise in together, coordinate their meals, time their snacks. How had they kept it up for so many years? It seemed as though the restrictions and careful coordination belonged to a different world she'd inhabited as part of a bubbled life.

Still, Charlie craved the routine, the steadiness. She liked being active, and enjoyed having goals and challenges – getting up early was still one some days. But even without Peter to set their plans, she was surviving. Barely, some days. But she was.

Walking into the kitchen, she looked at the watery morning light streaming in the glass doors. It was a lovely home, even with the spartan black and white and metal motif. How had he raised kids here for so many years without breaking the glass tables? Charlie still couldn't believe she'd taken Sam up on his rather insane offer to stay over for several days. She apparently was taking her mantra to do unusual things to heal quite literally. What would Peter say if he knew? Not that it was his business – he'd forfeited his right to care about her and have any control or say in her life a while ago – not that she blamed him. But she often wondered such things, even beyond her choice to spend time with Sam. What would Peter say to her exercise regime? To eating pizza? To drinking so much?

Feeling a bit careful, she opened the dishwasher. Everything was clean; she thought she might know where most things went. Having made the majority of the previous night's mess, she was able to unload most things without needing to seek each cabinet's contents, and the rest of it she guessed. The dishes clanked a bit, even with her trying to be quiet.

Then she unlocked the front door and slipped out, trying to let the heavy oak close slowly so it didn't make much noise. She broke into a run quickly.

Charlie was feeling a bit naughty, there was no denying it. Her thoughts raced twice as fast as she was running, yanking on the back of her eyes and pulsating in her mind. She'd said yes to Sam on a whim. It was a bit nonsensical of her, to decide to stay in a home with a stranger. Who did such things? Was she truly so desperate for companionship? For friendship? The only reason she felt it would work out safely was because they'd have his kids around to act as a buffer. That felt so much more earthy and realistic, almost a defense.

Still, last night had been freeing. Hopefully she had made a better impression on him. She had felt more herself and she had loved his enjoyment of the wine experience, his vehemence over his points of view, and the way his wide hands gestured wildly when he got into a topic. She could now likely tell the difference between a merlot and a cabernet with zeal.

Plus, Charlie thought Sam was handsome, and the fact that she'd get to spend some time with him was delicious. This week would probably be the best part of her time away from work.

She'd have to be careful, though. Last night's wine had made her feel her attraction to him keenly, and she didn't want to wreck their happy friendship. It was easier in the morning and the light to distance herself from it. Men had not been interesting to her in the past year - she had been too down on herself to care about finding someone to date. So many of her divorced friends said she should get 'back in the saddle' – whether that meant the bedroom or the dating scene depended on the friend saying it. And most of them were with someone new less than a year after their papers hit. Charlie couldn't do it. It still felt dishonest to the memory of what she'd had with Peter, to the love she thought was hers for always.

When she finished up the third mile, she slowed to jog the final bit of the driveway. It was maybe eight in the morning, she figured. The shadows were sharp grey against the early light. She opened the door, trying to be quiet yet, not sure if Sam slept in.

"Hey!" He turned from the counter. She was surprised to hear heavy relief in his voice. "You went for a run." He registered her clothing and the light sweat on her face and arms.

She shrugged. "I rise early."

"I thought you left," he admitted suddenly, the lines still dug deep into his forehead. "I looked in your

118

room and it looked empty and there was no sign of you."

"My car was still here," she reminded and he had the grace to look a bit sheepish.

"Forgot about that. Didn't even get that far."

She was immensely flattered suddenly. He was worried she had left! It was touching and a tad romantic if she let her mind go that way. He was newly showered and shaved. She smelled his slight shake of cologne, and took in the jeans and the striped blue shirt. He looked smart, handsome, fresh. Charlie felt her sweat stained outfit to be out of place and kept her distance, aware of the smell of sweat and bed on her hair and skin.

"Mind if I quick shower?" she asked, thinking ahead to the day and wardrobe she'd brought.

"No - go ahead," he was rummaging around the cupboards. "Do you like coffee?"

"Yes," she called over her shoulder. "That'd be lovely."

She checked the weather on her phone before pulling out clothes. It was to be unseasonably chilly, so she grabbed jeans and a loose, silk short sleeved patterned blouse. She found herself actually caring about what she looked like, as if Sam might notice. What an odd, awkward feeling – it was almost as if she was dating him.

The shower was fast, efficient, and effective. She knew how to move quick, and it helped she didn't often bother with make-up. Brushing out her hair, she padded out barefoot while she slapped on a simple watch. Sam was pouring fragrant brewed coffee into two mugs.

"What'll it be for breakfast? Eggs?" He was happy again. She was extremely touched that he had been so worried - almost upset - that she'd left. What had he been afraid of? That she'd had a bad time last night? That he'd said or done something to turn her off? She felt like she should put his mind at ease. The urge to communicate with him was overwhelming, as though she could give him all the corners of her mind, but she held back. She believed that that too much emotion and too much discussion could kill a friendship, a relationship or a marriage.

"Sam." He looked up at her tone from where he was rummaging for a pan below the counter. "I'm sorry I worried you. I would never leave without saying good-bye at the very least."

He gave a little grin, as if he needed to hear that, and nodded. Her dissembling finished, she dove back into regular conversation.

"Yes, to answer you, eggs. Let's do that and some toast and a bit of fruit and call it good, don't you think?"

"Sure." He was obviously elated, once again, to make a meal together, and truth be told, so was Charlie. She thrilled at cooking for two, and suddenly realized that she'd get to cook for two hungry pre-teen boys soon too, and the idea made her almost giddy. It was going to be fun. Except...

"Will your kids like me?" The question slipped out.

Sam gave a one-shouldered shrug as he continued to crack eggs into a bowl. "I don't see why not. You're great!"

She brushed off the compliment without acknowledging it. "It's not that - it's...will they be ok with a random woman hanging around when they wanted to be with their dad?"

Sam stopped, a hand poised above the rim of the bowl. "You want to know if they'll have hostility to anyone they might see as infringing on their mom's space."

She hadn't meant it quite like that, but it did get to the heart of the matter. "I guess that's what I'm asking."

He gave a little chuckle. "I'm forty-seven. I don't need to ask my boy's permission to have a friend stay over for a few days. And Amy's remarried, so the idea of their dad having a new girlfriend won't shock them. We've been divorced as long as Cole can even remember."

"Good. So they're used to this."

"Ahhh...I wouldn't say that, no," Sam went back to the eggs and started to beat them with a fork. He obviously had no whisk. She made another mental note and then went to the fridge to get out fruit, waiting for him to elaborate. Finally he raised his eyes to hers.

"I haven't dated much since the divorce. I just didn't want to - I had no interest in reengaging the dating scene. The few women I've met and dated briefly the boys never met."

She started to cut up the fruit, thinking of what she might do to entertain with them, feeling a little thrill of pleasure at his embarrassment to not have many girlfriends. The notion made her feel extra special. He was letting her meet his boys – even spend a lot of time with them. She was flattered beyond her initial expectation. But she was nervous just the same. Even though she'd always wanted children, and acted as auntie to the many kids her staff had, the idea of playing the part of a mother, however loosely, was not something that came naturally and immediately to her.

"What will you want to do with them? Any plans?"

Sam poured the eggs in the hot pan. "Not really. When they first arrive, they'll sleep a bit more than usual. Then they'll probably want to ride the horses, go for some swims, relax in the house and play video games. See friends. We play board games sometimes, watch a movie here and there. It's guy chill time as they don't have homework and things."

"Are they active in any sports?"

"Conner is. He does baseball, mostly because most of his closest friends do. Cole is not at all. No interest. Though he's more of a fish than his big brother."

Sam pulled out a toaster from below, from a large space on the island, and she finished cutting up the fruit.

"I forgot to ask - scrambled ok?"

"Absolutely."

They ate companionably. She asked what kind of food the boys liked and he dove into thoughts for menus, as if having someone to cook with invigorated him too. She couldn't get over his enthusiasm.

"How do you *not* entertain with all of your enjoyment of food and wine?" she asked him, feeling as though she was digging into his personality over and over.

Sam shrugged, sopping up the remaining bit of eggs over his toast crumbs. "It's not so much fun to plan menus by myself. And I…I tend to just get stuck in my bubble of contentment." She read between the lines a bit. He was lonely sometimes too, though probably didn't classify it as such. Glancing down at her plate, she dipped her finger into the remnants of breakfast, wishing she had the words to tell him how well she understood. No words came. She was stilted yet from the silences that grew between her Peter. Discussion could happen, but it was hard to really pry beneath the glossy sheen that most people wore. Sam's seemed to be nonexistent, and perhaps that is why she found him so appealing, why his earnestness was easy to believe. But if she started to talk about his feelings, then by default, she'd have to talk about herself.

As they finished cleaning up, she heard her phone ring in the bedroom. It had to be work - no one else would really think to bother her right now. She ran to grab it, and then slid onto the long black couch, the leather chilly under her forearms.

"Charlie."

"Hey! It's Amanda!"

"Yeah. What's up?"

"Look - I know you're busy on vacation and all, and I'm so sorry to bother you, but you know the Thompson renovation - the living room?"

"Yes."

"Well, when you handed over the portfolio to me, it was all perfect, but she's wanting to change out the glass elements for something else, and I don't know what to tell her - are you thinking crystal? It's so expensive!"

"No, no, let me think...are you still doing peaches, pale grey blues and ivories for the upholstery?"

"Yeah. She says the glass elements are annoying. I don't get it - she wanted a watery, clean vibe."

"It must be a bit too feminine though, I bet." Charlie thought about her client's nuances. "You know - what about mirrors? Add a deco vibe to it, or go European - see which she prefers - but I'm thinking take out the Louis writing desk and use a mirrored one, and then have some knobs in mirror, do something over the mantle, and maybe one or two small pieces - not the coffee table."

"OK - perfect. I'll keep you posted, if you care."

"If everything is fine, don't bother - I'll hear about it when I come back to the office in a few weeks."

"Having fun?" As Amanda asked, Sam appeared over her, handing her a revived cup of coffee wordlessly. He sat next to her, closer than they had sat last night, and leaned back with a fresh morning paper in hand.

"You won't believe it, but I've actually met someone who knows me. Or, sort of knew me – through you and your boyfriend – the one that you used to try and citify, I think was the term."

"Dean?"

"Sure, if you say so."

"Really?" Amanda's voice was lightly interested. "Well, that's nice. Small world. I hope you're enjoying the time away at least, then."

She grinned at the back of the newspaper; he couldn't see her. "I'm having the time of my life."

The paper came down and he caught her eye and he gave her a huge smile. She actually felt herself blush a bit. It felt good.

$\mathcal{C}$hapter 9

Her voice on the phone was lively, happy. Merry. Sam couldn't believe how much even the simplest creative topics made Charlie glow. When she hung up with her staff, he put the paper all the way down.

"You love what you do."

She twisted a bit of a smile. "Yes, I do. I'm good at it." It was said without defiance or ego, and he liked that she was proud of her talent - no apologies. He handed her a piece of the newspaper.

"I generally like to catch up a bit, and then I'm off to check the horses. Care to join me?"

"Sure." She had already snapped open the section and was reading it, coffee poised in one hand over her shoulder. He settled in comfortably. All they needed was a fire crackling and some music and he'd be in heaven. And he knew inherently that part of that was because he wasn't enjoying the mood on his own.

They read in silence for a while, and then she looked up at him, breaking into his paragraph.

"Do your kids like pasta?"

It took him a moment to shift gears. "Oh yeah."

"What about butternut squash pasta?"

"I don't see why not." Even if they didn't, he'd force them to choke down a plate if she was making it for them.

"Maybe then this afternoon I'll head out to the farmer's market and pick up some things for dinner."

"What farmer's market?" For all his enjoyment of country living, Sam didn't explore much. It was a task better done with others, and it was hard to get the boys enthusiastic about things like that. He stuck closer to home than he always meant to.

"You don't know you have a daily one up the road? I think it's a bit off the main streets, but yeah, every day until the end of November, I think."

"How the heck do you know?" He felt a bit foolish. First he'd missed the bed and breakfast and now the market. Charlie was resourceful. Or at the very least, she noticed things he did not. Did women just have a second sense when it came to finding lost gems, or was he especially obtuse? Her next words made him feel less so.

"There are signs in town for it, and a little blurb in the paper today talking about how the fall produce should start to show up." Her fingers traced the ink, smearing it just slightly.

"Well then. That sounds like a good idea. Maybe Cole will go along," he offered, thinking of how great it would be to get his kids out and about. It might make them like it more at the ranch, so when they turned eighteen they'd come and stay for good on their own choice. The notion always niggled at his mind, teasing and tempting him to play at favorites, even though he was entirely cognizant of the fact that he only hurt his kids by making them choose a parent through the amount of gifts each could buy. And he didn't want to give them any disadvantages.

"Good."

Another half hour passed and then he stirred. He didn't want to leave the cozy chamber now, but he really needed to feed the three horses. When he stood, she leaned forward and took his empty coffee cup from the coffee table, and took hers and his to the sink. He watched her walk, the way the soft blouse moved against her skin, and wished he could ask her questions, to discover more about her history so he could figure her out to move forward, wherever that took them.

They moved outside into the sun. It was going to be a windy day regardless of the sunlight - the days themselves would start to get finicky on temperature. The barns were still cool inside; the stone kept them so, and he clicked on the basic lights. A horse nickered; they knew he was going to feed them and then let them out in a bit. They'd started on the far pasture yesterday, and he'd put them out there again.

"Here's the feed," he instructed Charlie, showing her how to give each horse some grain and then started the hose so he could empty out and then refill the water buckets. It was a tranquil space, low ceilinged, and stuffed with straw. He loved it all. Even though he wasn't a big rider, having the animals to tend to was enjoyable in a lazy sort of way.

They brushed each horse down; she followed his lead, and asked a myriad of questions about the care of the animals' food, exercise, riding and hooves. She had a basic working equestrian knowledge, but not enough to move about the barn with confidence and wasn't afraid to say so. It garnered her additional props in his mind. He liked a woman that knew when to be humble and when to be confident.

"We need bridles, right?" She moved off to the side, peering into the gloom.

"Everything's hanging on the back wall, but watch for spiders."

She paused and glanced at him. "Oh yeah? A little afraid of the creepers?"

Sam cocked his head at her. "No – not necessarily. Just it's the perfect type of place for some of the poisonous ones to hang out."

Charlie drew her hands behind her back quickly, her eyes darting above their heads.

"Like what kind?"

"The usual. Black widows and brown recluses. Nothing you won't find under a bench at an old restaurant in, say New York," he amended.

"I think I will only touch the horses and leave the rest to you," she said, walking backwards until her back hit the horse's stall. Sam grinned at her.

"Now who's spooked about the 'creepers,'" he teased, and she smacked his shoulder, almost as if she was flirting with him. He felt young again.

Once the horses were brushed and cleaned up and fed, Sam opened the large door overlooking the pastures and took two of the mounts out, leaving Charlie the most docile. She handled the bridle with obvious clumsiness, a trip to her walk that made her legs look ungainly.

"We'll take them over and to the pasture we met the other day - the grass there is getting long."

"Okay!" She was, regardless of her uncertainty, enthusiastic, eager, and he was grateful because he knew she was a bit out of her element. There was straw and a swipe of dust along her shirt, and her cheeks were flushed and she looked like she was having a great adventure. He wondered if it would last.

They walked the horses to the land, and he let them go. She leaned on the fence and watched the animals amble, munching happily on the long stalks, particular with the long sensitive noses. One gave a steamy, heavy humph and rolled a bit on the grass, and he felt the usual release of happiness at making another creature feel good. This desire to always help and give more as he aged was one reason he had been both a successful business man and yet also never enjoyed the process. It had always been a calculated thing back in the old offices. Here it was all simple.

Next to him, Charlie bent and settled her chin into the hollows of her crossed arms, her face serene and open. Once again, he saw the freckles in the light, uncovered and free of cosmetics. A tenderness washed over him, and he remembered the day they'd met at this fence, when he'd offered a random bottle of white wine. Was that only three days ago? He pressed his body into the soft old wood and swallowed his breath before diving into his most curious question.

"What happened, Charlie?"

Her face turned toward him, but she kept her cheek cradled onto her forearms. He felt thankful that her eyes didn't narrow in anger or pain, instead focusing on him with the same thoughtful weighing she employed when he was talking about wine or his children. She was thinking and debating talking, he could tell, so he quickly amended. "You don't have to tell me if you don't want me to know. I'm just...curious."

Charlie turned away from the fence and gazed back over the land. At first he thought she was going to ignore him, and he'd have to accept it. She was quiet for a moment, then give a little shake to her head. "We'd been married eight years. No kids. I couldn't...I can't." She pressed her lips together at the admission. "Peter was supportive for a long while. I started the business in interior design, and he worked, and we talked about adoption...but he couldn't take the plunge. And he wanted children so...desperately. So did I...but...he...we grew apart, as so many people do," she waved a hand, and looked down at her legs, stretching them out and pointing the toes. He saw the long toned muscles of her calves and knees.

"There you have it." Sam raised his hand uselessly before dropping it back to his side. "You made the decision to end it, then?"

Charlie gave a little laugh. "No. He did. He knew he wanted biological children, and that I wanted to adopt. We couldn't meet in the middle, and so he thought we should both be free to find someone who could fit our needs...better. Thanks to social media, I see he's found that for himself. But no one wants a middle aged woman who can't have kids." The last was said with bitterness, and then she found Sam's eyes. "I'm sorry. I'm not usually such a rancorous person. Talking about my divorce brings back all my little insecurities. It'll fade."

"I'm sorry, Charlie. I didn't mean to rub something that was already raw," he said, guilt dropping into his stomach. There was more to what she said, but he got the gist of it. At the same time, he couldn't help but feel a little relieved that her divorce was, in part, a bit similar to his – no one had cheated, no one had deserted the other. But his heart ached for her. The flatness to her voice belied the hurt she still carried. He wondered how deep it went.

"I suppose you deserve to know by now."

"I didn't realize it was…that it was something so…" Sam struggled to find the words.

Charlie rescued him with her effortless redirection. "So, the one building is the barn. What's the other?"

Sam turned and settled next to her, their backs leaning on the fence. How could she shut herself away so fast? He'd spent enough time staring at her across the wine glasses to know that she was battling some sort of exhausted emotion at bringing up her divorce. But he could play the game if it put her at ease. He pointed casually. "That shed is where I keep the saddles and extra feed for the horses. And over there is just the gardening things for the vineyards. I keep some barrels in there too."

"Show me?"

He nodded and led her over, giving her a tour of the workings of his little ranch. Charlie ran her hands on the oak barrels that held some of his vintages, where they aged carefully. She touched the gardening gloves, fingered the saddles. He found himself waxing eloquent about everything, as if he was trying to convince her how great it was to stay here, that she'd been smart to postpone her meandering trip to hang out with him. And then he did it too to cover the unveiling that her dissembling brought. As they walked down to the vineyard, where he was going to show her the vines, she gave a long sigh.

"Am I boring you?" he worried, glancing at her. The wind was soft, cool, and her face was turned to the sun.

"Absolutely not. This is so relaxing, interesting...just perfect." He heard the merry note in her voice again, and was pleased beyond belief.

"You're OK?" he wanted to keep her from diving into the sorrow of her own memories, knowing he was at fault for dragging them up and out of the recesses of her psyche.

She exhaled through her nose, and her eyes crinkled at him. "More than you realize. Sam...look, don't feel bad about bringing up my divorce. Really – you've given me something beautiful these past few days. You don't care about my...my fertility or my work ethic or how much time and money I pour into adoption paperwork. You just want to know...me. It's been more healing than anything else. Thank you for that."

He was not prepared for the seriousness of her rejoinder, and was struck into silence long enough for her to transition into another topic.

"So are these all the same variety?"

"No. I've got some picpoul here, and some pinot over there, and I had temperanillo earlier." His voice sounded twisted, and he cleared his throat. He couldn't shake how much all of her reveals had affected him.

"Mostly whites or reds?"

"A mix of both," he touched the posts, where the vines grew thick with wide leaves and tiny curling feelers. He thought he might have to come and chew up the ground soon, cut a few things back. He would after the boys left - it was a chore and a half and he'd rather spend the time with Charlie and his sons.

She seemed to read his mind and glanced at her watch. "The boys will be here within the half hour,

Sam. Did you want to head back to the house? Start lunch?"

He turned to her, feeling warmth spread into his gut. The suggestion of domesticity in her comment made him suddenly, desperately want to keep it like this, that she'd stay until...who knew? That she'd be around to help with the horses, that they could work side by side while they cared for the vineyard, that they'd make food and drink wine and never run out of things to talk about. And if they did, they'd drink coffee and read the paper in comfortable companionship. He realized he had found a kindred spirit in her, that his attraction to her was doubly facetted - he liked her mind, her bearing, her translucent fragility. If she was going to be a friend, he wanted to make sure she stayed so always, and if that meant some serious bonding with the time she gave him, he was going to work hard at it.

"Sounds good. They'll be happy with something on the grill. I have some meat yet I think."

"Perfect."

They moved up to the house, and as they did, he felt her hand unexpectedly take his. It was a quiet gesture, once again careful and calculated, but he took more initiative and intertwined their fingers strongly, griping her. He felt connected with her, as if sharing the morning doing random tasks and talking made them closer. He was sure it did. She didn't pull away and he could feel his hopes rising. He was already hoping she'd let him into her life a bit more. Perhaps someday, maybe, there'd be a chance their friendship could be different.

But Sam knew that Charlie wouldn't date him unless there was something beyond it. She was too serious to go out casually, he understood that innately. Which was why he was waiting to go beyond this comfortable place – likely she'd meet him halfway. He wanted to know what he wanted from her - he had no intention of going through another divorce again, and it would have to be something pretty amazing for him to give up his curated situation. He didn't want to rework his entire way of living for a woman, no matter how pretty. He was too practical for that. But Charlie made him consider what it would take.

They reached the house, went in, and released their hands. The air that hit his palm tingled. He went to the doors and opened them up, letting the cool breeze clear out the cavernous space. Soon there'd be two extra bodies filled with energy bouncing around, and he was very excited to see them.

Charlie had pulled out the hamburger, and was rummaging around the fridge for sides. He grabbed buns and chips from the narrow pantry, and then went to the kitchen island and started to make the patties. He thought about pulling out the Playstation so Conner could find it, and that he should probably get the saddles prepped for a ride or two, and the pool could do with being heated a few more degrees since it was a bit chilly.

"Do you want some onion in them?"

Her question interrupted his pleasant thoughts of what he wanted to do with the boys when they were here. He looked up. Charlie had an onion opened up, and was poised to chop it. He hadn't thought to do that and it sounded delicious.

"Yeah - they'd love it. Extra flavor."

"Hold on then." She chopped half of it roughly and quickly. He scooped them off the cutting board and put them in the bowl with the meat. Just as he started to mix it up, the front door banged open.

"Dad!"

Cole came racing around the foyer corner, tanned, thin, his blond hair bleached with sun and water, his face more peaked than Sam remembered due to what was obviously a growth spurt.

"Hey!"

He dropped the wooden spoon and grabbed up his eight-year-old heartily, giving him a huge bear hug.

"Hey Dad." Conner followed more casually, dropping his bag on the floor and ambling in at a slower speed. He kept his hair longer, more styled, and Sam noticed the shadow of facial hair starting on Conner's upper lip. My God, how fast time had flown even just this summer.

"Hi you." Sam was careful not to be too enthusiastic here, and gave his older son a one-armed shoulder squeeze. "How was camp?"

"It was fine." A standard pre-teen answer, he knew, but he couldn't help feeling a bit disappointed. He loved the excitement Cole had for things yet, and he knew the monosyllables were all a sign of Conner getting older.

"Hey, guys - this is Charlie." He drew them into the kitchen, where she was finishing up the hamburgers now.

"Hi." Cole said automatically, and Conner just wordlessly watched her. She didn't stop moving, and smile at them all warmly. Sam realized she was

143

nervous. It was a bit endearing, that she wanted so badly to make a good impression.

"Hey." She nodded. "You guys up for burgers?"

"Okay. Hey Dad, did you know I got to waterski? It was so cool. I wonder if we could practice somehow in the pool?" Cole didn't seem to really meet Charlie's face, as if he didn't know what to say to a strange woman in his father's kitchen. Maybe this was going to be harder than Sam had expected. Too late now. He swallowed his own spiked nerves and answered his youngest.

"Um. I think the pool is a bit too small for any type of skiing practice, but maybe at the pond by Jake's, if they still have all the equipment." Conner was still staring at Charlie, and Sam took both of his boys by the neck lightly.

"Why don't you both go throw your bags in your rooms and come back out for lunch?"

They listened wordlessly. Cole took off quickly, but Conner moved slowly, almost languidly. Sam stood with his hands on his hips, watching them disappear down the hall.

"They're good-looking boys." Charlie's voice was soft.

He glanced at her, where her hands didn't stop moving. She'd patted the meat ready for the grill, sliced up a small plate of veggies with a bowl of grapes and the chips. He went over to her and surveyed the island.

"A little feast. You're quick."

"I have no idea how much -."

"Dad, I'm starving." Cole had already returned, eyeing up the food on the counter.

"Burgers will be ready in ten," Sam tussled the dense hair on his son's head. "Can you wait?"

Cole hopped on one of the bar stools and Charlie quietly pushed the bowl of grapes at him.

"Yeah." He grabbed a bunch of the grapes. They were still wet from the wash she'd given them.

Sam took the plate of meat and headed out to the patio, but heard his inquisitive son asking: "Why are you called Charlie? Isn't that a boy's name?"

He chuckled. He'd actually been a bit more worried about Cole, who was sensitive. He'd wondered if Cole would be too shy, or not like the idea of his dad dating. Maybe Conner was the one he should have worried about instead. Camp seemed to have made Cole a bit more outgoing, which was good given his normally quiet and artistic nature. Or maybe Charlie didn't come off intimidating, which Sam figured was also part of it.

The grill warmed fast, and he flipped the burgers on. As he waited to turn them, Conner wandered out and stood next to him.

"Dad - is she staying here?"

"Yeah."

"For how long?" There was pure curiosity, not really defiance in the question, and Sam tried not to respond with anything but casualness.

"I think a week."

"Oh."

Conner was definitely becoming a teen. He wondered what his son thought of a woman in the house - after being divorced for so many years and not bringing many girlfriends around, he knew that this new arrangement struck his kids as odd. But he also didn't want to shelter them from how life could be - that someone could be a friend, be generous, and have a good time. That sometimes things just were like this.

"So, camp was good?" Sam spoke into the silence. Conner nodded absently again, and went back inside where Cole was opening up animatedly to Charlie.

By the time the burgers were ready, she'd enlisted the boys to carry the food out to the table on the patio. They did what she asked without complaint, mostly because she was a stranger and they didn't have the vocabulary to disagree. Sam rarely asked them to do many chores on the ranch; he wanted their stays with him to feel relaxing, like little vacations. He had them so rarely during the year that he wanted them to love coming out. He knew it wasn't exactly the best thing to do - that he wasn't teaching them much on responsibility - but he wanted his kids to like his place and he didn't know how to do that while still incorporating heavy discipline.

"Thanks guys," Charlie said happily, pouring water in all the glasses. She hadn't brought out any wine. He realized he didn't miss it - that having his boys back home was all the euphoria he needed.

Charlie started to ask more questions of both of them, getting more than one word answers out of Conner every once in a while. His oldest was checking his cell phone often on his knee, but Sam was just too happy to have them home to harp on any habit this first day. Cole was full of memories, activities, ideas, and more alive than Sam remembered him. He could get used to this new vibrant edition of his youngest son.

The meal went almost too fast, as if the conversation made it all fly by, and she casually wondered if the boys could carry in a few things. They did it without question, as if her words were easier to follow because she hadn't demanded. Sam wasn't sure if they were still a little in awe of him having a woman in the house, or just caught up in the endless stream of chatter she managed to keep going. She was still merry. He was starting to think that this was more her - that the sadness she'd first held was stemmed from the loneliness she felt so acutely at her divorce's anniversary.

Cole started to help load the dishwasher without any prompting; he was the most involved in conversation with her. Sam saw Conner flop on the couch with his phone and furious texting happening. A twinge of annoyance crept into his consciousness. Well, it was the age, he reasoned. He supposed there would be a lot more friends coming over now anyway, and there would be plans to make.

"Well, since you guys had such a great time in the water at camp, you should have a pool party or something here," Charlie was suggesting to Cole, who lit up.

"Oh yeah! That would be awesome! Hey Dad, can we?"

Sam carried the last of the food over and met Charlie's amused eyes.

"We'll see."

"Oh, Sam, it'd be fun. I have some good treats that might be perfect for the boys and their friends."

He was hugely touched that she would offer this - to help him chaperone a bunch of kids and to make it into a full fledged party. He hadn't done anything quite so extravagant with the boys in years. There wasn't even any annoyance on his part that she would come up with the idea.

"Alright then."

"Yes!!" Cole pumped a fist and glanced at his brother. "Conner! You hear that? Dad is letting us have a pool party!"

"Yeah." Conner hadn't stopped with the phone. Sam wandered over, wondering what could possibly be so important, but his son shut it off hurriedly and stood, pocketing the phone. He frowned. The secrets were not cool, but again he didn't want to press the issue right now and decided to say nothing for the moment.

"Well, let's start planning tonight at supper. In the meantime, I'm off to the farmer's market. Cole, Conner, who's coming?" Charlie broke into the post-lunch lull.

"Me!" Cole was immediately in the foyer, slipping on his shoes. Conner looked ready to decline, except Sam wanted to go too, and didn't want his oldest alone in the house, or left out.

"Let's all go."

The definitive note in his voice brought up Conner's head, and he wordlessly followed his brother and the two scuffled out to the jeep.

Charlie shot him an amused look. "Lots of energy."

"Can you handle a week of this? And a pool party to boot?" he asked. Now that he knew the crux of her marriage's breakup, he hoped his children didn't constant remind her of her empty, childless life.

"Oh yes. I think I can," she laughed. He pulled out some rarely used reusable bags for the market.

"Thanks for being so great about this," he said to her, handing her the purse from the sideboard in the foyer. She took it as he found his keys, but he was completely, utterly unprepared when she put a light hand on his arm, leaned in, and placed a whisper of a kiss on his cheek.

"You're the one that needs thanking. This is the happiest I've been in ages."

She proceeded him out to the jeep, and he was glad, because he was sure he'd blushed and his heart felt like it was going to blast out of its cavity.

Chapter 10

Charlie put the finishing touches on a plate of melon kebobs. The boys' friends would be arriving in two hours, and she only had the hamburgers to prep before getting to relax a bit. She thought she'd go check on Sam, who was pruning the vineyard. He truly seemed to love all the chores that went with the ranch. It was as though he was still a western cowboy deep inside, let loose on the land after decades of city living.

It had been a great week so far. The past five days had completely flown by – and while they'd spent every waking moment together, the children kept them from really talking or having any type of overt romance. But they'd had a special time at the farmer's market, and she and Sam had gone back twice already for other meals together, meandering through the stalls and exchanging kitchen hacks. They'd made some great food, and Conner was finally starting to get more involved in the process. Charlie figured the older boy was having a harder time with her presence, and felt guilty that he continued to stand off from the fun because of her. But with only an hour or two each night without younger ears in the room, she never knew how to bring up her worries with Sam. Then again, she and Cole had had a wonderful time making a tipsy cake the other night, which Sam had deemed a bit ugly but completely edible and then some. At least she was making some headway with one of the children.

She noticed Sam rarely asked the boys to do anything, preferring to let them relax. Charlie didn't have kids, but inherently knew they did better with some structure, so without trying to step on Sam's parenting, she started to ask the boys to help around the house. It was a trick she'd seen some of her friends do who had toddlers and older children or step-children with relatively successful results from what she could garner. It was nothing obvious or with any nagging, and she always tried to make her requests something easy, nonchalant and fun. Cole really warmed to it, but Conner was still a bit sullen. He was often glued to his phone, which she again felt was probably something with his age, though he didn't let anyone in on what he was always doing on the device. She hoped it wasn't something naughty, and almost didn't want to be the one to find out.

She had an idea for an art project for her and Cole, but it would take a lot more than three days, and she figured her week was about up. It was important for Sam to have time with his sons without her there, even though she thought she was fitting in pretty seamlessly. And Sam definitely was someone she enjoyed being with no matter the task. It helped that he was friendly and gentlemanly, and his modulated response to her made her realize how attractive she found him.

After kissing his cheek before heading to market, he'd only taken her hand a few times when the boys weren't around. She wasn't truly sure if it was because he was shy about showing affection in front of them or because neither of them really knew what was going to happen between them. They started to sit closer on the couch at night. Part of that was lack of room with two more bodies in the sitting area, and the other because it was a nonverbal way of slowly giving each other permission to consider lightly flirting. She rather liked his nearness. She liked the smell of his cologne, the brush of his shirt on her arm, and, last night, the press of the side of his thigh next to hers as they all watched a Batman movie.

Charlie didn't know if she was just happy to not be lonely. Perhaps it would not matter who she was with if only they'd fill the holes of her life, or if there was something special between her and Sam. It was difficult to know, and near impossible to discover. Either way, she didn't want to over think it right now. Everything was just really great for the moment, and she wasn't going to rush in to upset the balance. It'd been too long since she'd felt any type of normalcy in her life, and this illusion of an elusive lifestyle was dreamy.

"Da--oh, hi Charlie." Conner wandered in.

He leaned on the counter and watched her put plastic wrap on the tray of kabobs.

"Cool. Those look pretty good," he commented. She smiled at him.

"Good. I hope all your friends like them too."

He didn't respond, and she turned to pop them in the fridge.

"So, are you dating my Dad?"

The question, served to her back, was filled with wonderment, as if the idea was extremely odd and foreign. She turned around to meet his frank face.

"I don't know. I don't think so. Not really."

"Then why are you staying with us?"

She sighed and went to pour herself the rest of the morning coffee. It was going to be a little bitter, but Charlie liked the heaviness of an old roast. She eyed him up, and wondered if this was a time she could break into his shell. It was worth a try. Holding up the pot, she cocked her head at him.

"Want some coffee?"

The adult question made him sit up a tad straighter and he yanked part of his hair away from his eyes.

"Ah. Yeah, sure."

She took down another cup and poured in half full. She hoped Sam wouldn't mind her giving his son caffeine like this. Well, she could argue innocence.

"Milk? Sugar? Both? Neither?"

Conner was looking in the cup confusedly, and Charlie realized he'd probably never had coffee before but liked that he was getting to drink what he probably thought was a bit taboo. He likely wouldn't even like it.

"Um..."

"I figured you'd like milk like me," she rescued him, and he nodded again.

After fixing their drinks, she leaned over the kitchen island near him, and mulled over his question. She didn't want to give him a watered down answer, one that he would obviously see through, but even she wasn't fully able to comprehend what to call the arrangement. And there was a high chance that whatever she said could get misconstrued, repeated to Sam, or understood incorrectly. Charlie had no idea how the minds of twelve-year-olds worked.

"I'm staying here because your Dad asked me. We met when I was having a rough time getting over my own divorce and we got along really well. Instead of me spending money at a bed and breakfast, we thought it'd be nice and casual if I stayed here instead. That way we could get to know each other but he'd be able to hang with you boys too, and I could meet you as well."

"Sounds like dating."

"I guess...it sort of is," Charlie amended. "It's the way us older folks who have been married before think of taking it slow, maybe. It's very unorthodox, but I think it's working, don't you?" She liked that she was being honest with him. It felt like the right thing to do. He was looking at the counter and

158

glancing at his phone, and suddenly she realized why he was asking so many questions about dating.

"What about you? You dating anyone?"

The guilty jump of his head was all the confirmation she needed, but he tried to play it cool for a moment.

"Um. I don't know. Not really seriously." His brush off made her want to smile, but she knew it would be considered inappropriate by him. So Conner had his first crush, a first flush of young love. Sam had been right.

"Is she pretty?"

Conner started to nod, then remembered he was supposed to act uninterested in the topic. "Um. I guess. I mean..."

"I'm sure you met her at camp." Now was not the time for twenty questions.

"Yeah, I did."

"You didn't invite her to the party."

"Naw - only dudes are coming anyway," he stirred the coffee with the spoon and took a tentative swallow. He put it down quickly, and she stifled another smile.

"That's true. I'm sure none of them know about her anyway." She was completely guessing in unchartered territory. Not only did she have no idea what to do with babies and toddlers, but handling the early stages of a young child's dating life felt like trying to learn Russian. She could only go with her gut and hope she did it right.

"Well, no. It's pretty new and all. None of them have girlfriends."

"Maybe, maybe not."

She didn't want to press the issue, but this was something she'd have to tell Sam about so he could understand why his son was so attached to his texting and more quiet, perhaps, than usual.

"Did you want to invite her over some time? Like...we could all cook dinner together?"

Conner's eyes met hers finally and he appeared excited for the first time since he'd arrived back from camp.

"Oh - do you think so? That would be pretty cool."

"Why not? Maybe tomorrow or the next night, if she's free. Check with her and see, and I'll just tell your father the basics." As Charlie said it, she felt her nerves string straight in her neck. Had she just gone over Sam's head? What if he didn't want his son dating so young, or having a girl over? Was she trying to win Conner's favor? Why did it matter – there was a good chance she might not see them much after she left the house in a few days. There was no reason to build trust, or create a bond. But she felt driven to do so, inherently wanting to have a relationship with this moody teen. She wanted to help Sam.

"Yeah, ok. I will." He was already pulling up his texting, and she finished her coffee.

"I'm going to go check on your dad."

He barely acknowledged her departure, and she took off towards the patio. In the distance, she could see Sam's white shirt against the greeny yellows and browns of the land. The deeper shades of emerald and purple of the vines flickered around his shoulders. He was hunkered into the dirt, and his faded jeans hugged his legs and calves. She was more attracted to him every day. The more they talked and shared memories, the more she felt as though she belonged on the ranch. She only wondered if he felt as comfortable with her taking up space in his otherwise orderly and bachelor-infused lifestyle.

"Hey!" He stood and wiped his brow with his forearm. He looked dirty and a bit sunburned around the neck and absolutely happy.

"Hi. How's it coming?"

"Just going to finish this line, I think. What's the time?"

"Figure they'll start showing up in an hour and a half maybe."

She was a little nervous about it, now that they were going to have eight boys running around the pool, but she was also excited with the activity. It was as if she had her own kids, in a way, or at least a taste of parenthood without the strings. And she loved every minute of it.

"Perfect timing."

He bent back to the vines, and she watched him in silence for a bit. The buzz of insects, the clip of his shears, and the ruffling of the grape leaves in the wind was comforting, basic, simple. She moved the pail over to make it easier for him to discard the pieces he clipped. The weight of the bucket was heavier than she was expecting.

"I was having a nice chat with Conner."

"Conner?" He continued to move along the line, but she could tell she'd gotten his attention.

"Yeah. He ah...I thought he could invite his friend over for dinner tomorrow or the next night."

"Really." There was an expectation to the comment. Was he annoyed?

"It seems you were right. Girls were right around the corner. They've arrived in fact."

"Oh Jesus." Sam didn't sound relieved that they'd gotten to the root of Conner's despondency.

"Well, at least now you know why he's been all strange, maybe. Young love and all that."

"I know, I know," Sam was almost done with his pruning, and he paused, finished the last snip and straightened again. "It's just now I have to have the really serious birds and the bees talk with him. He's that age."

"Oh." She hadn't thought of that. Parenting was still beyond her on so many levels. Here she'd just handed Sam another problem instead of a solution.

"I'm so glad you found out," he said, placating her worried frown and managing to putting her mind at ease. "Now at least we know, and I can talk to him before he does anything stupid."

"He's only twelve," she started, but Sam shook his head and picked up the pail of clippings, and started to walk to the barn.

"That doesn't matter. Old enough to know enough not to get into trouble with girls."

She sighed, and followed him. In the shadow of the old thatched roof, Sam put his tools away carefully, and she emptied the pail into the brush he kept for compost. It was cooler in the old walls, the smell of old stone and mortar and wood filled her nose. It was as though the dust was always damp in the building, the age of the rocks permeating the essence of the air.

When Charlie stood back up, she saw Sam was near, and looking at her in the soft light of late morning that filtered through the chinks and the doorway's low arch.

"What?"

"You're pretty amazing, you know," he said fondly, and brushed a thumb along her face, grazing her

164

cheek. It was the most intimate gesture either of them had ever given the other, and it made her a bit short of breath. Charlie remembered the flushes of first love herself – the rush of heavy desire that choked breathing, the pooling of need, the overarching consuming one person felt for another. This was not unlike that, but deeply tempered with her own misgivings about marriage, about men, and about her own failings.

"You think? I just found out your oldest has a little crush on a girl. And I've invited her over for dinner without asking you first."

"Who cares? It's not just that. They're having a pool party in an hour, because of you. My boys are having a great time at the ranch, and they're even getting involved in some chores and the cooking. This has been a total blast, and I can't help thinking I'm the one that got lucky having you stay here."

"The feeling is mutual," she said, and turned to him. All of a sudden, she realized he wanted to kiss her. The idea was electrifying, a bit terrifying, and overwhelming all at the same time, and before she had another moment to think about it, he had grasped her face tenderly and leaned in. His lips were warm, sensual, and heady, and her eyes closed with the deliciousness of it all. She hadn't realized how much she had wanted to kiss him too until it was happening, and it wasn't scary at all but wonderful. The kiss was more than a short, gentle trial, and he released her face to gather her near, his arms around her waist. Her own snuck up his shoulders and went about his neck. His tongue was soft and hot at the same time. Charlie hadn't kissed anyone in a long while, and it was better than she remembered.

When they broke apart, breathing hard, he rested his forehead against hers and gave a light laugh.

"That is a way to say thank you."

"Who's the one saying thank you?" she quipped, and stood on tiptoe to peck him on the cheek airily. "Will you kiss me again?"

"Absolutely." He bent into her, crushing her close, as if both of them hadn't realized how much they had been waiting for this moment to happen. Their kiss was needy, yet careful, as if they understood that a kiss was all it could be, that this would have to be digested and thought over after it happened, and what it would mean moving forward. They had broken their tentative, prudent friendship and had smashed their shared sense of delicately constructed carefree companionship.

But when he kissed her, all Charlie thought about was the heat of his hands on her back and waist, the smell of his cologne and the earth on his skin and the soft hair on the back of his head.

Finally, she pulled away, and put a hand up, lightly tracing a thin beam of sun slashing on his cheekbone. "Wow."

"I'll say."

She pressed her lips together. "How am I going to stop from kissing you now all afternoon?"

"The boys will keep us hopping. Making sure no one drowns and all that."

"Oh God," she hadn't really realized that whole responsibility. "Do we make them all wear life jackets?!"

Sam laughed and released her completely. "No, no, they all know how to swim. Don't worry - it'll be fine."

They walked out, side by side, into the late morning sun. She wanted to hold his hand, but was worried about moving too fast now. There needed to be time to digest that kiss. Still, the space split between them, tantalizing and thick.

"Sam..." She wanted to say something, anything, before they were back with the boys.

"Mm?" He was examining a little cut across the back of his forearm from the vines as they entered the cool shade of the patio.

"I'm glad you kissed me."

He looked up at her as they paused outside the kitchen. "I'll be sure to do it again." The smile lit his face, but they heard feet pounding from the back of the house and moved as one indoors. But not before he ushered her first, a hand lightly on her lower back, hovering, careful, but there just the same, and it was enough to make her blush all over again.

They each went to their rooms to shower and change, and Charlie pulled on her suit. She was nearing that forty mark herself, but the days of the two piece were not quite gone. It was, perhaps, one of the small silver linings that came from not having had children. Still, she didn't want to display too much skin just the same with a bunch of pre-teen boys. Opting for her one-piece, she yanked on a gauzy cover up and slipped on sandals before going back into the kitchen to finish those burgers. The activity was balm to her spirit, that at least she knew.

Chapter 11

Sam sat on the edge of his bed, elbows on knees and face in his hands. He was all set in his swimsuit and polo for the party, but he had to take a few seconds to breathe. It'd been a spur of the moment kiss - something he'd been aching to do for days - and he was torn between worried and headily aroused. He hoped Charlie wouldn't put distance between them now. He was relatively sure he hadn't ruined anything. He figured they both were managing their rooming arrangement with the understanding that whatever was brewing in their bodies would eventually fizzle, grow bigger or stay platonic. Sam had taken it away from the platonic option. Nothing was left except for them to see where things led or to ignore it all and she'd walk away from him and his boys in a few days. And he wanted her more now. God, badly. He couldn't remember wanting a woman this much, at least not in any type of recent memory. Before kissing her, he could wonder about it all in his imagination, but the real thing was almost more difficult to put in the back of his mind.

"Dad?"

It was Conner at the door, and his young face looked both older and yet vulnerable. Sam straightened.

"What's up?" He knew better to fake nonchalance in front of the older boy; his son had just caught him looking more than a bit troubled.

"Are you okay?" Whatever question Conner had originally planned to ask was gone. He was staring in consternation at him, but all Sam could think about was how in hell he was going to have the sex talk with his twelve year old. He wondered if Amy had already done so, and had a moment of hope that the whole thing would be redundant and unnecessary.

"I'm fine, Conner." Sam wanted to get it all over with, but knew making his son uncomfortable moments before his friends arrived was less than ideal for a good conversation. "What did you need?"

"Uh. Um. Charlie mentioned I might have a...friend over for dinner?"

He was glad his son still thought to clear it with him. "Yeah, she told me. It's all good, Conner."

"Cool. Thanks, Dad."

Sam was interested to meet her, wondered what she was like, to have made his video-game-playing, moody son interested in her. At least he'd get a chance to meet her, gauge whether she was raised well and kind or simply one of those horrifying visions of sexualized femme fatale that everyone gossiped about on the internet. He hoped she was a nice girl, more wholesome and simple. Like Charlie. Damn. There he went, thinking about her again.

"Hey, Dad," Conner paused at the door and Sam looked up once more.

"What?"

"I like Charlie. She's nice." It was the widest compliment Conner would give at almost thirteen, and Sam cracked a grin.

"Thanks. Glad you like her."

With barely a nod, his son disappeared into the gloom of the hallway. He heard pans and noise from the kitchen - either some of the kids had arrived or his sons were joining Charlie in the final preparations. God, he loved having her around. She made a huge difference in the entire atmosphere, from how enthusiastic the boys were about everything they did to his own mentality day to day. Sam had forgotten what a woman brought to a household. He liked getting up in the morning, sharing meals and plans and chores. He was quite aware of the fact that the rosy glow of newness would eventually wear thin, but he was also seasoned enough to know that there was just as much chance that even without the newness they'd still be compatible enough that their relationship wouldn't ever end.

He wandered out to a sight; both boys were slapping together burgers, elbowing each other to get to the bowl of chopped onions and haphazardly sprinkling salt and pepper on the finished patties they made. Charlie was moving about with a leftover grin on her face, trying not to jump in on how things were being created, and instead pouring bowls full of potato chips. She'd made dips the night before and Sam had helped. They'd talked about politics over a bottle of white while doing it, and the boys had ignored them by playing one of the more recent PS3 games. Sam tried not to stare. Every morning, Charlie ran, but this was the most naked he'd ever seen her. A pale blue one-piece swimsuit was covered with a see-through navy dress that went to her knees. The bodice was wide, so it sloped off a shoulder and her hair was whisked up with sunglasses. She looked delicious.

"Sam!" she spotted him. "Can you help me carry these out to the pool?"

The layout for the pool wasn't the greatest from the kitchen, almost as if the previous owners had added it as an afterthought. It was a step down from the porch, a short walkway, through a gate to an area where there were chaise lounges, some basic chairs, a table and entertaining sideboards. He'd set up some pails earlier that needed to be filled with ice, sodas and waters.

"Sure." He watched her fill a tray, and then another, and then mentioned to his boys casually,

"When you're done with those, don't forget to each grab a case of soda to bring down, okay?"

"Okay, Dad." Conner responded automatically, still mixing his burgers with the onion. Cole didn't even nod, but Sam knew he'd take his older brother's lead. He was amazed at how painless that was to get them to do what would normally be considered a chore. Would they moan if Charlie wasn't there? Or did they really want guidance, rules and expectations here on the ranch? If they did, Sam knew he'd feel as though he was raising them better. Was it really as easy as that?

Charlie gave him a bit of a knowing smile, and he realized she had seen what he did. So what? It was her lead and he liked it. He took a tray from her and followed her out so he could get a look at her backside. Jesus. He was supposed to look at her all day and not touch her?

They slid the gate back and started to unload the trays on the sideboards. Sam went to the cooler and pulled out the bags of ice and opened them up. Charlie came over to help him, and he stopped ripping open the plastic and stood, pulling her up to his body in one movement.

"Sam!" she half whispered, and he shushed her.

"Shh. Sound carries pretty good. I just had to..." he gulped in air briefly before diving in for a kiss. Now that he'd tasted her, he didn't seem to be able to quit. The gauze of her dress felt like watery gossamer, as if he was nearly touching her skin but not quite, and the sensation was ungodly sexy. He wasn't sure she was completely ready for his overtures, but he couldn't wait again to kiss her, and the opportunity was too perfect.

She leaned into him, making it difficult to stop until they heard the excited sound of voices pour through the house. They broke apart and grinned at each other before she left him to go up. It was unspoken, unnecessary. He would finish the ice and she would greet the kids, and the ease of it was a beautiful thing to Sam, who had not had such a seamless marriage the first time. Had Peter really given up this woman for the chance to have a biological family? The idea was foreign to Sam, but maybe it was because he'd already had his own children. He still felt as though he was missing part of the story. Was Peter really so blind? The whole notion didn't make sense: why start fresh on the hopes you might get a better chance at children? How would one know that parenting styles would match? Well, he wasn't one to judge. Sam still felt like he was swimming underwater where the boys were concerned half the time. He shook his head and finished up the ice.

It wasn't long before he heard the chatter of excited voices pattering down the stairs and toward the gate. He looked up and was surprised to see Conner and Cole both carrying soda cases, and two of their friends bringing the rest. He wondered if they'd remembered on their own, or if it was Charlie's prompting. Either way, he was immensely pleased, and thanked the boys in the most manly, unobtrusive way as possible.

They nodded with his praise, but turned to their friends immediately. Even with raising the heat in the pool, Sam knew that it would feel cold when they pummeled in. Thankfully, the sun was warm enough, now that it was almost noon, and they were young boys who didn't care about any chill in the water. Before long, music was blaring from the sound system, cannon balls were constantly smashing and shattering the water's cratering surface, and Sam was heating up the grill he'd dragged inside the pool gate.

Charlie appeared with the stragglers who'd arrived after the others, and the rest of the boys made short time of getting into the water. She grinned at him.

"Wow. I had no idea what I was suggesting."

"It's awesome. They are in heaven." It was. This happiness was what he was always striving for with having his sons around, and this was the epitome of it all. There was no way Sam could explain his euphoria. It was a constant nag, even years after his divorce, to create a boy's haven here, but he knew they sometimes took advantage of his nature. Still — they were his children and he wanted them to have an uncountable number of good memories from their childhood out on the ranch.

She'd brought down a white wine, chilled, and some plastic pool glasses for them. He'd almost forgotten he had them — she must have had to dig around the far reaches of his cupboards. The notion of her head-deep in his cabinetry only served to make him appreciate her more.

"As long as we don't get sloppy, I thought we could nurse this. What is that music?" she glanced over at the stereo system, and Sam gave a half shrug.

"Whatever is hip now, I guess."

"Wow, am I out of touch. Here I thought I kept my finger pretty good on the trends."

"I have the boys and I can't even keep up," Sam said, and gestured to a chair by the bistro table and near the grill. She sat and started to open up the bottle. He checked the heat and started to layer on the haphazardly built patties.

"I'll pour and bring out the cold food in a bit and we should be set." She swung a leg over the other and finished opening the wine. The condensation on the bottle left water on her thighs, and Sam couldn't help but stare at the leanness of her legs and the tan of her skin.

As she left, Conner came over, dripping wet. "Food almost ready?"

"Yup."

There was a brief pause, but long enough that Sam turned expectantly to his son.

"Dad, she can come tomorrow."

"Wh--oh. Yes. Good." He nodded and Conner spun back to jump in the pool. Dear God. He was more nervous about meeting this girl crush and not doing anything stupid to embarrass his son than he was about the fact that Charlie slept a few feet away every night.

When she came back with a few trays of food stacked together, he went to unwrap them with her, murmuring under the music:

"Conner's girlfriend is coming over tomorrow for supper."

"Okay." Charlie was methodical about folding up the plastic wrap, but he could tell she was trying not to grin.

"You eat this up, don't you?" he asked playfully and she turned to face him. "You like all the hustle and bustle of kids."

"I really do. It's what I always thought I'd have."

He saw her face soften at the idea, and wanted to touch her, but the burgers were sizzling and there was a call to change the channel on the radio. They

178

moved apart simultaneously and Sam had a sudden realization that Charlie had become a partner. She was part of his house, his lifestyle, and even a parent. They were playing the two sides of a marriage without even having to try. Had it once been so easy with Amy too? Sam couldn't remember. He knew they'd already been stiff with each other before Conner was born - she'd had the first baby to keep them from drifting apart, and when that didn't work, they both thought another would keep them together. But it still hadn't worked. Maybe they'd always been prudently cautious with one another. He certainly didn't think there was ever the effortless ease of Charlie's seamless presence. There were lots of hazy memories of emotional train wrecks, outrageous demands and unhappy silences – and a lot of the time he felt that he had no idea what had caused things to unravel or what he could have possibly done wrong. Amy's emotional upheavals had certainly been a thing to behold, not to mention her supersized demands on living the big life.

Sam didn't have much more time to dwell, because the boys were lining up for lunch. Without another moment to breathe, he was busy doling out burgers and helping with condiments, and Charlie was whirling around with the rest of it. They didn't have a moment to speak other than shoot comments about the food and serving until over an hour later, when the boys were back in the water and all the perishables were put away.

"Time for a second glass of that wine. Take a seat," he ordered her. She didn't protest, and peeled off her cover-up to lay out on one of the lounges. There was an inordinate amount of splashing going on, but Charlie didn't even flinch as the water rained on her body.

"I will work on my tan a bit, then, if you don't mind." She took the glass of wine he offered, and pulled her sunglasses over her eyes. "But I'll still help keep an eye on the kids. No sleeping on the job!"

"I'll join you in a sec." He wanted to wheel the grill out of the way, but he couldn't help sneaking a look at her completely exposed legs and the deep plunge of the swimsuit's neckline. Charlie wasn't large chested - he knew a lot of it that came from the exercise she did almost daily - but she had some curve and a lot of lean muscle. He moved away, knowing he was a few seconds away from being outrageously obvious, and scrubbed at the charred bits of food with a tightly wired brush.

Sam took the grill back to the patio, scraped it down one last time and went back to the pool. He took off his shirt, feeling only mildly self-conscious. He was glad he hadn't gone completely to seed yet, even though he knew he could do with trying to lose a few around his gut. Came from drinking all the wines! He reclined in the chaise next to Charlie and took up the vintage waiting for him. The extra pound of flesh was worth it for the grapes.

"Still good and cold," he commented, then pushed his sunglasses up his nose and sipped the pinot. It was drier than most, and he liked it.

Charlie nodded, and they spent a lazy hour just watching the kids and generally half-sleeping. She flipped once to get sun on her back, and he worked extremely hard to not look at her behind. Not that it would be obvious he was doing so with his sunglasses on, and her back to him, but he was worried about what his own attraction would be. He wanted to squeeze her to him - he didn't even need to make love to her to get what he wanted, which was her body nearby, close enough to have small sensual connective comments in their own casual intimacy.

After another hour went by, he stirred. How had he just spent two hours in Charlie's company without chatting her ear off? Was that a good thing that they could exist in the same space and ignore each other?

"Boys - everyone want to take a break and have something to drink?"

Cole leapt out of the pool and came running, followed by his friends. Eight year olds were so much easier. Their enthusiasm was still infectious and genuine, unconstrained by social norms or posturing beyond boyish play. Conner and his buds stayed in the pool and focused on some type of blind polo game they'd made up.

When Sam came back after distributing soda, he found Charlie turned on her back again. The heat of the sun over the past few hours had made her tanned skin a red bronze. She didn't really need sunscreen being so dark already, but he hoped she hadn't gotten burned.

"So...what do you want to do for dinner tomorrow?" she asked him. Over the past week, she had transformed from a gloomy divorcee to a glowing, animated woman and she asked the question about Conner's date night with the same excited tone she used for nearly everything. He again reminded himself that the initial impression of her was not really Charlie. The Charlie he first met was her at her most depressed. This woman now was bright, open and enthusiastic. He'd seen her at both ends of the most severe mood swings she probably ever took, and it'd all happened in a week. Still, this bright, gleaming version of her was magnetic.

"I don't know. What do you think?"

"Pasta," she said decisively. "That's easy and everyone likes it. A pasta bar, maybe, since we don't know what she might prefer. And the boys can help. And we'll need to pop to the market for a few fresh vegetables."

"I have a morning coffee with my investment manager," he remembered. "But I'll be back by ten or so. Can you wait for me?"

She flashed him a grin and reached over to hold his fingers with hers. "Of course we will."

She assumed at least one of the boys would go along, he saw, and thought suddenly that Conner might have a keen interest in it all anyway. God, she was good with the kids. How did she do it? Was it because she knew it was temporary? Or because she genuinely had a growing connection with them? Sam wondered where all these questions and sorting would lead him. He knew he was weighing her, judging their future, considering his options and what he wanted. It was natural, he supposed. Even if he was stimulated by her, he certainly wasn't about to jump into anything without thinking hard about it. Too many things weighed on his choice: his sense of solitude, his peaceful ranch, his children, and his expectation of what he had planned for his future.

They spent another hour out in the sun and water before winding everyone down. It was long enough, and Sam was grateful the parents were prompt in picking up the kids. He knew most of them by sight, and some by brief conversations here and there that added up to a decent idea of their children's raising, parenting styles and all that. One of the boys came from a divorced home much like his, and he was good friends with Tom, who got out of his car to come and find his boy.

"Hey, Sammy!" he hailed. Sam raised his hand in welcome, and waited for Tom to make his way into the gate. Tom's son was already changed and talking animatedly with Conner and Cole and one other twelve-year-old who was still waiting for his parents.

"Tom."

"How are you, old man?" Tom worked in winemaking too, like so many did in this region, and his hands were always stained. He was a hulk of a man, and towered over Sam by half a foot, his large meaty arms and shoulders pulling at the faded t-shirt he wore. Tom was a good-natured sort, one more prone to a beer than the wine he made, but Sam liked him because they were both bachelors and had kids. There weren't many around with younger ones.

"I'm great. And you?"

"Can't complain. Oh. And hello." There was surprise and appreciation in Tom's tone, and Sam turned to see Charlie rising from her recline. She looked... Well, Sam realized, she looked hot and sexy. Next to him, Tom was hurriedly closing his gaping ogle and was reaching out to shake her outstretched hand. Sam jumped in with introductions, unused to making them.

"Tom. This is Charlie, my...friend," he finished lamely. He wasn't sure what to call her. She was indeed his friend, but he'd almost popped out with *girl*friend and they hadn't really made any decisions about their relationship. Friend sounded about right.

"Good to meet you," she said warmly. "Your son had a great time."

"I'm sure they'll all sleep well tonight," Tom said, and then turned to Sam. "Hey, will you be coming to my shindig next weekend? I'm bringing in a pig."

Tom always did a great party the weekend after his kids went back to the city, and if Sam had the boys, he usually passed because it was their last weekend together. But this year the timing worked so that he was free and alone, so he nodded affirmative.

"Sure."

"Good, good. And you're welcome to come too, Charlie," Tom said generously. "A week from this Saturday, starting in the afternoon about four."

"Thank you! I'd love to come," she said, without committing one way or the other. Sam suddenly realized she was still planning to be gone by then, and felt himself feel the first whispers of panic. The thought came, unbidden and as spontaneous as every reaction he had had where Charlie was concerned: *He'd have to convince her to stay.*

Tom nodded and called to his son, who came running. As he waved, the last car pulled up and the final remaining friend disappeared into his mom's jeep and in a moment, it was just the four of them.

"Whew." Charlie fell to the chaise lounge. "Well, I hope you boys will be hungry again in an hour or so for dinner. We have a lot of leftovers to eat up."

"No problem," Conner said. He seemed the most relaxed Sam had seen him since arriving back from camp. Cole was bouncing to the music, and in a spurt of unfiltered exuberance, Sam picked him up effortlessly and tossed him in the pool.

"Gotcha!"

"Dad!" Cole came sputtering to the surface, but barely got a breath before Sam jumped in next to him, walling him over with a wide wave of water. As they both wiped their eyes, there was a hoot and Conner was cannon balling over their heads to land with a smack against the surface of the pool. It was an instant wrestling match, and Sam found himself under attack of bony arms and legs and elbows, both boys ganging up on him in good-natured fun. They finally all took a moment to rest and he saw Charlie sitting in a chair along the pool's edge. She looked happily amused, and he waded over to her.

"Care to help a guy out? I don't think I could win a game of water polo alone."

"Sam!" she chided, laughing.

"Kidding..." he eyed her legs. "Here, help me up." He reached out a hand and she grabbed at it automatically. He yanked her in quickly, pulling her across the water and half into his arms as the water engulfed her entirely.

"Oh! You!" She sputtered as he released her into the water, and he wondered suddenly if she'd be annoyed that her hair would be ruined and her body soaked. He didn't get another second to think about it, because she sent a gigantic splash at him before diving under the surface and coming up near the polo game. "Conner and me against you and Cole, then."

He should have known better. It seemed a reflex to expect the usual feminine response from her, and she generally surprised him every time he questioned what her reaction would truly be. Of course she'd want to join in, and was happy to do so. He should know that by now. Regardless of whether her enjoyment of her sons went further than skin deep, it's all she was showing him, so he'd have to run with it and assume she meant it.

They spent another fast hour in the pool together before getting out, the boys combatively fighting about nuances regarding points given or retracted. They all went in, dripping wet, to change for supper. He rinsed quickly, feeling elated with the ease and success of the day. Pulling on jeans and a shirt against the coming night's chill, he went to re-heat the leftovers.

As he walked down the hall, the guest bath opened and Charlie spilled out of the steam in nothing but a towel. It showed even less of her than when she'd been wearing a swimsuit, but the suggestion of her near nakedness hit him hard. She blushed a bit, and brushed past him quickly to her room and shut the door, but Sam was stuck rooted to the spot for a few seconds. He would have to figure out how to kiss her again tonight.

$\mathscr{C}$hapter 12

Charlie found a fresh glass of red wine waiting for her when she met Sam in the kitchen. The boys were still chatting away in their joined bathroom down the hallway, and they had a few moments to themselves. Sam was pulling out leftovers, and she went to set the table on the patio. When she came back in for the water and glasses, Sam mentioned off-handedly,

"You really should go to Tom's party next weekend. I mean," he met her eyes. "I want you to go. With me. My date. If you want." The last was half-apology, half afterthought.

She felt herself grow excited, all nerves long forgotten since they'd shared their first kiss. "I'd love to go with you, Sam." She remembered how he'd introduced her to Tom and the obvious awkwardness of their situation. It was silly to pretend they were anything other than what they were. "On one condition."

Sam stopped moving and eyed her up warily. It was a way of speaking she didn't normally use, and she could tell he wasn't expecting her to make demands.

"What?"

"That you call me your girlfriend, not just a friend. If you're okay with that."

It'd only been a week, but Charlie wasn't going to beat around the bush with where things were progressing. She'd been married before and knew what she was doing. They were adults. If it didn't work out, they certainly knew how to end things before anyone took a walk down an aisle. And she wanted to belong to him, somehow. It'd been hard not to touch him all afternoon, with him walking around in nothing but swim shorts. He was still incredibly handsome for someone who didn't exercise and was hitting the far end of forty. She had enjoyed her view.

Sam's smile went wider. "That's an easy deal to make."

"Yeah?" she couldn't believe he was agreeing so easily. Maybe he really did have a serious interest in her.

"Yeah, but I have another favor to ask for that, then."

"What?" she couldn't imagine what else he could ask for at this point.

"Stay until then, at least."

It was the one thing she didn't think she could stay yes to, and something she was certainly not expecting, and felt her face fall. His matched hers. "What? You need to leave?"

"No, I don't *need* to, Sam," she sighed, and pulled out the rest of the leftovers. He matched her, piling the burgers on a plate to reheat in the microwave. "I just think you and the boys should have some time alone without me here. I'm not family, and you should get your bonding with them before school starts and all."

"Charlie," he said softly, but didn't elaborate. He knew she was right, and he couldn't press the matter any further without making overtures both of them knew were too early.

"What day do they leave?"

"Friday afternoon I take them into LA," he grimaced, thinking of the traffic.

"I'll show up Saturday morning, then, and we'll have a weekend of it with Tom's party. Does that seem alright?"

"Does it have to be just a weekend?"

His question, a half-whispered plead, drew her up. He was asking her to continue to stay, almost as if it was an indefinite offer. The idea caught at her consciousness, warmed her stomach, and made her head tingle. To stay with Sam until they decided it wasn't working - or crazier still, until they stay together forever - was a wonderful, heady notion. She almost wanted to sit and start hashing out possibilities with him, but Cole bounded in, starving already for food. She couldn't believe how much food eight and twelve year old boys could consume — the amount was staggering.

Still, his arrival meant she could ignore Sam's question, and he didn't seem to need an answer anyway. Perhaps he was just being overly hospitable anyway.

They busied themselves, and started to plan out tomorrow's dinner. Conner was actually enthusiastic about her pasta bar idea, and she and Sam promised to help him find good ingredients at the farmer's market the next day. The only glitch in the entire operation was that Cole didn't understand why he couldn't bring his own friend over, not reading his brother's nuances. The fact that the dinner guest was going to be a girl didn't seem to register on the younger one's radar, and he thought it only was fair that they would each have someone to talk to.

"Cole, maybe next time," Sam placated, but Charlie jumped over him, not realizing she was overriding her newly minted boyfriend in the process.

"Well, maybe it'd be alright. Both boys having a guest and all."

Sam shot her an annoyed look, but one glance at Conner made his expression soften. Conner was looking anxious, as if anything that would be out of the ordinary would leave him to eventual merciless teasing from his younger brother, and Sam gave in. Charlie had realized much faster than he did about how Conner desperately wanted to play the new girlfriend thing as quiet as possible. If that meant keeping Cole in the dark for even a few more weeks, the older boy would do anything, even if that meant having an additional bratty eight-year-old at the table tomorrow.

"You're right. It would be fun."

Charlie relaxed into her chair, and Sam shot her an amused glance, as if surprised she could understand the politics of young boys better than him. She didn't know how she could, but she was glad it had worked out. Hopefully Sam wouldn't be truly irritated with her.

Cole bounded out of his chair after eating to phone Tom's boy, and Charlie gathered up the plates.

"Conner, maybe you could grab everything off the table so your Dad can wipe it down before you settle in?"

Conner moved without a word, and Charlie was pleased her casual, cobbled together parenting method seemed to work with the two. Cole came back in as they were finishing up the easy dishes. "Jamie can come."

"Good. Thanks, Conner," she said casually, as the older boy stood by the counter with his hands dangling free, surveying. He'd done what she'd asked in a round about way, but wouldn't automatically pitch in with the dishes and that was all she'd prompt from kids not her own. Sam didn't seem to mind the way she got them included, and until he verbalized anything with her, she was going to treat them the way she would her own nieces and nephews.

Thinking of the little toddlers made her pause. She hadn't seen any of them since the divorce.

Once the Playstation was in full force, Sam brought over a bottle of red. "Care to join me on the patio?"

She wiped her hands on her jeans and nodded. She was tired after a day in the sun and all the activity, but not tired enough to turn in directly after eating. Sam had already uncorked it, and she brought the stemware out. His kitchen was almost as familiar as her own now - at least with the basic cooking and every day living. She didn't even know how many times she'd loaded and unloaded the dishwasher. So this is what it would have been like, before, had she moved in with Peter instead of marrying him first. It was truly like playing house, and had it been her first time around, she would be nervous about it. But not this time.

She gave an involuntary sigh as she sank into the cushions on the loveseat next to Sam. He shifted, surprised perhaps that she made the choice to sit so close to him - usually they sat on separate chairs to give each other space. But his shift was only to free his arm, so he could drape it over her shoulders lightly, along the back of the seat.

"What a wonderful day," she mused, clinking her glass with his.

"Agreed."

He drank deeply, and she followed, not realizing how bold and strong the wine was. It was delicious, and she took another simple sip.

"This is divine," she raised her glass to the light, peering at the color. It tasted as if it should be opaque, almost black, but it was lighter than she expected. When she brought the glass down, she saw Sam staring at her with a smile. "What is it?"

He gave a little half shrug with the arm that held his wine. "You care about the little things."

"I try to. It's all in the details with my line of work."

"Speaking of," he shifted in their shared seat, and his thigh was once again pressed against hers. Now that they'd shared a few kisses and an embrace, Charlie found herself extra sensitive to his nearness, but made herself focus on him and his words.

"Your work. You are based out of LA?"

"Yup. Though I'm still on sabbatical. Only two weeks in. I figured I'd take a solid six or eight weeks, as if I'd had my own baby."

"Twelve, actually, is the standard," he corrected her. "Especially since you own your business — you could take as much as you needed in that respect, I suppose, as long as your clients were covered and you could be reached by phone or email."

"Is it really twelve? That seems insane."

"Oh, trust me, it goes quick," he said, and she wondered if she could actually take that much time off from the office. He seemed to follow her thread of thought. "But that being said...you could always start back in remotely."

"Sam," she had to head him off. He was jumping ahead to months, and she wasn't sure he was doing it because he felt beholden or because he was truly eager to keep her around. It had only been a week, and she had no idea what his motives were, but she had to make certain they were on the same page. "I am leaving for a week in a bit, and I'll be back Saturday morning. We can talk about how long I'll be in your space after Tom's party."

"Don't you get it, Charlie?" he admonished lightly. "I'm trying to tell you I want you here, in my house, hanging out with me. Work from here if you can't stand a full eight or twelve weeks completely unplugged. But stay. I don't want this to be a long distance thing yet."

199

She didn't either, but she wanted to be practical.

"I can drive up from LA any time, really."

He gave her a skeptical look, and she glanced away. He was right in disbelieving her. Life – and work especially – could get in the way very easily.

"Or…" she thought. "Don't you come down for meetings? To get the boys? We could get together a lot."

"I suppose you're right," he was gazing out over the yard, and his jaw looked taut. Had she displeased him so much with her hesitation? There was a freedom in being with him, unlocked by fertility issues or hugely differing lifestyles, but the notion of staying with him for the next two or three months made her head feel light. Was it a bad feeling? She couldn't tell.

"I mean…oh Sam," she looked down into the garnet and black wine sloshing in her glass. Her hand was shaking a little and she set down the stemware carefully. "I have loved this whole…experiment. I think…I'd like to agree with you, and stay on for a while. But…"

He turned to her, and she read only earnest hope in his demeanor. The attraction that tensed and pulled and tingled between them was shut off: his goal to convince her to stay seemed to be motivated by something other than sex. What could he possibly hope to find in her? There had to be other women he'd dated, whole women, women without broken bodies.

"But what? You'd rather scurry up and down wine country alone? Stay in bed and breakfasts with other couples instead of cozying with me?" He was playful, but she sensed his urgency, his wish.

"Well, no," she admitted. "But…I know how I disrupt your life. There's no way I'm not."

"Charlie, I know we haven't known each other very long," he rationalized. "But I don't say things I don't mean. If I didn't want you to come back, I wouldn't have invited you to return and stay past Tom's party. I wouldn't have…agreed you are my girlfriend." The twinkle in his eyes was infectious and she laughed lightly, the seriousness of their conversation lessened by his attempt at brevity.

"So…you'd like me to stay for…almost three months?" The notion was catching, exciting. She wanted to say she would. Why wouldn't she? What could possibly happen?

Sam nodded, but stopped talking, and she was glad he'd let her sit and think without the pressure of his constant badgering. She could feel him willing her to agree, but pushed it off, trying to make an objective decision.

Well – what *would* happen? They'd grow closer. They'd get to know one another. They were too old to pretend to be something other than themselves, so they had that going for them. They'd drink a lot of wine. She smiled to herself and glanced at her quickly emptying glass. She'd probably learn more about country living than she'd ever expected, and thought about the horses and the vineyard. The notion of getting her hands in the earth had a distinct appeal.

But they could tire of each other. Get annoyed. Have disagreements and arguments. Fight. Would Sam care that she liked to exercise and eat healthy? Would he put his whole life on hold for her while she stayed? How could she shut him out to work from the ranch?

As she mused, she realized all her arguments against staying on weren't superbly strong. She would have her own car, and she would have the ability to leave if things got weird.

So, there was truly no reason not to try this out, other than her nerves and her worries – all of which would exist even if they dated from afar. Her voice sounded crackly and she cleared her throat. "Okay. All of this is on the condition we stay honest? We've both done the whole marriage thing and divorce thing, so we know how to do that, right? Stay honest with me."

"If you mean communicate with you, I can do that," he promised.

"Yes, that," she nodded. "I think that was something I lacked with Peter – the ability to put my emotions into concise words. All my worries and fears. And he kept his from me, too. I think it's something – I *hope* it's something – I've learned how to do better."

"Well, we can probably both keep that top of mind," Sam concurred.

"Then…to the next several weeks…to us and to honesty," Charlie picked up her glass, raised it toward Sam and then finished the last drops. The black, grainy residue from the grape skins at the bottom of the globe stuck to the edge of the rim, and she wiped them off.

"You want honesty?" He poured them both more wine, finishing the bottle. She saw the label – a Paso Robles cabernet sauvignon with a Foxglove label. "I honestly couldn't stop staring at you today. I want some time to make out with you without quitting for a long time. I wish you'd spend the night in my bed, in my arms, one of these nights. I won't pretend that's something I'm hoping for eventually. I don't give a damn if you keep on all your clothes, but I just want you near."

His admission was entirely unexpected, but Charlie felt herself glow with all of it. She wouldn't have gone quite so far as admit she wanted all of these things too, but to have them said gave them a voice and made them her desires as well. But just as quickly, she felt herself draw back internally just a bit. What if she started to pour her feelings into this man and his children and it ended up a failure? She'd feel even worse about herself, more so than she already did, still, deep down, for being unable to do what Peter had always wanted. Being less a woman stayed with her more than she liked to think.

The wine was making her a little tipsy - it must have been a full day in the sun and water to give her such an effect already. It made her feel shivery and hot, especially where Sam's own body was hovering. Leaning into the crook of his shoulder and arm, she fell into his side, where his heart beat.

"I'll stay, Sam."

"Good." This was said without relished satisfaction, but with resounding relief.

"Do you suppose we should be covert about the whole sleeping thing?"

He pulled away from her just enough that he could get a read on her face. She stared into her wine, and tried not to grin up at him. In his pause, she wondered why she was offering. Maybe he hadn't completely meant his thoughts. But instead of the hesitating backtracking she waited for, his arm came around and he pulled her tighter.

"You'll sleep with – *next* to – me?"

She nodded silently, and felt his heartbeat speed up a bit.

"Damn. Is it time for bed yet?"

"Sam!" She felt herself blush even with the cool of the night against her face. "I'm serious though. It's not like there's going to be sex, and I don't want to upset Cole or confuse Conner. How do you want to play it?"

She was earnest in her worry. She didn't want to leave the wrong impression with his sons, nor give them false ideas to take back to their mother. The thought of Amy tackled her and she couldn't help but have a pang of trepidation. She'd never thought of meeting and dating another man after her divorce. At least, not quite yet. And it had not been a factor in any half-formed daydreams that her next boyfriend would come with an ex-wife himself, or pre-pubescent boys.

But all of those considerations only flipped on her consciousness. Charlie had a sneaking suspicion she'd need at least a solid hour of kissing Sam before she could fall asleep tonight, but he had face to save. And she really did not want Amy to know that after a week of playing house together that she and Sam were sharing a bed, however platonic it was.

"Let's wait until they're in bed. We're usually up before them anyway, and we'll play it cool and careful. Thanks for thinking of it, though." There was a heartfelt sincerity to his words, and she couldn't help snuggling tighter.

They finished the bottle of red speedily, but opted out of another. Sam gave her a hard look, and said bluntly again, "You wanted honesty? Another glass or two and I won't be able to stop with just kissing you tonight."

She appreciated his candor, and gave him a little peck over the kitchen sink while pouring them ice water. He slunk an arm around her waist and hip and pulled her close as they surveyed over the great room. The boys were in a half doze in front of the Playstation already, and Sam patted her side before releasing her and going to put an end to the game. It was after nine thirty and she knew the boys were usually in bed by now.

They were certainly tired enough not to fuss as Sam instructed them to shut things off. As the boys went to their bathroom to brush teeth, she and Sam did the house chores that were becoming so normal. Taking out garbage, closing and locking doors, shutting off lights. They had a rhythm that came naturally, and Charlie knew she loved the routine of it. If she stayed here for weeks, it'd be incredibly difficult to leave it. Her apartment felt unnaturally sterile when she thought of the place. She determined not to think of it, at least tonight, and instead followed the lights down the hall to her own bathroom.

She brushed out her hair and washed her face off again. Going to the guest room, she looked at her pajamas. Thin cotton pants, a camisole and a cardigan sufficed, but it felt utterly naked so she left on her bra. It was nerve-wracking, yet exciting, to be getting ready to spend the night in Sam's king bed. She couldn't wait to kiss him, and be held by him again. She wanted him - badly - but she also didn't want to jump any faster than things were already moving. This was certainly no time to be foolish.

In the hallway, the running water had stopped, and so had the pattering of bare feet on the tiles. She padded out herself, being cognizant to shut her door lest one of the boys wake early in the morning, and followed the narrow beam of soft light at the end of the hall. Sam was up and waiting for her.

Chapter 13

Sam turned around from turning down the covers when Charlie gave a quiet knock and slipped in. He was already in his pajamas; pants and a t-shirt, but she looked soft. It wasn't as if he hadn't seen her in her pj's before, but knowing that she'd be in his arms, wearing them, made the idea of nightclothes sensual and tactile, regardless of how covered up she was. He'd left on one lamp near the bed, and her skin glowed against the quiet pale creams and greys of her clothing.

Without waiting for her to say anything, he walked up to her and pulled her close, sighing into her neck.

"Oh my God." Her voice was a whisper as her body gave in to his, folding into the curves and hollows of his own. He kissed her collarbone, her shoulder through the fabric, and then up her jaw until he found her lips, holding her face in both of his hands. He kissed her gently at first, holding back his craving, but soon he couldn't stop and pause. He felt as though they'd always kissed, as if they belonged together here, in this room, in every moment of the day. His body was connected to hers, even when they were a room apart, or across the kitchen. He was aware of her at all times. Every time he met her eyes directly, he'd feel an excited, raw thrill in his gut. And now that they were together, alone, all that tautness relaxed and he could kiss her languidly, and then hungrily.

He didn't know how long they kissed, but they eventually ended up laying next to each other, arms loped around one another as the kisses became less frenzied. Sam ran his fingers through her fine hair, brushing it over her back, trailing a hand across her shoulder blades. She gave a soft breath, and ran a thumb along his lips. The light was still on in the room, casting fuzzy grey shadows in every curve of her face and along the harder edges of the furniture.

"Why can't you?" The question popped out, unbidden, and he hurried to explain further. "Have kids, that is. What is it?"

Her expression grew wistful, but she didn't seem as pained as he worried she might become at his wondering. Her eyes trailed down his chest and stomach, and then came up to meet his squarely.

"My eggs are bad. I mean, they're very poor quality. Nothing can change that, no fertility drugs, IVF, nothing. It's like...like as if a man was shooting blanks. My eggs are empty, if they come at all."

Her explanation was simple, distilled, plain. He felt a surge of pity for her, and then realized she didn't need any, that she was already full of sadness and his own wouldn't help matters. There was no answer to such a response, so he drew her close, snuggling her head under his chin. He felt her hand come across his belly, and then up his chest. It felt divine to touch her so freely; he suddenly wondered how he'd keep himself from jumping her once they had the house completely to themselves. He'd have to, he vowed. If he wanted to try and do this right, they'd have to be smart and wary, however badly they wanted to jump fully into something physical.

"Did you spend a lot of time with doctors?" he asked. Her inability to have children was such a yawning hole in her - it tainted her personality and made her who she was. He wanted to get the crux of it all, to figure how it had changed her, and likely had dissolved her marriage. The notion of being completely unable to have children made him founder. What would it be like, to be told he could never have made babies? The idea was foreign, impossible.

"Yes. Lots of specialists. We flew to several states, even, and I did so many tests... A doctor in Atlanta finally spelled it out for us. Peter was more crushed than I was, if that was possible."

"A man wants his own children," Sam said, knowing it sounded trite, and not sure if he should defend her ex. Not sure how he would react if it had been him. He liked to think he'd be supportive. That he would bolster her instead of falling to pieces himself.

"Oh yes. I don't blame him for that." Her response surprised him. He thought she'd be more bitter toward the man who had been so uncompromising. "I'm the one who failed him."

"Stop that." He half sat up, prompting her to shift away and sit too, facing him. Her face was empty of emotion, as if she accepted she was not enough, that she was less a person, and less a woman. It ate at Sam, and he was inherently irritated that she didn't see it the way he did. *Let me have the right words*, he begged the universe.

"You asked," she said, spreading her palms up. He grabbed them, and held her hands tightly, staring at her hard.

"Look." He paused, gathering his feelings about the matter, knowing that one wrongly placed syllable could shatter their friendship. "I know you aren't purposely dwelling in self loathing, but you'll never get past your divorce if you don't realize something very important."

She started to shake her head, and he knew what she was thinking. Every divorce, every relationship was different and had a different effect on each person involved. And every side of the divorce was felt and handled differently. He understood that, but that didn't change the deep issue he saw here. He released her fingers to put a hand on either of her shoulders.

"Charlotte." At his use of her full name, she faced him, realizing he was in utmost seriousness. "You need to realize it was Peter who failed you in this. He promised to love you through sickness and health. You can't mourn a love that..." He paused, thinking how he wanted to frame his feelings on what he thought he understood about her ex-husband. "When he gave up on you, when he didn't want your marriage to last because of this, you have to realize – *believe* – that his love for you wasn't strong to be begin with. If it was not your fertility, it would have eventually been something else. There was always going to be a catalyst with the same ending. It just happened to be this."

She was staring at him, and he suddenly wondered if he'd been too forward. They'd only known each other a week, and maybe he was being too pushy. But her self-worthlessness was apparent to him, never more so when they talked about her ex, and Sam prudent and shrewd enough to know they needed to get over this hurdle if they were ever going to try and work as a couple. Charlie would never be able to really care for him, or give their relationship a full chance, if she didn't start to feel herself worthy of unconstrained, unconditional affection, through and through.

Without warning, tears spilled from her eyes, and she covered her face with her hands, silent sobs wrenching from her gut. Sam was aghast. He hadn't meant to make her cry, and this was a far sight from the romantic night of kissing he'd been fantasizing about all day. She was holding in the deepest of her cries, as if purposefully trying to stay quiet for the sake of his kids, and he was overwhelmed with her, unsure what to make of this. Was she dealing with the same feelings that had plagued her for years in her marriage and divorce? Were these cleansing tears? Would she ever get over her sadness? He didn't give a damn that she couldn't have kids - in fact, having a baby at his age seemed a bit daunting anyway. She had nothing to fear from him. And he was, in a way, glad he didn't have to endure the test of loving a woman through fertility issues. He could care for her without the pressures of starting a family.

"Charlie, I'm sorry," he murmured, pulling her close. "I'm sorry."

She shook her head against his shoulder, one hand still covering her eyes. He held her tight, feeling the sobs convulse her, her breath coming short and shaking. It felt like forever, and guilt started to eat at him, but thankfully she pulled back after only a minute or two and finally removed her hands from her face. Her skin, even under the deep tan, was blotched and stained with red. He reached forward, taking her head in his hands, and kissed her forehead, then her mouth, tasting the salt of her tears. He felt awful, but they were words that needed to be said, and earlier was always better. He'd learned that the hard way.

"Don't be sorry. That's the most wonderful thing anyone has said to me in a long time."

Her confession drew him up. "You can't be serious."

"You know how it is. Everyone dances around the divorce topic, and unless you pay for a shrink, no one ever is quite so bald about the heart of the issues. You've...well, it's something to really think about, but my God. You've just given me back a piece of myself."

He wouldn't put it that way. He'd only been honest - something they'd promised each other to be. It was refreshing to know his honesty had not gotten him into too much trouble, though it definitely broke the mood. Sam pulled her close again, and she curled around so they laid, spooning platonically, as they drifted off to sleep.

When he woke in the morning, they were still in the same position as when he'd fallen asleep. Charlie was breathing lightly, and in the dim light, he went up on an elbow and gazed down at her. She was classically pretty, but not what anyone would call drop dead gorgeous. He personally considered her a bit of a knock out, but that was probably because he knew her, and her personality stood out bold and bright in his mind.

As he looked at her, he lazily thought about the day. Today he had his coffee appointment with his investment banker, then they'd head to the market for food, and Conner's little love interest was coming over tonight. Crap. He still needed to do the whole birds and bees conversation with his son. That was not something he was looking forward to doing. Maybe he should wait and see how everything lined up tonight - if things were pretty young and innocent, he'd wait.

Oh…who was he fooling? Boys were boys. He remembered being almost thirteen. Girls had been mystical, sexy, exciting and one never admitted to knowing less than what one did. No. He'd have to chat this week. Maybe Charlie would give him ideas on how to broach the subject.

Sam stared at her as the sun crept into the bedroom. She'd become such an integral part of their lives so fast. How would he talk to his boys once she was gone? Get them to admit their feelings? Do the same chores around the house with such ease? He felt panicked at her leaving tomorrow, but he knew she was right. He did need the time with the boys alone, but he wasn't looking forward to seeing her leave for a week.

She sighed, half stirring, and he felt himself ache with her nearness. Her body was warm in the morning, still soft. He couldn't believe he'd managed to spend the night without waking often to touch her. How easy it was, to be with her.

"Oh…" She woke with another sigh, her eyes opening, then closing before opening again. His arms instinctively tightened around her, and she gave a small smile before turning to face him, her hands coming up to cradle his face, with its day-old stubble already grown. "Good morning, Sam."

"Hi," he managed. He hadn't had a woman in bed for quite a few years. Kids did that. There wasn't much time for dating, not that he actively looked for it, and he was never really into the full intimacy anyway. Charlie had seamlessly fallen into place, which was what he'd always told himself he'd look for: something – some*one* – that would not disrupt the perfect little solace he'd created out on the ranch after his divorce. Having her here, close, in his sheets, was such a cozy tableaux that he didn't want it to end.

"How did you sleep?" Her voice was muddled with morning.

"Wonderfully," he admitted, and brought her tighter. "Though waking up was better."

"You think?" She pushed closer, her breasts grazing his chest, and the nearness of her thighs was enough to arouse him in the morning. He shifted away, not wanting her to get the wrong idea, but he forgot that Charlie'd been married a long time and wasn't anywhere obtuse where men were concerned. She got a crazy little half smile on her face and wiggled closer to kiss him.

He couldn't help giving a small moan of pleasure, and when she broke away after only a moment or two he didn't let her go. "You can't do that to a guy and leave him hanging. I'd like a proper good morning kiss, if you please."

"Sam!" She actually giggled, and he playfully tackled her back down for a deeper kiss, where her legs somehow got intertwined with his, his hand went up her shirt to caress a bra-clad breast, and he forgot all about shielding her from his erection in the heat of their embrace.

It was the obvious slam of a door down the hall opening up that stopped them this time, and she gazed up at him from the tousled sheet. Could he classify her gaze as fond? Loving? Wistful? He gave a rueful laugh, taking care to be extra quiet. "Damn. Kids are up."

She reached up to brush his face. He wondered if he was as flushed with desire as he felt. She looked utterly kissable again, but he knew their moment was over. Thankfully the day's activities would keep him from daydreaming too much, though he knew he'd be rewinding these snippets of sensuality all day in his mind.

"There's the real wake-up call. Time for me to sneak back to my room, or the bathroom at the very least."

"Who cares if they catch you?" he found himself saying stoically. He was already planning his life with her in it as his girlfriend, and his sons were old enough - at least Conner was - to understand how some of this all worked. They lived in reality, and he wasn't going to insult their intelligence about him and Charlie for too long anyway. He appreciated that she wanted to be careful about their activities, at least this early on, but there was no denying the fact that at some point he'd have to talk to his sons about his relationship. Hmm...maybe he could use some of what was going on between him and Charlie as a way to explain things to Conner.

"You really wouldn't mind?" She sat up, and straightened her light sweater.

"Well, maybe Cole we could wait a bit to tell."

"You go check first then - make sure the coast is clear."

Sam stared at her, surprised at the amount of affection he felt welling up for her. This could really be something, if they let it grow. He got up, but then thought better of it, and bent to kiss her swiftly. "It's kind of like being naughty teenagers again ourselves, sneaking around the parents."

Charlie gave a choked chortle as he moved out to the hallway to make sure she could get out safely, and found himself grinning, as if he'd done more than sleep next to her all night.

Chapter 14

It was Friday. Charlie couldn't believe how long the week had dragged since Sunday morning, when she'd taken her leave of Sam and the boys. Cole had given her a hug, and Conner a wave and a grin. The night of his girl crush had gone over smashingly successful. They'd ate, cleaned up as a group, and played board games until her parents came to pick her up. Shelly was cute, pert, with freckles and innocence. Cole and his friend had joined in cluelessly, and Conner had seemed more at ease with Charlie ever since. She felt a bit awful leaving when things were going so well.

Charlie wondered if Sam ever got around to having that "birds and bees" discussion with Conner. She found herself wondering about all three boys constantly, as she wandered north up California's interior, stopping aimlessly at wineries. She took a rental horse ride through vineyards at one, and all she could think about was riding out with Sam on his horses.

Somehow, somewhere, she realized that she had it bad. That the few nights they'd spent kissing and sleeping next to one another were not enough, that she needed more of him. More kisses? Of course. More of...*him*? His steadiness? His calmness? His humanness? Her mind would go haywire if she really started to think what it could all mean. Had she really found someone she felt fulfilled with? She'd thought it was over after Peter, but then again, she'd felt over about herself then too.

Sam had changed that. She spent the time alone to mull about what he'd said to her last week. As she sampled wines, took a bottle to sip back to her bed and breakfast, or ate simple meals out, she thought about his words the first night they'd laid together. He was likely right. Perhaps Peter had not really loved her enough to see their marriage through the thicks and thins of their vows. Something, somewhere, would have driven them apart. Perhaps it would have been their work, or their interests, or children themselves had they come along. All Charlie had known was that she couldn't have babies, and then Peter had looked elsewhere for his perfectly planned life.

If she stayed off social media, she felt better about herself. She couldn't be tempted to check his profile, to stare at photos of him with her, of their flushed cheeks, the crumpled racing bibs crushed between them. If she stopped checking Instagram, she wouldn't see the elegantly manicured salads he was making, the delicately balanced diet and morning sunrise runs.

Charlie'd gone along with it all. She did like to run. And she did like to eat well; living in California made it next to impossible to ignore the food passions that swept the nation. Afterwards, when Peter had found a replacement...a very possibly fertile replacement...she had forced herself to stay with the habits that she had curated during her marriage.

But sometimes it was divine to eat pasta. She might skip a run some mornings. And she filtered and wondered over Sam's declaration that Peter wasn't good enough for her. That he had failed her. The concept was novel. Charlie had never spun the argument the other way. She had always focused on how she had failed to live up to Peter's expectations and hopes and dreams. Even though it was something completely out of her control, she felt that she had done wrong, that he was within some sort of twisted right to find a woman who could give him the family he so desperately desired to put his life in order.

But Sam thought otherwise. He didn't believe she should beat herself up about not being good enough. He believed that *Peter* had not been good enough.

She felt herself come back into her own, slowly, nearly imperceptibly. The time apart from Sam was good for reflecting. She could digest her past a bit in the light of a future that gleamed with possibilities. After calling into Clear Studios, talking to Amanda about where things sat, she did the math and realized she could take the next nine weeks off yet without too many pattering pangs of guilt. The reasons rained around her whenever she weighed them. Besides, she needed the breather and she craved the time with Sam. After that, they'd have to talk about the next steps, and time would wear them, and see where they really wanted everything to go. She didn't feel panicked about it, but was anxious to see what might really happen between them.

God, she missed him, and even missed the boys. She was looking forward to heading over to the ranch tomorrow morning, even though she'd arrive after the kids had already been returned to their mother. They'd be back the following weekend, and maybe even excited to see her. She could only hope she'd left a good enough impression with them, and then wondered in the same moment what they might end up telling Sam's ex. Well, nothing to be done.

As she checked in to her last bed and breakfast, her phone beeped. Sam. They texted maybe once a day, usually to say good night. The abstinence from long phone calls was unspoken. They were purposefully putting time and distance between each other, and neither wanted to be the one to violate. She looked over at her phone screen. This was early for him.

cant wait to see you

She smiled to herself as she read the message. The feeling was mutual, and she responded in kind. As she let herself into the small little room, she breathed in the scent of old floors, earth and flowers. Because she finally had someone in her life again, she didn't feel so lonely doing this little trip up and down the wine country. It was refreshing, and if she saw something fun and unique enough to tell him, she'd usually text him a photo. He would always respond with enthusiasm, and it was enough that she could share her trip.

The phone chimed again. *i miss you, come early.*

The sentimental side was a touch unusual, but she was glad he was so forthright. She pulled up the screen as she flopped on the bed.

Can I call? She was finally ready to break the taboo and hear his voice.

In answer, the phone began to ring, and she took the call with a grin. "Hey."

"Hey." His voice sounded tinnier on the line, but there was utmost happiness in the tone. "What's up?"

"Oh..."she trailed off. She didn't know really why she asked to call, only that a text message hadn't felt enough to connect. "Wanted to hear your voice."

"Did you?"

"How quiet is it there now?"

"Well, the boys have been gone for roughly an hour, and I'm bored stiff already."

"I find that hard to believe."

"You're right," he admitted, and she could hear the contentment in the warmth of his rumbly timbre. "I have a ton of chores to do. Might not get them all done in time, even."

"Well, don't rush them for me. I'll help you when I get in tomorrow."

"What time?" he didn't even bother to mask his eagerness, and she felt herself fill with excitement and wonderment. Even with time to think, he'd take her yet; he wanted to be with her too. She felt giddiness well inside her, even though she tried to push and shove and batter it down. The hopeful happiness clenched at her stomach and tickled and cracked along her nerves.

"Not soon enough," she laughed easily. "But early, I should think. After my morning run."

"I'll be up," he promised. "I can't wait."

When they hung up, all Charlie could do was continue to lay on the borrowed bed and think about him. She desired him. When she thought about kissing him, she got hot, flustered, desirous. They'd be together, alone, most every day, even once she started working again, and with only brief interludes of the boys around. How would she possibly stop from giving in completely? They'd end up in bed together, she knew this. The question was how soon? And how soon did she want it?

Funny how after marriage, the taboo of sex went away. She'd been careful about intimacy before Peter, as if some vestiges of childhood rules held her from diving into any type of explicit promiscuity. Now, though, she knew what she was missing. She knew that she could have sex with Sam and it wouldn't have to be tightly personal or last forever. There was both freedom and safety in the notion, and while she didn't want sex to change what was churning and growing between them, the attraction between them sat heavy and physical in her empty womb.

Charlie barely slept. Half-formed thoughts swirled in the twilight of sleep. When she woke early, she did a long run, trying to put on miles so she did not hit the road at an ungodly time and turn up at Sam's in the wee hours. She knew he didn't lay in bed, that he was often up with the horses, the ranch chores, the other little things that came in running a small vineyard. But still, there was something to be said about not being overtly eager.

She'd gone up the middle of the state and doubled back, so that she was near enough that the drive was about an hour. Taking Sam's advice, she'd hit up the area north, trying all the tiny little 'garagiste' wines and spending some time in Paso Robles. It had been fun, but she decided the next time she returned she wanted him to join her. There was nothing exciting about sampling wines and have no one to gush to about them.

As she pulled up the long driveway and spotted his jeep, her heart gave a huge lurch, battering and bouncing in her chest. What should she do? Run to him? Be casual? Kiss him? She found herself still nursing insecurities, but now they didn't stem so much from self worth as much as playing this new relationship cool.

At the sound of her car door, she saw him emerge from the barn, looking already a bit rough around the edges. He must have been in the vineyard early, finishing any pruning and getting ready for the bit of harvest he'd planned.

His face lit up at the sight of her, and he walked quickly up the pathway. She wondered if she looked as delighted as he did; she felt that way, at least.

And then suddenly it was as if she never had to doubt what to do with Sam, because it fell into place. His arms shot out and pulled her tight, and she wrapped him up into a hug, their faces buried in each other's shoulders. It was a bear hug, full body impact, and Charlie breathed in his scent, accented with the smell of earth and wet greenery from the vines.

"Wow. I missed you," he said, pulling away with a wince. She checked at his grimace.

"What?"

"I did, I missed you!"

She shook her head. "Not that, I believe you about that. I mean...are you ok?" She didn't think she'd squeezed him quite that tightly.

"Nothing, just a little stomach twinge. Not used to giving out big hugs and all," he said lightly, pulling her close again, but more gingerly this time. She frowned a bit, but then he chased away every other thought in her mind by bending forward and kissing her hard.

It blew her way, his kisses. They were all encompassing, overpowering, and she almost wondered if they could make her pass out sometimes. She brought her hands to his face, where the sheen of sweat covered his skin and pulled away abruptly. He gave her a strange look, perhaps wondering why she had stopped their kiss, but gave another grimace, as if his body was tense.

"Sam," she couldn't help but feel worried. "Are you sure you're alright?"

He pulled his hands from her waist and rubbed his gut and chest. Her head immediately went to his heart - *what were the symptoms of a heart attack again?* She couldn't remember. One look at his ashen face though and she jumped into action.

"Come on – inside, now."

She got him into the house without a protest and bade him sit on the couch. She'd imagined walking in and feeling happy to be back in the huge cavern of the space, the coolness of wood mixed with modernity, but instead she was only a bit frantic. What if something was truly wrong? What would she do? How could she cope? Pouring a glass of water and taking it to him, where he sat, mindlessly rocking slightly, she started to think this wasn't a heart attack. That didn't make her panic any less. What was going on?

"Sam, honey," she put a hand over his. "What is it?"

"I'm all tensed up, Charlie," he said, and his voice sounded tight, breathless. "It came on so quick, just now. I can't..." he paused, trying to get in air, and his pale face started to turn reddish, as if he couldn't breathe properly.

She gripped his hand and then stood. "Let me go out to the car and get my phone. We have to call someone."

Sam shook his head and pointed to the counter, where she saw his own cell sitting on the cement kitchen island. The fact that he didn't want her to leave him made her even more scared. He gasped out his password and she poked the screen, pressing overly hard to ensure the numbers stuck.

"I'm calling the hospital," she specified as she dialed. The nurse who took intake calls took in the initial information speedily, asking for Sam's weight, age and condition. It wasn't necessarily the ideal way to find out those kinds of stats about a boyfriend, but Charlie didn't give a damn.

"Yes, he's wheezing. Yes, and light-headed too," she looked to him for confirmation. He nodded very slightly.

"Yes. And rocking. Mmm...No, no pain in the arm."

"Charlie – " She glanced over to him. He was indeed gripping his arm, but at the same time she saw the red mark on his skin. That was no heart attack.

"Ma'am? It sounds as though Mr. Gaffney was probably bitten."

"Bitten?"

"By a widow or a recluse. Can you have the spider? It helps to know which species bit him."

"What?" The notion hadn't even crossed her mind, but she suddenly realized it had probably happened in

234

the vineyard, or more specifically, in the barn somewhere.

"The spider. The folks in the ER will want to see it if at all possible."

"No. That is to say, we didn't even think of a spider until just now. Do you need to send an ambulance?"

"No ma'am." The nurse was crisp, certain. "Just bring him into the ER immediately, and put an ice pack on while on your way. The nearest hospital to your location, according to the GPS, is a good ten miles."

"Okay."

She shut off the phone and turned to Sam, who was looking ashen again.

"Sam..."

"I heard," he gasped. "Spider. Probably from the barn - I was cleaning."

"We've got to go in to the ER."

He looked waxen. "I think I'm going to throw up," he managed hoarsely, before losing his breakfast on the hardwood floor around the coffee table. He didn't look any better afterwards, and she suddenly feared worse, that he might be having an allergic reaction to the bite, or something along those lines. Her mind raced. She grabbed the ice pack from the freezer and a towel to wrap it in. Stepping over the gobby, watery puddle, she hauled him up.

"We have to take you to the emergency room. Do you have your wallet?"

"Back pocket," he rasped. She was glad he was coherent.

"Okay, off to my car."

"What if I get sick again? Oh Jesus, Charlie, I've gotta clean that - "

"Forget it, I'll do it later. Come on, Sam, please." She urged him, grabbing his house keys to lock up behind them. She was at once thankful for her familiarity with him and his belongings. She didn't even want to think about what would have happened if she wasn't there. An ambulance, she reminded herself. They'd have sent one.

He got in stiffly, and she plugged the hospital information into her car's GPS as fast as she could, sneaking glances at him all the time. Sam did not look good, as if he'd been hit with a horrible bout of the flu. While driving, they located the bite location exactly, a red searing under the skin along the underside of his right arm. He pressed the ice to it, lips tight, and laid his head back on the seat.

"Hold on, babe," she muttered, and drove them off as fast as she dared. She wondered if she'd get a speeding ticket if she pushed limits and decided she didn't give a damn, and she'd make any officer give them an escort to the ER anyway.

But they didn't get pulled over, and suddenly they arrived. Admittance was ready for them, thanks to the 911 dispatcher calling in ahead of time.

"Sam Gaffney," Sam stated, leaning heavily on the counter. He was still sweating heavily, and breathing hard. She took his hand, surprised at the rigidity in the fingers. Charlie didn't have much for run ins with black widow spiders, especially since heading into LA to live, but she had a vague recollection of what could happen from her childhood in northern California.

"And you are?" The admittance nurse looked over her glasses at Charlie, who focused but was at loss for words. She wasn't family.

"Charlotte Paggo." Her voice sounded as though her name was a question.

"My girlfriend," Sam finished, looking at the nurse defiantly, who didn't actually seem to care, just wrote up her name on a visitor's badge.

"Thank you, head on in with the nurse." The woman in scrubs behind the desk came around to usher them through the doors with a clinical, iodine whoosh. They were taken to a small room, and he was told to lay down. The nurse checked under the ice, re-asked the same vital questions, and through it all, Charlie was getting more and more anxious. Finally, she exploded.

"I'm sorry. Excuse me. I'm new at this bite thing. But shouldn't someone be just…making him feel better?"

The nurse gave her an annoyed glance, and then looked back at Sam. Charlie ground her back teeth. She detested being given the run-around by hospital staff. But then, she was heavily biased against most things medical.

"Did you happen to get the spider?"

"No. Didn't even realize I'd got bit." He wiped his face, and Charlie went to his side, took his hand again, and noticed a flush along his neck.

"Well, you've got a fever and your blood pressure is up. The doc will check on you in a bit, not sure if we need the antivenin, but maybe some pain killers for a few weeks."

She walked out briskly, leaving Charlie feeling winded. Sam griped her hand and she glanced down at him. He looked pained.

"Thanks for trying to stick up for me," he rasped.

"Where does it hurt?"

"Well, the bite area itself is pretty awful," he admitted. "But it's my chest - all tight, and my stomach, and all my muscles ache. I wouldn't recommend this."

"Oh darling," She couldn't help the endearment, and pushed back his hair from his forehead, where the sheen of heavy sweat still laid.

He smiled at her. "Sorry. I'd planned a better day."

"Well, we're together at least," she soothed. "At least you weren't alone to drive yourself here."

His response was cut short when the doctor walked in, staring at the chart. She flipped the paperwork on the counter and washed her hands.

"Hi Sam, I'm Doctor Schinel. So you've had a widow bite?"

"So they tell me."

"Let's take a look at the bite location," She propped dark glasses on her nose and bent over Sam's arm. Charlie watched, backing up against the wall until the inspection and slew of questions was over again. Being in a doctor's presence that was not about her fertility was odd - so many times in the past she'd been under the lights for herself. Strangely, now that that part of her past was gone, it was harder not being able to do much for Sam. Is this how Peter had always felt? Every time?

"Okay, Sam." The doctor pulled the clipboard toward her. "You've got the nausea, sweating and breathing we usually see. Be thankful there's no tremors. We'll have to watch the blood pressure and fever." She also looked over her glasses at Charlie, but her demeanor was friendly.

"Can you monitor his temp? Take it about once every few hours and make sure it goes down in a day or so. If not, call us back."

Charlie nodded, relieved to have a task and be included. The doctor didn't stop there. "You'll be staying with Sam?"

"Yup." Sam had enough gumption to say that with conviction, and reached for Charlie's hand again.

"So I'd expect the pain around the bite to last another seven to twelve hours, but some of the symptoms may continue for quite a few days, possibly weeks."

"Like what?"

"Oh, the nausea, the sweating should be gone in a day or three. We'll want to see you back in two weeks to check the blood pressure. If breathing gets harder, or doesn't get better in two days, we want to know. And if the pain doesn't get progressively better, starting tomorrow, we'll get you some muscle relaxers. In the meantime, some basic prescription painkillers is a good place to start."

She jotted down a few things, and then handed Charlie the prescriptions.

"Okay?"

"Thanks Doctor Schinel," she managed, and the doctor gave her a brief, clinical nod and smile before walking out.

She turned to Sam, who was carefully, gingerly getting into a seated position on the bed. He managed a wane grin.

"Romantic, ain't I?"

She went to sit next to him. Now that they had medicine and solutions, she felt herself a bit shaky, as if the adrenaline was thrusting itself out of her pores.

"Most definitely," she said, touching his leg. "Let's get you home."

He wasn't any better, really - still sweating, breathing hard, and faint with pain. Thankfully, they got the prescriptions quickly, and she had him take them down on their way back to the ranch.

Glancing at him often, she found her heart pounding with worry and thankfulness that she was able to be there with him, and take care of him. He looked awful, and the heavy sweat had soaked through his shirt.

"Let's get you to bed." It was just hitting midday, but that didn't mean he should push through the day. Plus, she wagered once the pain pill hit, he'd be out cold.

She parked, got him out and into the house again without issue. As they hobbled past the great room, the smell of the mess on the floor hit them, and Sam groaned.

"Ah, shit. I forgot about that. I'll -."

"You'll get into bed. I can clean up a bit of puke," she said firmly. His bedroom was familiar, filled with his scent. She'd forgotten about how cozy the large bed was, even in the steel and black of the house decor. He sat on the edge and popped his shoes off with his toes so that he didn't have to bother bending to take them off.

"Your shirt too, Sam, you've soaked it," she said, and then moved to unbutton it without waiting for his response, automatically taking over the situation, filling the role of caretaker without thought. Under his shirt, his skin was flushed and hot, but solid and tanned. Even with him ill and clenching in pain, she still fought her attraction.

"How's the pain?"

"Better already," he said, but laid down without any further argument. "I'm so sorry, Charlie."

"What for?" she was picking up his shoes and bundling his shirt for laundry.

"I'd had all kinds of great ideas, some wine chilling for tonight's supper, and now it'll take days for me to recover. Charlie - it's not what I'd planned for us."

"Sam," she smoothed his hair back again, and used his shirt to wipe down his brow a bit. "I'm going to be here as long as I can - at least the next nine or ten weeks. We'll have time."

His eyes lit up, even with the pain and fever. "Really? You haven't changed your mind?"

"That's my plan, at least," she put lightly, bent to kiss his forehead and stood quickly. "Now try and sleep a bit. I'm sure those painkillers are making you drowsy."

She went back out, tossing his things in the laundry and foyer closet, and then set about cleaning the mess on the floor. Two scrubs of bleach, soap and water later, and she thought she had it all taken care of. It was now middle of the afternoon, and she realized that they would definitely not be making it to Tom's party. She wondered if she should call.

Going to the bedroom, she saw Sam sprawled out, sleeping heavily. Well, she was not a long term girlfriend - she couldn't go to his phone and find Tom's number and ring him to let him know.

Granted, he'd given her his password. The idea of looking through his phone felt sacrilegious and a breech of his trust. She decided against it. Tom would just have to deal with two no-shows.

Sam looked peaceful, at least, and she was glad he could sleep with all the tensing of his muscles. As her eyes traveled over his back, and the jeans he still wore, she felt herself get a bit teary. She'd missed the intimacy of having another in her life, even with all the nitty gritty that came with it. This wasn't the welcome she'd envisioned either, but she'd take it. Being with him was enough.

Chapter 15

Sam woke up and stretched, wincing only slightly. It'd been three days since the spider bite and he was finally feeling more himself. At least he hadn't puked again. *God, that had been awful.* He glanced around. Charlie had gotten him in shorts and a t-shirt eventually, and he'd been sleeping in that and lounging around in them for the past two days. Likely he stunk. He sighed, glad the nausea was gone, and the sweating too. The fever had receded, and he figured the blood pressure had to have gone down. They'd know next week. In the meantime, the pain in his chest and his breathing was better. If he was truthful, he was not back to normal completely. But he'd take it over what he'd been feeling the past 48 hours.

He got up and wandered into the hallway. Charlie's bedroom door was wide open, and he peered in. She was curled onto the far side of the bed, half covered with a sheet. Sam still kicked himself for the whole episode. What were the odds he'd gotten bit? He knew better than to poke around the old buildings without a long-sleeved shirt, and he felt foolish and vulnerable. How was he supposed to woo Charlie while she was in his house if all she did was take care of him and his ranch? How long would he feel like crap?

The great room was cool, the morning light dim. She'd kept on one of the soft lights in the ceiling and he shut it off. The kitchen was shining, clean, even though she'd been bringing him meals in bed and looking after herself. She'd kept him abreast of the animals too - he was thankful she'd helped him let out the horses a few times so she knew how to keep them fed, watered and happy. She even had caught the spider they suspected had caused the whole issue, tucked in a corner of the barn where some of the tools were kept. That was in a small mason vessel on the kitchen table, busily trying to spin a web onto the glass walls it was in. He picked up the jar and peered at it. It was almost like a trophy. *Damn thing.*

"Hey. I thought I heard you."

Charlie was up, and she was watching him from the threshold of the hallway, sizing him up from across the space. She looked tanner than he remembered, now that he could really see her, and the pale color of her pajamas accented it. He put the spider down and went over to the coffee maker.

"I could use some. You?"

"Absolutely." She followed him over and went to get out the coffee cups. He made the brew stronger, and then went over to pull out toast and fruit. She'd kept the fridge stocked up, going to the farmers market and making hearty pastas. Any longer of laying around in bed, and he'd need to start going with her on those morning runs to take off the extra squeeze around his middle.

"How are you feeling?" she asked him, as she started to wash berries.

He shrugged. "Still a bit stiff and painful. I stopped taking the pain meds, but I think I should take a half a pill."

"Sam." She stopped the water and looked at him seriously. "Take it easy on yourself."

"I will," he put lightly, but in truth he was so anxious to get back to normal, and start to enjoy her stay. Nine didn't seem like that long of a time to have her on his property. He wanted to relish every bit of it. As he pulled open the doorway to the patio, and the rush of cool air spilled into the house, he felt himself shiver.

"Careful." Charlie was at his side, a coffee cup in hand. "I don't want you to overwork your muscles."

"Oh, I'll be fine," he brushed off her worry, but took the hot coffee gratefully. He sat down on the cushions, and gazed out at the morning on his property. Everything looked the same, but he still felt his vision go soft and woozy. Not that he'd admit it.

"I'll bring out the toast and things." She squeezed his shoulders and disappeared into the kitchen once more. He heard the homey sounds of her tinkering around in the sink, and felt a bit at peace, as if everything was right and organized. He shivered again, and rubbed his hands around the mug. He still felt lethargic, but he was feeling loads better than earlier in the weekend.

"Here we are." Charlie brought things out on a tray; she was forever finding things in the kitchen that he'd forgotten he owned. "So, did you..."

He looked up as she trailed off, staring at him. Suppressing another shiver in the chill morning, he gave her a wan smile, wishing he could have his energy back.

"Sam, you look terrible. Let's get you back in before you get a fever again or something."

He shook his head, determined to enjoy the morning with her. "I'm fine."

"You're literally shaking, babe. Get up."

He could tell she was worried, and didn't like making her upset, so he stood at her insistent pull on his upper arm. As he stood, he stumbled, feeling like an idiot, but the shakes didn't seem to stop. It hadn't seemed that cold outside. *What the hell?*

She propelled him back into his rumpled bed, and he laid down before the room could spin any more. He heard her coming back in and opened his eyes. She had the breakfast tray balanced with their coffee and a little smile on her face.

"Breakfast in bed instead, how about?"

He propped up pillows and waited for her to come around and join him. The toast was a bit cold, but it was still cozy and fun, and he so appreciated her company and her companionship during this whole silly ordeal. Who knew how much a spider bite could knock him down?

"That sounds even better."

251

It was a bit of a chore to be chipper, but he did it for her. Not even to keep up appearances, but to try and make her stay worthwhile. He didn't think she'd be the type to run off if things weren't going perfectly, but who wanted a vacation taking care of a new but sickly boyfriend?

"I um. I was reading *Food and Wine* magazine," she offered, trying to pull him into conversation. He felt the familiar prick of excitement at her words, thinking of what he wanted to do with the grapes in a few weeks.

"Yes?"

"They did some article on Riojas. Mixing tempranillo, graciano and garnacha. Don't you have some of that in the cellar?"

"No," he shook his head. He tried to wink at her, but the effort to be very light was too much. "I have grenache."

"It's different? They all sound the same," she admitted, smiling at him as if she was relieved he was talking. Well, he hadn't been very chatty, he knew that much.

"Yeah, they do," he put down the last of his toast. She picked up the edge of his crust and started to eat it, the easy comfortableness between them settling and swirling around them. "It's the same grape, just a different way of pronouncing it depending on where you live. Garnacha is what they call it in Spain, where it is grown in a different climate and soil, so some might argue it's a slightly differently composed grape than the Grenache. Grenache is French and American."

She shook her head. "I feel like I know nothing when it comes to wine."

Sam laid his head back against the headboard. "You know more than you realize."

She wiped her mouth of crumbs, and picked up the coffee, pulling up her knees. "You're feeling better then, at least in bed?"

"Oh yeah," he said, and took her hand. "Charlie. Thank you for everything."

"Call it pay back for taking me under your wing to begin with," she said gently, and looked up at him. She frowned, and he wondered what was wrong.

"You look a bit feverish. I wonder..." She got up and took the tray up, leaving him with his coffee. "I'll be back."

He laid back against the headboard and pillows once more, and closed his eyes. These symptoms would have to go away sometime.

Eventually, she was back, still in her pajamas, her phone cradled in her ear, and a box of over the counter meds in her hand.

"Uh huh. Okay. Hold on." She looked at him. "I'm on the phone with Doctor Schinel's nurse. They think you might be having a bit of an allergic reaction."

He was surprised she'd even bothered to call the hospital, and appreciation flooded through him again. She cared enough about him to worry, to research. She disappeared, finishing the conversation in the hall before coming back in with a water glass and Benadryl.

"We're supposed to try this and then monitor your breathing and heart rate. You aren't feeling short of breath yet again, are you?"

Sam thought about his morning. It wasn't any worse than yesterday, so he shook his head. She sat next to him on the side of the bed and handed him the medication, as well as the ones from the doctor again. "Take the pain meds, see if they make a difference, okay?"

He sighed, but there was definitely a part of him that liked being nursed by her. It was a welcome thing, a change of always being in charge and managing the place. Not that he was in need of relaxation, but he liked not having to worry of the next meal, or the chores for a few days. He did as she asked, and then closed his eyes. He was still a bit tired, and wondered if he was younger if he would not have been so struck down. Maybe his age was catching up with him.

"I'm going to hang out in the kitchen and read so you can sleep...will you be alright? I'll have my phone. Don't get up to get me."

Sam nodded and heard her leave and shut the bedroom door behind her. He drifted to sleep for a bit, but woke almost immediately. He wasn't so tired, and the medicine was really starting to help. Sitting up, he looked at his crumpled, crumb-crusted t-shirt and thought about cleaning up. Did he have enough energy to strip the sheets off? That seemed a bit too much. So he took a hot shower, and went back into bed to read the news on the computer. Outside the bedroom, the patio doors slid open.

Charlie came back to check on him later than he expected, looking a bit worn. He felt another stab of guilt. She was supposed to be on sabbatical and taking a break from life, but instead she was caring for an invalid, managing horses, a ranch, vineyard watering and meals for two. He thought about when she'd been gone, he had daydreamed of kissing her, and in the hopes that things might go a step or two further, he'd gone ahead and bought a box of condoms, just in case. Now he wondered if their budding romance had come to a total halt, that the earthiness of taking care of him had stilted her feelings for him and he'd lost the chance to build something more than friendship with her.

He thought about her ash he followed her back into the kitchen, where she surveyed him in the brighter light.

"You look better!" she commented immediately, as she poured herself a tall clear glass of water. The relief on her face took away the worn worry she'd come in with. "I was hoping we wouldn't be looking at another trip to the ER or an ambulance."

"No - I took the medicines you gave me, you know. They've helped a ton. I think I'm even breathing better," he said truthfully, refolding the paper.

She drank the water hungrily, and poured another glass. He watched her drink heartily, and when she finished the second glass, she poured a third but left it, instead sinking to her elbows to look at him across the island.

"Sam...I'm so glad it wasn't any worse than this."

He looked at her fully, taking in the lines of her face, the angle of her chin and nose. There was something almost fragile about her still, to him. Maybe she'd always be someone he wanted to take care of, like he had the first time he'd met her. Maybe that was why this arrangement felt so strange to him - that she was taking care of him and his.

"Me too," he said, and reached for her hand. "But now that I'm feeling better, do you want to try and cook tonight together?"

She surveyed him critically. "Maybe tomorrow. I don't want you overdoing it."

"How about I just manage the grill, and I'll even promise to sit down while the meat cooks?"

She smiled at his familiar light humor, and gave a nod. "Fine. Deal. Now, I'm off put on long sleeves and such see to the grounds."

"I'll wait and come too, hon," he put lightly, and turned back to a newspaper. The medication really was working wonders, because he watched her out of the corner of his eye, her short runners skort skimming the backs of her thighs as she moved down the hall, and he felt the new desire well in his stomach. Oh yes, he was feeling much better if he had the energy to get a little amorous again.

She was back as he was pushing the paper into the recycling bin, looking refreshed - the haggard look she'd had in the earlier part of the day was gone - and he had a fleeting thought that she'd spent the entire morning worried sick about him. That maybe it wasn't just the managing of his household, but that she cared so much about him. He liked where that led - he wanted her to worry for him, just as he did often for her even on the littlest things.

"So the boys will be here this weekend?" she was asking, as they strolled back outside to the barn.

"Yup."

"Good. I can't wait to see them. Do you think they'll mind I'm here again?"

"Are you kidding?" He gave her a sideways glance, then reached across the distance and took her hand.

"The boys were better...happier even, when you were here. They missed you."

She gave a laugh. "I made them do chores, though."

"And they're all the better for it," he told her sincerely. "I mean it, Charlie. It's good for them to have you around."

"What do you think they told their mom?"

Sam hadn't actually thought that far ahead, but he wasn't surprised Charlie's thoughts had gone there. Women always tended to think of such things if memory served him right. "Probably that I have a girlfriend." He hoped that was still true. "Amy will be fine with it. Probably even happy for me."

Charlie didn't answer anything back, but they'd arrived at the horses so talk turned to the animals. They spent a lazy rest of the morning taking care of them and the barn. He was happy he could keep up with her, and only got short of breath towards midday, not that he'd admit it to her.

As they walked back to the house, he took her hand again. "Want some wine with lunch?"

She gave him an appraising look. "Are you sure you're up for it? All those pain meds?"

"I think they're wearing off a bit," he said, weighing his internal clock. At least, he thought that was true. "I'd rather have a bit of wine than take another batch of pills to take the edge off."

He thought about her lean legs in the jeans, the toned arms that were hidden by the light long sleeved shirt she wore, and he wished he could strip her of the clothing, see her in nothing but a bra and panties, touch her skin, and kiss her slowly. He wondered if she fantasized the same way.

"If you think you can..." she trailed off as they went into the kitchen. "How's BLT's and white wine?"

"Sounds very good," he said, and before she pulled away to start the meal, he kept her hand and yanked her into his arms.

"Sam!" Her exclamation was half finished before he kissed her. God, was it better because he was still floating on the end of medication, or because he'd missed it? Kissing her was actually a hot thing, underlaid with calmness. It was a fitting feeling, as if this was a good place to stay forever, with her in his arms, kissing her. He knew he wanted her, but even having her in his house was enough. If they spent the entire time together doing nothing but kissing, Sam would feel as though he was lucky. He didn't know how to put a word to it, but this was something better than he'd ever had in a woman, and certainly different than his marriage to Amy. At least, he thought so – if he went with his gut.

He kissed her long, unbridledly, tasting her, touching her slowly. There was no reason to rush it, and he didn't. The best part of the kiss was knowing he didn't need to do anything other than kiss her, that she would be happy just kissing him too. And under it all, he was relieved, for the second time this morning, in that she obviously still had feelings for him, because she kissed him back, and with a bit of abandon.

They ate, and he actually forgot about being under the weather. The wine helped. As they mingled over the bottle, he watched her caress her glass, the wetness of her fingers. Why was that so sensual? She'd muddled around her wine glass before; it was almost a nervous gesture or one she did without thinking. Suddenly, Sam realized the pain medication and alcohol were mixing a bit.

"Charlie..." he took her hand at the kitchen table. She looked up at him. They were finishing up. "You are really wonderful."

Her eyes narrowed. "Are you feeling okay?"

"Why?" he certainly felt the drink, which was a bit odd for him so soon in a bottle. But it felt deliciously warm compared to the chills of earlier, and he felt his body yearn to have her near. Still, Charlie was all practical.

"Because your eyes are a bit dilated, and you are flushed."

He didn't feel so awful, but he let her pull him up and back to the bedroom. The bed looked inviting, but not without her.

"I'll go back to bed, but not alone," he murmured, pulling her to his side, caressing her hip. He felt full of lust, surprisingly so, as if he could not crush her close enough.

"Samuel." She used his full name. "I knew the wine was too much."

He didn't care, and wound her into his arms. All he could think about was bed and wine and Charlie. It was so singular. Damn, those were mighty fine drugs!

"Just lay with me a little while, honey," he pleaded, yanking them onto the bedding, which was still unmade. He felt warm, but not feverish. He should have thought about wine earlier; any pain was gone from his chest and stomach. It was as if he was drunk for the first time in years.

"I shouldn't. You should sleep."

"Forget sleeping." He curled his body around hers, reveling having her in bed. "Let me kiss you more."

"Sam, seriously."

He could tell, through the haze, that she was still worried about him, perhaps especially so, now that he was enjoying her nearness. Her body was a bit tense on the bed, so he massaged her arm and stomach slowly. Her skin was softer than he remembered, smooth, almost hairless. He wanted to kiss it. He quickly lifted her shirt, revealing her stomach and the bottom of her peach and lace undergarments. How odd the smallest details were apparent to him.

"Sam, you should sleep, I mean it." Her voice was muffled by the pillows, and he leaned over, moving her fair hair and kissing her neck and ear and jaw.

"I don't want to sleep. I want to touch you," he admitted. "I want to have you nearby, and I want to kiss you, and maybe take off your bra." The disclosure felt good, freeing. "Maybe kiss your breasts."

"Dear God." She griped his hand, and the strength of her fingers jolted him, but not enough to stop him from kissing her shoulder through the fabric of her shirt. She tasted like…like sun, he decided. And tanned skin, if that was a taste. And of…coffee?

"I rather like this," he said, feeling heat fill his body even more. "I like being less restricted with you."

"You won't remember this once you wake up," she warned. "I'll go clean up."

"No," he demanded. The thought of her leaving his bed suddenly seemed awfully, incredibly impossible. "No, stay, please, Charlie."

"Kissing only then," she amended. "Just kiss me."

"Happy to," he said, and he flipped her over to meet him halfway, so he could kiss her hard, the way he wanted, and she let him, and even reacted to him, her hands roving his arms and back. He let his hand go under her shirt, under her bra, filling his palm with a breast. She moaned into his mouth, and he was undone. The bra came apart with a flick of his wrist - even after all this time, he could still remember how it was done.

"Sam," she broke off the kiss. "Careful."

"Just let me," he begged her, feeling himself be carried away on the booze and the drugs and enjoying the sexy bliss of it. "Let me love you."

She yanked away from him, as if he'd hurt her, and the motion was enough to jerk him into reality.

"Stop it, Sam." Her voice was rough. "I'm leaving."

She pulled herself away, her hands quickly finishing up her bra, and she fled out of the room. He flopped back again on the pillows. His head was swimming, but Sam knew he hadn't lied. He got it. He didn't play games, or wonder. His head and his heard were completely decisive about this one. He knew what he wanted and what he saw happening. He loved her. Shit. He loved Charlie. Charlotte Paggo. He loved her.

Chapter 16

The boys both gave her hugs when they arrived, and they spent the two and a half days playing outside with the horses, harvesting a few grapes for Sam's cellar, and playing bocce ball in one of the pastures with low grass. Sam was constantly worried about keeping them in long sleeves, as though he could ward off spider bites simply by covering all skin.

As they walked back toward the house, Cole went racing ahead with Sam trailing behind. Conner lagged back, and Charlie turned to wait for him. The mid-afternoon sun was warm, buttery yellow, and hit the highlights and ruddy flush of his cheeks. Having seen the handful of photos on Sam's dresser, Charlie knew he was starting to lose the soft roundness of twelve and was morphing into a streamlined, stretched teen.

"Alright, then?" she asked.

"Yeah…"

They walked side by side in silence for a beat, before Conner cleared his throat, no doubt to whisk away the newly developed pitchiness. "I…um. Shelly and I are…official?"

His reveal caught at her heart, and she wished she could pull him into a half-hug, or at least pat his shoulder, but instead she kept her voice neutral and her hands at her back. "Really? That's great."

"Yeah."

Conner wasn't one for many words, even now that he was comfortable with her. She had decided not to take it personally once she noticed how inarticulate he was with Sam too. Maybe he was more chatty with his friends, or maybe he was going to be the silent type. It was obvious he was sensitive, just like Cole, but his aged made things more difficult. The fact that he had decided to tell her a big piece of his personal life struck her hard.

"Well…that's cool." She would like to gush, but knew innately that it would embarrass him.

They caught up with Sam and Cole on the edge of the yard. Sam had recovered well quickly after the episode in the bedroom. He'd passed out a bit afterwards, and she checked on him often to make sure he was breathing fine, but his body seemed to have finally managed to shake the poison. In the afternoon, the grey in his hair sparkled, and the warm glow around his eyes matched the roses under his cheekbones.

"I'm almost out of breath from the walk," he chuckled as they turned together to go inside. "I think I'm really officially going to seed."

"There's a remedy for that," she teased. It had become a bit of a joke between them – how she ran and he wanted to...but never did. He claimed he'd slow her down. She pushed that it was worth going slow if it meant having a running partner, but it was a consistent stalemate. She knew running was not Sam's thing, and to be honest, it didn't bother her one iota that he wasn't a fitness fanatic.

"Dad, can we do pizza tonight?" Cole was at the patio door, peeking out. Conner had already disappeared into the black depths of the house.

"Um..." He looked to Charlie for affirmation, and she suppressed a wide grin. How had she become the keeper of the kitchen meals so quickly? Did he realize how much he included her, asked her to join in the decisions? "Maybe?"

She shrugged. "I didn't have any ideas for tonight. But I want to do something fancy for their last night."

"Yeah – pizza!" Sam called up to Cole. "We'll start the oven in a bit." It seemed like the boys were starving for food always, and supper was devoured as soon as it was served at five.

"Sam," she touched his forearm, stopping him from heading up the stairs. He swung to look at her, his eyes soft. She battered down her bubbling questions and instead focused on her role as quasi-mother to his boys. Without her own children, she never knew the right rules. She assumed Conner told her about his new girlfriend because he was too shy to tell Sam, but she couldn't be sure it wasn't some sort of test he'd given. Was he checking to see if she reported everything to his father? Well, he hadn't asked her to keep it a secret, and her instinct was to share.

"What is it? You look serious," he said lightly.

"Well…it's. Conner. He confided that he and Shelly were officially dating. I just…thought you should know."

"And he doesn't want me giving him grief, I'm sure," Sam grinned a little ruefully, and rubbed a palm along his temple. "I won't say anything, but thanks for telling me. Did you want to work at all before we eat?"

She nodded. "Yes, please. Just two hours to check on things. I'll do a bunch on Sunday after the boys leave."

They walked up the patio together, his hand on the small of her back, and the touch brought to a boil the anxiety and nerves.

Those nerves stayed at bay with the busyness of entertaining two bouncy, energetic boys. But when the house went silent on Sunday afternoon and she pulled out her computer and scrolled through her emails, her heart and head demanded time to digest.

She kept going back to what Sam had said nearly a week ago. *That he wanted to love her.* He'd been sick, his eyes dilated, his speech soft. But he'd been so definite. He had said he wanted to love her. She didn't necessarily know what that meant. She'd been so lit up by his obvious want for her that she had almost allowed him to do more. But when he'd said that, she'd snapped. It wasn't that she was upset about it, or that it had made her angry. It was the automatic words that had nearly spilled from her own lips. She had almost responded in kind.

Was it reactive? Was it obligation? Was it the desire to have some order back to her life?

As she answered emails slowly, she reflected. Charlie was still smarting from her divorce. She still felt like she could never find someone to fit Peter's role in her life, regardless of how he'd treated her. To start again building history seemed too great a task at this point. Besides, what if it all failed again?

To know that Sam had any kind of feelings for her at all was scary and wonderful and amazing all at the same time. But it was too unnerving. The unspoken and spoken drifted between them, nibbled at their silences and slept on the bed with them. It was something she needed to get away from, if even for a few days. She'd been able to hold it together since the little moment on the bed, and Sam hadn't said a word either, so she wasn't sure he even remembered saying such a thing to her. Maybe he had been too drugged up to comprehend what he'd said. Maybe he didn't mean it like...*love* love. Maybe it had been just sexual.

But she should go back to LA. See her staff, visit a client or two. Think. Things slipped too easily into place with Sam, and Charlie felt there had to be a catch somewhere, somehow. That it couldn't happen again, that whole illusion of forever. She knew she could work from the ranch. She knew she could make food and play with his kids until they left to have their own lives. She wanted to sleep with Sam, and touch him in all his nakedness. But she was too scarred to let it all go, and be able to accept where life had been heading these past few weeks. And really...why would he want a woman who wasn't...even a full woman?

When Sam came back from dropping off the boys, they made supper, and drank a red wine. He didn't need his pain meds anymore, and the wine didn't mix the way it had five days ago. But she waited until they were chilling on the sofa to bring it up.

"I think I need to run into LA," she said quietly, into their reading silence. Sam lowered his magazine and raised his eyebrows. Now that she'd said it and created her little escape hatch, she almost wanted to take it back. In reality, she knew she didn't want to leave the ranch or spend time away from him, but she almost felt she had to, to clear her head. That staying here without taking a day or two to breathe would lead her to jump into this relationship with both feet.

"When?"

She bit her lip. "Probably at the end of the week - leave Wednesday and back Friday so we have the weekend again."

Sam put his reading down entirely and looked at her squarely. "If you need to...or want to, I guess...you should."

She could tell she'd hurt him a little, but she was nervous about him, about their evolving friendship, and how quickly everything was happening, and how easy. Easy. It couldn't be this easy.

"Just need to see some clients, visit my best friend. Just so they don't think I've completely disappeared from the planet."

He sighed, and put his elbows on his knees, hiding his face in his hands, rubbing his forehead. "It's what I said, isn't it? You're running away from me. Shit. I'm sorry, Charlie."

His voice was raw and rough, and she immediately slid on the leather sofa to his side, putting an arm around his shoulders. She put a cheek against his back and closed her eyes. Why should she run from this comfort, this ease? It wasn't the heady, over the top romance that she'd had at first with Peter, but it was a real thing, a true, adult courtship. He wanted her, and she him, in so many ways other than in the bedroom. Why couldn't she just take what was being given?

"I could say I'd take it all back," he said through his hands. "Though I don't think that would make you any less likely to not leave for LA, and it wouldn't be true anyway."

She opened her eyes and stared across the room into the dim kitchen. So he did remember what he'd said, and he meant it. Sam loved her. Well, there was something. Could she say the same thing back? It was instinctive to do so, that she should return it. And she did, but she wasn't sure it was the right kind of love. It was so different. So quick. So comforting. There wasn't the hot spark of young love, nor the passionate lustful obsession. It was companionable. Cozy. What would it mean if she declared her feelings? What would it change?

She squeezed his shoulders, the thoughts coming slowly. "I'll go but I'll be back, Sam. You haven't chased me away."

"No?" His head came up, and she saw his eyes were a bit bleary. Did he really want her to stay so badly? The idea made her feel wanted, desired, special. Her thoughts curdled and melted into the desire for him to hold her, to just exist in the same space.

"No. And I've got to pack more clothes - I hadn't planned on taking so many days and weeks of

sabbatical, and I'll need late fall sweaters and such."
The rationale developed as she said it.

He smiled at her, relief coming across his face. She
was also relieved that he hadn't stopped her, begged
her to stay, or worse of all, asked for a declaration of
love back.

"Well, you've got a point." Lightness was back in his
voice, and she was glad for it.

"Then I'll leave Wednesday. Keep your phone on
you. I might need to call often as the hours pass, as I
miss you."

"I hope you miss me," he leaned back and pulled her
into his arms. She curled next to him, her head under
his chin, and an arm around his belly. They sat
quietly like that, listening to the soft sounds outside
and the whisper of wind through a few open
windows. Charlie was looking forward to
experiencing fall out here, and getting to know Sam
even better. Now that she'd secured a few days away,
she knew she didn't want to really be gone for good.
And knowing that gave her a few inklings of what she
really wanted.

She didn't realize she'd drifted to sleep until Sam
shifted under her. She looked up at him, and he
squeezed her tight.

"We're getting old," he joked. "Falling asleep on the couch before ten. Bed?"

"Yes."

They got up, and moved together down the hall. Sam paused at her door, but she gave a little shake of her head.

"I don't think I'd like to sleep alone, if that's alright?"

He smiled again at her and leaned in to kiss her forehead. "It's absolutely alright. I'll be waiting."

She pulled on her pajamas and brushed her teeth, thinking about Sam constantly. Maybe this was love, truly, when someone took over thoughts and ideas so utterly. She'd maybe forgotten how it was. And oh, she thought about him, and wanted him to touch her and she to touch him. Maybe she'd let him go a bit farther tonight.

He was in bed when she wandered in, lights already off. Climbing in, she curled into her familiar place, his chest touching her back, her buttocks skimming into his hips, their legs parallel to each other.

His fingers danced on her stomach lightly, tracing shapes. She sighed into the night, but she was more awake now that she'd had a little nap on the couch. They were quiet and still, until he spoke into her hair.

"Charlie...I'm sorry I've spooked you."

"You haven't." She turned in his arms to face him. In the pale moonlight coming through the cracks in the drapes, she could just make out part of his face.

"I think I have," he pressed. This conversation was easier for them both in the dark, she realized. "Please..."

She found his lips blindly, touching them with her fingertips. "You've done nothing but made me reflect on how I feel about you. I'm still sorting...but it's not a bad thing. I'm glad you told me."

He sighed against her hands and brought her close. There was a moment of hesitation, and then they were kissing, passionately, fully, desperately. This kiss was more than anything else before - it was emotional - and she let herself fall into it. He was kissing her as if he needed her to affirm his declaration, though he kept his hands in chaste places, something that for once was driving her crazy. Where was his lust? She wanted his hands on her breast again, and under her pants. She didn't know what she wanted beyond this but she decided to follow it. She knew where it could lead, but suddenly that didn't seem important. What were they waiting for?

She kissed him harder, grasping his face, running her hands through his hair, and then down to unbutton his pajama top. Once she'd freed it, her palms ran down his chest and stomach, around his back. His skin was thick, hot, masculine. Still he resisted touching her, though his kiss was like fire.

Finally she pulled away from his mouth, gasping. "Sam. Touch me."

His hands were tentative, and he hesitated still. "You want me to?"

And even in the middle of her yearning for him, she recognized what had happened. The last time they'd touched so freely he had professed his love for her, and she'd bolted away from him as if she didn't want to be intimate. Charlie realized he was afraid to scare her off again. She would have to repair this little rift in their relationship. It was perhaps like building his trust again, showing him that her desire for him had not abated.

She pressed her body to his, feeling his need for her even though he was refraining from acting on it. "Yes. I want you to touch me. I want...you."

His arms came around her, pulling her tight. "Come here, then."

He commenced kissing her again, but this time his fingers wandered, and she melted as he pulled off her shirt, bending to kiss her breasts as he peeled off her bra. She sighed into his mouth as their chests touched, feeling their stomachs rub together. It'd been a long time since she'd been in bed with a man, and the fact that this one loved her as well made the entire thing more sensual.

The kissing became deeper, and she took the initiative by running her fingers along his waist, pulling a bit on his pants. This felt so easy, natural, right. She knew she wanted him all, that she needed the sex suddenly, as if her body couldn't stop. The need for him pooled in her belly, made her breath come short, chills and heat interchanging throughout her spine. As she yanked down his pajama bottoms until he could kick them off, her hands brushed over the front of his pants and he jerked.

"Charlotte!"

Her name was a gasp, a gulp of air, rasped and rough.

He kissed her hard then, keeping his body apart, as if afraid to allow himself to let go. It was odd for Charlie to play the part of the needy, the aggressor, the amorous one. But she felt she needed to give him something now, especially since it was still too difficult to tell him how she felt. And she wanted him. She touched him purposefully, reaching to caress his stomach and anything else she dared. Touching him so intimately, finally, made her feel the ache. His arms grabbed her up, squeezing her bottom, sliding under her own pants, as if he'd given up and decided to let go. Her head fell back, and he kissed her neck, her collarbone, his hands massaging her hip. She quivered and cried out when he finally touched her in turn. He was a skilled lover, and she had a moment when she wondered how many he'd had before and after his divorce. Did it matter anymore?

"Do you want all of this?" he murmured as she shuddered under his careful massage. She started to nod, forgetting he could hardly see her in the darkness, and her voice was strangled.

"Please. Sam."

"You want all of me?" there was a light tease in his voice, even though it was husky and desirous.

She reveled in the way he was so obviously wanted her, the way he desperately needed her.

"Yes...make love to me." She wanted the sex. She'd missed sex. And she knew inherently it was more than sex for him, and even for her.

They moved together then, swiping away the last of their clothing in a hurried pace, eager to feel the nakedness between them, and Charlie could not contain her voice as he filled her, held her, took her until her back was slick with a fine sweat. They ended gasping, folded into each other, their limbs entangled in the sheets and clothing. It was quiet, suddenly, completely, and in the dark, she heard him sigh.

"What is it?"

"We forgot a condom."

She started to giggle. "If you're worried about getting me pregnant--."

"Not that, Charlie," his voice was light. "It'd just be the common courtesy, you know."

"To offer? I would have said no. Unless there's a reason you need one." She was fishing for answers, knowing now was the best time to get them, when they were still panting with spent desire.

She felt him shake his head. "No, no. Haven't had many partners. Two before Amy, and one right after

282

the divorce." He'd had fewer sexual encounters than she'd expected of a man his age. Though perhaps kids slowed things down, and made it more difficult to have casual affairs. And Sam, as much as he liked people, liked the simple life. Women could complicate it all, and she had a feeling he wouldn't have even had her stay on if she disrupted what was important to him - kids, ranch, wine and quiet peace.

"What about you?" His hand was on her stomach, caressing her skin, as if he couldn't stop touching her now that they'd gone all the way. Her own womb was swollen with aching pulses.

Charlie sighed. "There was my college boyfriend, then one right before I met Peter, and then Peter. And now you."

She got a kiss when she finished with that, but she continued. "I'm glad we don't have to use a condom, Sam. It was good to feel you."

He buried his face into her shoulder and nuzzled her neck. "You're telling me. I'm so glad you wanted this. I thought I...I thought I'd gone too far, too fast."

She saw her opening to make her explanation, that she could repair her hesitation to his initial try at deeper intimacy. "Last time it wasn't the touching. I have always found you...hot." She ran her hand down his belly. "It was that you were out of it, and still fondling me and telling me you loved me. I didn't want the first time to be while you were sick, that any touch or word might not be remembered. I wanted it to be more real..."

He pulled her tight to his body. The heat on her skin had cooled, and his flesh felt good next to hers on the sheets. She wanted to sleep naked with him, and found herself feeling drowsy.

"It is real, Charlie. It's real that I wanted you, still want you. Real that I love you."

His bald declaration made her close her eyes in the dark. She was glad he couldn't see her face. How could he be so sure and certain of it? Didn't he second-guess love, now that he'd had a failed marriage?

How could he even say it? Believe in it? What made him know? Did he mean it...for always? That he wanted to be with her? Or that he simply loved her now, as a woman, and perhaps he'd always love her, but not enough to marry her?

It'd been a while since Charlie had had to wonder about a man and his feelings. The game felt fresh, the insecurities were wild. Instead, she griped his hand, moving it so it rested under her breasts and curled tightly next to him.

"Thank you for loving me."

Chapter 17

The drive back to LA was tedious, a familiar headache that forced her to concentrate on the road and the myriad drivers that swirled and dodged, honking, speeding and swearing across the lines. It was made worse by the fact that she was completely second-guessing her departure. Did separation really make the heart grow fonder? What if Sam decided he liked having his house back to himself? What if...he shipped her handful of items back, angry that she hadn't told him she loved him when they'd kissed goodbye?

She could still imagine him, standing in the middle of the driveway, the brightness of early morning crowning over him as the coffee in one hand curled a smoky stream of steam and the other hand was still raised in farewell.

What had possessed her to think she should leave him? She should have offered to have him join her. She should not try re-entering her life right now, when things were so fragile and uncertain, herself included.

Well, there was no changing it now, she reasoned, swerving away from the inching traffic off to her exit.

Deciding to tackle work, to dive back in full force, she voice dialed Amanda and waited.

"Charlie?"

"Yeah? What's up?"

"Oh! Um. Nothing. Work. The usual." Amanda's voice could sound like a smile even over the line.

"I'm back in town."

"Already? Something go wrong?"

"No, no." Not really, anyway. *Wrong* wouldn't be the right word.

"Well...is there a client complaining or something?"

Charlie sighed inaudibly. "No, nothing like that. I need...fall clothes. And wanted to check the apartment and things."

"Oh, sure." Amanda accepted the explanation and then started into a litany of updates, even though Charlie hadn't asked. The names of her clients piled around her, burying her in the familiar sort and attack of managing a service-based business. Small fires, complaining customers, particular and picky people who felt they knew something about interior design, but still wanted an expert to tell them their ideas were right.

"Oh, yeah, and there's an invite on my desk. Big gallery opening. We should go and see – I bet it will be a great option for prints and originals. They have all ranges."

The thought of slipping into a cocktail dress and socializing was both entertaining and abhorrent. There was something about wearing jeans and exercise clothes every day that was getting addicting. But then, sometimes dressing up could be fun.

"What time?"

"Starts at eight. Want to be my date?" Amanda quipped. She was in between boyfriends, her own ex-husband on his third wife, which Amanda often said absolved her of any guilt.

There was not a single reason to mope in her empty apartment all night. Pressing her lips together in an attempt to steel herself, Charlie nodded once silently and then answered her friend. "Sure. Fine. I'm in."

The cocktail party meant the languidly lazy night was going to be replaced with champagne, sparkles and chit chat, but it would likely be good to get out and mingle, exchange stories with Amanda, and see if she would really miss much of it by spending her time out in the country. Would she miss networking? Would it be better to have Sam along?

Her apartment smelled stale as she pushed open the sterile door. Everything felt empty and plain after Sam's dark woods and black metals. Her aesthetic seemed to have made a temporary switch, and she swept through the space, adjusting lights and nuance until it started to feel like the place she'd left.

All the whites, the beige, the watery blue and soft grey. Charlie stood in the middle of her bedroom, surveying the bed. It had always been a lonely piece of furniture since moving out of the house, but now it was worse. Why did she really need to come back? She wasn't running, she knew. She just needed to...check.

Her phone pinged, reminding her that she had very little time to get ready before meeting Amanda. Maybe she should pop a cork and have a glass to get her in the mood. The glance at the depleted wine rack reminded her that she'd failed to stock it when she last ran out, as her plan had been to come back from a long sabbatical in wine country, laden down with bottles and crates of unique wines, tastefully cured and tested. She hadn't done much in the way of saving vintages. She and Sam had drank most of what they'd bought.

She had to stop thinking about Sam. *Focus.*

The cocktail dress slid on her skin, a soft silk she'd bought herself in the early days of divorce, when the purchase had been a fit of financial rebellion against her new single status. But the price tag was worth it. Turning in the mirror, she smiled, and if she was careful about it, her smile looked nearly genuine.

Piling up her hair into a twist, blasting her face with the usual regime of make-up, and spraying on some perfume, she was just packing up a purse when Amanda arrived.

"Let's go!" Amanda was dressed for a party, her vibrant dress plied with appliques and tall heels. Charlie followed her out, feeling as though she could

not catch up.   She should have had something –
anything – to drink.

*C*hapter 18

"Char?"

The voice caught at her ears, a visceral response that hovered and chewed at her from the inside out. It ripped her from concentrating on a beautifully rich painting, one she was considering for Sam.

"Charlie!"

It was impossible to ignore. The mellifluous tenor, the way it was obviously her name. How could she possibly act civil?

"Char – this is great! I want you to meet Erin."

"I...Hi." Where was Amanda? How could she possibly have been left alone long enough to be trapped into a conversation? And what were they doing here?

"Why are you at a gallery opening? It's not really your thing, Peter," she managed, still avoiding direct eye contact with the trim young woman on his arm.

He shrugged, his own eyes darting around the whitewashed walls. "Erin thought we could use some more color on the walls and this has been really publicized. She got us in – she works in public relations." He glanced down at her with the same calculated consideration that Charlie remembered from those last painful months before he'd asked for a divorce.

"That's...nice." What did he expect her to say? Were they supposed to make small talk? Her head reeled, and the liquor sitting in her stomach curdled and stung. Desperately, she wished for Sam. She wished he was there, holding her hand, giving her solidarity.

But he wasn't there. He may never be. She had to face this alone.

"Yeah. You've been well, though?" He looked her up and down, the small smile on his face that betrayed his inner earnestness, his careful tendencies, his strident particularness.

"I've been fine." She was, now, anyway. At least since she'd been to wine country.

"That's great to hear." He seemed to genuinely care.

"I...I should find my friend. She left for the bar...Nice to see you, Peter. Erin." Nodding briefly, Charlie edged away against the blank wall to her right and walked briskly away. She had no idea where the bar actually was, but as long as she walked with purpose, likely they wouldn't figure out how badly she was running away.

How could Amanda bring her to a place that Peter would show? Obviously, she hadn't done so on purpose, but the shock of seeing him made her feel faint and short of breath, shaky and shocked. The inadequacies flowed through her body, a river of self-flagellation and reminders of how Peter had changed everything.

"Charlie?"

Damn it! He'd followed her! She jerked up from her partial fold against another wall. It was very apparent now that she was not getting a drink.

Peter didn't comment or point out her lie. That surprised her. Instead, he leaned next to her.

"Where did Erin go?"

"Bathroom," he said shortly, his eyes gazing out over the crowd. It was nosier by the minute, but it felt as though they were trapped in a silent sphere in their own bubble of miserableness. Why had he chased her?

"She's very pretty." Charlie didn't have to elaborate. Young. Nubile. Probably fertile.

"Thanks." Peter took the compliment in stride.

"And you're happy?"
Please, let him go away!

He glanced at her, and sighed. "Charlie, I know we haven't spoken in a while. Since the divorce was final. And I...I've thought of you a lot."

"Natural, I'm sure."

The reminders of their initial romance, their solid marriage in the beginning danced across her mind. Of course Peter would think of her. She'd thought of only him, until recently. Of what it could be. Of what it might have been.

"I just...I miss you."

"Oh…I have…missed you too." She didn't much anymore, but it felt the right thing to say. Should she tell him about Sam?

"Don't you miss what we had?" His voice went wistful, and it took her a moment to gather her thoughts properly and to cut the rancor from her rejoinder.

"I did, but I assumed you didn't want what we had. Isn't that the whole point of our marriage ending? That we didn't…have enough?"

"You know how I felt about having a family," he reminded, his tone at once flying into irritability.

Damn it, where was his girlfriend? *Make him leave!*

"Yes, you made that very apparent by the end. I'm surprised you haven't file for an annulment on grounds I couldn't provide you with heirs." There it was, the touch of rancor. Peter didn't even flinch.

"I don't know if that would be grounds," he mused. "But regardless, I feel like there was more there – we had a lot of history and common interests."

"We likely still do," Charlie reasoned. "But of course, you are happy with your Erin. And…speaking of…don't you have a little one by now?" The mention of the illicit lovechild hung between them, briefly, and then broke and scattered. The idea of the baby was one Charlie rarely allowed herself. It was too raw – too much a physical reminder of how much her own body didn't work.

Peter sighed. "Never happened."

"She lost it?" There was no sympathy lost, but she tried to sound at least contrite.

He shook his head. "No. I mean…pregnancy turned out to be false. One of those…'imagine so hard you're pregnant and you'll seem pregnant' things."

Her mouth was open, staring at him. "Wait…you mean…the baby that was the final catalyst for our divorce…the woman you were sleeping with to try and father a baby on the side who carried your blood and your name…doesn't exist?"

"Oh, no, no. Erin exists," he waved a hand, where her bright brassy blond locks could be seen slowly making their way back toward their wall. "But the baby didn't." There was bitterness in his own voice now. Charlie was glad. Now he knew a small taste of what it felt like. She didn't know whether to feel jubilant or depressed. And none of it really mattered anymore. It was over.

"But no baby? You stopped trying?" She couldn't believe her ears. Her stomach was starting to hurt. She needed...she wanted...she wanted to be back home, at the ranch with Sam.

"I haven't!" he stood up, anticipating his girlfriend's imminent arrival to their tete-a-tete. "But...I can't believe nothing's happened."

"I have no idea what to say, Peter." She didn't.

"We've been together a while," he reminded her. "And I...miss you, Charlie. I wish we could...look at reconnecting."

Erin arrived, her face looking fresh and glowing, a youthful plumpness to her skin and a curve along her limbs and hips. She was indeed pretty, and obviously adored Peter. Perhaps she felt as if she'd won him — had beat Charlie out of a husband. Her smile was kind, but it was tight around her eyes as she held out her hand for Peter.

"You have to see what I've found, Pete!" she gushed. "These beautiful watercolors!" Whether in her excitement or her youth, she brushed past Charlie without a comment, and in way, she was grateful. Trailing her, Peter turned and shot a low reminder.

"Just think about it, ok Char?"

And then his head popped and floated with the other men in the room, melting and disappearing in a sea of dark groomed hairstyles.

She couldn't breathe. She couldn't think. What was she supposed to do with all of this? How could she process it?

Could Peter mean it? That he wanted to get back together? That he missed their marriage?

Goodness knows, she missed marriage too. She missed the past she shared with Peter, the intimate vibes of understand that had once passed between them. Was there any possibility she'd have that comfort again?

But then – comfort had happened with Sam. A new comfort, a real one. Perhaps more real than the illusion of what she was remembering from a dead marriage. A marriage, it seemed, that had ended on a lie, a farce, a possibility. The knowledge that Peter had cheated on her, had decided his desire to achieve just one more goal in his life, had always eaten at her. She believed, however, that she had failed him. It was her inability to serve him children that had led him to look elsewhere. She'd never expected the girlfriend to be so conniving, or to wish her pregnancy so badly that she would convince her body to produce the hormones that looked like a pregnancy.

And now...to know that there was no pregnancy. There was no baby. What should she do with that? Where should she go?

Well, it was obvious she couldn't stay here. She had to find Amanda, get an Uber, and then get out.

$\mathscr{C}$hapter 19

Sam drove into LA on Thursday night. Charlie was meeting him for dinner and then they planned to head back to her place. He frowned when he remembered their last conversation. She'd been different, a bit distracted, unlike herself. He didn't know her long, but he thought he knew her well enough, and he was worried.

They'd made love so many times after their first experience in the sheets that he'd lost count, which was pretty good considering they had only had three days of it. Once the door had been opened, neither of them were inclined to beat around the bush. They'd found themselves getting passionate in most rooms, in the vineyard, the barn, the patio. He was overwhelmed with her physicalness, her interest in sex as an act, as an emotion, as a conversation. He'd never had a partner so attuned to him, his body, or his preferences. Sam was desperately in love with her, and found himself loving her more every time he thought about why he did.

She had left later on Wednesday, and he knew she had been right to leave the ranch for a few days. She should stay connected to her business, and also of course pack more clothes for a longer stay. He felt like bouncing off the walls all evening and Thursday morning, trying any type of random chore to stay busy, but he knew he simply missed her. He missed their talks, their quiet reading evenings, the sex, the food. He worried about what it would be like when she was gone for good – back to the city and away from him for months at a time. The notion struck him as unlivable.

Then Charlie had called in the afternoon. She had been bumming around some of the old decorating haunts and found some pieces she thought might fit the house perfectly. Would he like to come in for dinner and browsing on Friday?

She didn't have to say it - he knew she was missing him too - but she'd also been a bit short about it all. Something was wrong, and he was anxious about the possibility that she was having second thoughts about their relationship. As much as she'd moved on from Peter, even since the short time he had known her, Sam knew Charlie was still more emotionally fragile than he was. It was why he didn't dare press her for love, why he was just glad he had her time and person to be with. She would offer what she wanted, when she could. There was no point in pressing her. He had time.

They met at a restaurant on the north side of the city in the Granada Hills area. It wasn't the most posh neighborhood he could think of, but it saved having to battle traffic until later in the night for him, and she was already nearby in Burbank seeing a client.

He arrived first, glad he'd thought to wear a blazer over the polo and khakis, as the restaurant was still pretty nice. She'd picked it, knowing the area a bit better than he did. Sitting, he spun the spoon and sipped the ice water and mulled, worried and fretted.

When she arrived, his breath nearly stopped with relief. Her face lit up tremendously, and she looked utterly sublime in a narrow black skirt, a ballet shirt and heels. It was the most dressed up he'd ever seen her, and he vowed to take her out more often if it meant getting to see her so dolled up. She had her hair pulled back in a knot and make-up on, and even wore jewelry. While Sam didn't need all of that in a woman every day, it was special to see the one he loved look so divine. He knew she was turning men's heads, and couldn't help but be a bit smug that she was coming to his table.

He stood as she neared, his eyes devouring her face. She was still smiling, but as he reached and kissed her lightly on the lips, he detected the same offness that he had heard on the phone. *What was it?*

As they sat, and she folded the napkin over her lap, he decided to act on his belief that he wasn't going to have a relationship like his marriage. That if he was going to be with Charlie, he was going to talk about everything. That was how they would keep interested in each other's lives, how they'd make sure they never grew apart. He hoped he could find the right words.

"Charlie, it's good to see you," he said first, as the waiter came to take their wine and appetizer order.

She gave him another smile, but waited for him to order them a bottle. "Thank you for coming down, Sam. It really is good to see you. I needed to see you."

Her comment was forceful, and Sam felt a horrible forbidding. Something had happened. Was she telling him she wouldn't be coming back to the ranch? She'd decided, in the quick time apart, that they could only be friends? He couldn't lose her. He thought he was done with dating and women, had found peace in his home and ranch and sons, and that was that. And then she'd stumbled into his life and it didn't feel quite right now without her in the house.

When the waiter had left, he focused on her, but she didn't meet his gaze, instead picking at the tablecloth and glancing around the decor, as if she'd never been in the restaurant before. Her lack of engagement alarmed him.

"Charlotte. What's wrong?" He used her given name on purpose, so that she would realize how seriously he wanted her to answer. He took her hand for good measure, to stop her nervous plucking. She brought up her head and her eyes were full of worry and glossy with pain.

"I saw Peter."

His heart sank. She *was* saying good-bye to him. "I see. When?"

At least she didn't pull away her hand from his, and he held onto it tightly, as if by keeping her close, touching her, he might not really lose her. He fought his own building panic, forcing himself to listen.

"Wednesday night, at a gallery opening. I was going for artwork for you, actually," she said, and he remembered the whole premise for him to come down into LA, to see things she'd found for him. Maybe it wasn't all lost. She still cared enough to think of him, to fill his house as if she wanted it to be nice. He clung to the straws of hope.

"And Peter was there?"

She nodded, looking a bit miserable. "I...he made overtures. He said he missed me. Alluded to being together. I was shocked, surprised, overwhelmed. It was as if all my thoughts of marriage - that I was only supposed to ever be married once, to one man - were true, that we could forget this had all happened. All of that, I thought...in a moment."

Sam hoped he could hold it together. Anger, devastation, sorrow. It all hit him in the gut, and they stared unhappily at each other across the table as the waiter silently brought the wine. They let him open and pour the bottle, silence sitting like fog between them. Once they were alone again, Sam took his hand from her fingers, but she surprised him by grasping it again with both of hers. Why did she hold onto him right as she was asking to leave him?

"Sam, listen to me."

He shook his head, wanting to get up and go, feeling a fool. He shouldn't have given her so much; he was getting soft in his age. He shouldn't have even started to hope. She hadn't been ready for him, for his life or is love, or even the pretenses of romance. It should have been obvious to him from early on, but somehow he'd been blinded by his belief that she was durable, that she was healing. He should have known better by now.

She was clenching his fingers, her nails almost digging into the skin, pinching the lines of his knuckles.

"Samuel Gaffney. I'm trying to tell you everything."

"I don't know if I want to hear it all," he told her lowly, sharply. "Just tell me you want to be with him, and I'll head out."

"*Oh my God.* No! What I'm telling you is that I thought all of that, and I spent Wednesday night wrestling with all my old insecurities. He'd said his current...girlfriend, I guess...had been trying for several months to get pregnant. And it wasn't working. And he missed what we had had. But I have been so happy with you, Sam."

"I understand, Charlie. He's the man you married. You're entitled to miss him, and want to be back with him."

"I thought about that." She was tense, tight. "But all I felt was insecure if I thought about going back with him. How would I know...what if he ever got tired of me once more, or angry again that I couldn't give him kids? I couldn't trust him, even as I entertained the what-ifs."

"Are you going to give him another go?" Sam wanted this over with. He couldn't listen to her talk about her decision to get back with Peter, and he was angry she would even consider it. He'd thought her stronger.

"No, Sam. I called him later Wednesday night to tell him that I didn't appreciate what he'd said to me, that his actions in the past could never been undone, and I did not love him any more. But he never picked up. I got a text this morning. His girlfriend got a positive pregnancy test. What are the odds in all that timing?"

Her voice grew hard, bitter. "Just goes to show I *was* right in my decision. That I couldn't go back to him. He'd never really be happy with me. He would have left me a second time. I don't belong with someone who doesn't love me. I'm finally over him - I don't miss him anymore."

"Are you…sure?" It pained him to ask, but it had to be said.

She nodded. "More than sure. I…I'd always put my own failures next to him, and what he did to me, to us and our marriage. That the choices he made were my fault, in some ways."

Sam recognized an opening and pounced, keeping his voice and his face as casual as he could. "What..what did he do, Charlie? He left you?"

"Yes," she looked across his shoulder, her eyes unfocussed for a moment. "Yes. He left me for his mistress. The woman he'd been sleeping with for a while...even though we were still married. Erin, her name was. Is. Is. He's still with her. She'd told him she was pregnant, and that's when he told me that he wanted out. That he was going to be a father by another woman."

Sam didn't know what to say. Clearing his voice, he inhaled sharply. "So he got his wish."

Charlie shook her head, an a rueful laugh escaping her. It was a sour, angular sound, almost as if it wasn't her laughing. "That's the best part. There was no baby."

"Excuse me?" Now she just wasn't making sense.

"Exactly," she squeezed his hands. "She wanted to be pregnant so bad that...she thought she was. What's so awful is he probably knew it was a false pregnancy when he signed our divorce papers. It was long enough to know whether or not Erin was truly pregnant. And...he signed them anyway."

Sam felt the wind go out of him. So she hadn't wanted Peter after all? Dear God, she could have gone about telling the story a different way. He stared at their hands, and then their untouched wine, and then her face, which was etched with lines and harried worry. She had had a lot to deal with alone, and the familiar protectiveness washed over him.

"Charlie. Honey." He brought his other hand up, so they were joined at all four points, handfasted over the tabletop. "Look at me."

She found his eyes, and he wished he could lean over and kiss her.

"I'm sorry, Sam," she whispered. "I'm sorry I doubted what we have, and what you were offering me, to even consider Peter again. I feel so...free. I never need to wonder again."

Sam wasn't sure if he should be relieved or not. He understood that Charlie's emotions were not his fight. It was why he never asked her how she felt about him, and why he knew inherently that she wasn't much ready for a full commitment to him. He hadn't realized how tentatively she was delving into these new waters with him, and was absolutely shaken that he had almost lost her.

"Were you wondering? About being with Peter?"

She shrugged. "Once or twice. Not much at all since meeting you. I don't know, Sam. You've been at this longer. Do you wonder what life might have been like had you stayed with Amy?"

"No, not really. Maybe here or there, but few and far between," he said truthfully. "I had a good divorce. We agreed we were not happy together, that we didn't have enough between us to keep us together. We talk. We have to, I guess. But it was mutual."

"Well...I always have wondered how my life would be fuller, or different, or better if I'd been able to hold onto Peter. I wasn't able to get past how awful I felt about being unable to give him what he wanted."

"We've been over that," Sam reminded. "He wasn't good enough for you. He didn't love you enough – or at least, the right way."

"I know you're right," she sighed. "And being with you...I forget about all the what-ifs. I don't think of Peter. It's why I needed to see you again. This whole stupid roller coaster made me realize I was happier, and felt like I belonged in my skin better, when I am with you."

Sam exhaled and squeezed her fingers before releasing them and picked up his wine. She watched him, and did likewise.

"To us," he toasted, and she touched her glass with his, finally smiling at him.

They started to eat the appetizers then, and Sam reflected when he could about this whole issue. It had been hard to talk about, and made him worry that she might never trust him completely either. He didn't think Charlie was the type of woman who would hold a grudge and apply it to everyone, but he realized she was more emotional than she let on. Well, then he'd just have to make sure he talked with her, and he was glad she thought to tell him all of her mind and communicate what she'd thought and worried about over Peter. It showed that she was willing to be open about everything - even difficult topics - and that, once again, gave him hope.

They were able to finally put Peter to rest. By the time the bottle of wine was gone and the food was eaten, Charlie had been able to better articulate that she was about finished with mourning what she'd always imagined her life to be like. She'd had expectations of a marriage that would last decades, children, grandchildren, and a traditional way of doing all the milestones. Now all of that was gone. He didn't blame her, and he knew saying good-bye to that kind of expectation could take a while. He wondered how quickly she'd be able to really move on from it all, but her cheery self was soon back, and he realized she was closer to closure than he understood. If Peter had really shaken her core, she would not be able to brush it off so easily. In fact, maybe Sam had to thank the man. He'd just proven to Charlie that she did not belong with her ex, that he was fleeting, unable to commit to anyone or to see past his own plans and goals. A chance meeting with Peter had opened the path to Sam.

He followed her as best he could through late night traffic to her apartment. After the harrowing drive through cars and managing parking, they found themselves in her space. It was a loft style, with open concept walls and exposed ceiling ducts. He could see why his own home didn't bother her, since she had a modern taste herself.

"Do you like it?" she asked, swinging around after plopping her purse on the side table.

She buzzed around, turning on lights, rejuvenated with wine and, perhaps, his presence. He watched the lamplight hit her skin, and she pulled the knot out of her hair, threading her fingers through the fine strands. In a strange moment of clarity, he pictured what it would look like when it was white.

"Can I get a tour?" he heard himself ask, as if purposefully distracting his mind from wandering too far ahead of everything. He had to remember that she was not nearly as committed to their relationship.

"Let's start here."

So before he could get that tour, she threw herself into his arms for a hug that quickly turned sexual. It was as if it had not been two days since they'd last touched, and he consumed her body on her couch, forgetting, for several wonderful moments, how upset he'd been earlier. How he thought he'd lost her to her ex-husband.

When they finished devouring each other, he curled her hair around his fingers. She laid naked on top of him, her body twisted around his, and her head on his chest. He felt the thin sheen of sweat on her back, and her breath was soft on his shoulder.

"I love you."

It was a whisper, a half sigh, and Sam felt himself freeze. Had she really just said what he thought he'd heard? He considered the possibility that he was hearing things, and he couldn't ask her to repeat it. His heart restarted, pounding hard, and her head came up.

"I can feel that."

"What?"

"Your heart rate. I can't tell if you're glad or not that I...care for you." It seemed she couldn't say it twice anyway.

He clutched her close, feeling his skin react to her, his body stirring against her thigh. Gods, couldn't she feel and see what she did to him? And that by telling him her heart he was moved all over again? Sam wasn't the type to get teary or overly sentimental, but her admittance struck him hard. Here he'd thought he was the odd one to fall so quickly, that he'd spend months - maybe years - waiting for her to perhaps feel the same. *To know she loved him...*

"Charlotte, my love. I'm more than glad you love me."

He bent up to capture her lips, and their kiss turned into something more frenzied, until he felt his need for her rise up and he could take her again, pleasuring her until she was dizzy, riding on a waves of release. She called his name many times into the dim room, kissing him as he let his release ride inside of her, thrilled they didn't even have to worry of condoms, that his skin could slide with hers in every way.

They dozed afterwards, until she roused him so they could fall into her bed. She did not have a king mattress, so the space was not so luxurious, though they didn't need the room because they slept so tightly together. Sam enjoyed it - he knew that even in a happy marriage such lusty nights did not happen as often as in the beginning - but he was content to live it up. He fell into a deep sleep, grateful she was still his.

In the morning, they made breakfast and then whisked off early to a few small places that Sam would have never gone for furniture and pieces for the home. Charlie had discovered some wooden chandeliers that would be perfect over the dining table and the kitchen island. She had found better, softer blanketing for the guest room and his room – whites and greys, navy and camel colors. There was a gigantic 'found' wood trestle table for the kitchen that he absolutely loved, and matching chairs. He was thankful she hadn't gone insane with cost - everything was fairly priced and he took them all.

She worked with each furniture store, as if she had long-standing relationships with them, discussing packaging, delivery, any final finishes. He stood back and watched her work and negotiate and plan, and felt a welling of happiness. She was good at what she did - finding these pieces and working with the vendors - and he was bursting with pride that she was his. He stood quietly to the side, hoping other customers saw her finesse, wishing he could brag to them all that she was his girlfriend, and that she loved him.

When they'd finished with the table and chairs, she turned to him with a little smile.

"Before we escape back home and get out of the city for a good while, can I show you the art I thought you might like?"

He took her arm in his, feeling lucky and utterly touched she called the ranch home, and bent to kiss her lightly. "Let's go. Where's it for?"

"On the south wall, by the kitchen table, right before the patio doors open up. You know?"

He nodded, thinking of the tall, barren dark grey wall. It did need something, but he hadn't found anything that felt like the proper match for the space, and truthfully had stopped really looking.

They arrived at the art gallery, and he held her hand as they walked in, knowing that she had difficult memories from Wednesday. She was confident, though, surprisingly so. Had she really just finally shut down her worries from Peter? Sam found it hard to believe that it could all be over, that she could move on so easily. Or maybe he had been the catalyst in her life - she would have wallowed in self-pity and insecurities the rest of her days if she had never met him. He liked to think that that was so, that they could make each other better people.

"This is it."

It was a mix of old master and impressionism, the brush strokes closer to Van Gogh than Bronzino. But there was a rich mix of dark and light, as evening crept through afternoon over the rolling hills and vines in the distance to create a cozy tableau in the foreground of a languid, half finished picnic. There were no people - she had been right to choose something that was landscape just a still - but there was evidence of them, and of a good time, just deserted to perhaps go pick more grapes or play a game. He was struck by the colors, the shadows, the detailing.

"It's amazing."

"It's by a new up and coming artist - one of his first few pieces he's showing, so it's a good price."

Sam shook his head, gazing up and down the canvas. It was a good size for the space, the right directional. It didn't even need to be framed, as it had been finished properly along the edges.

"I don't care about the price, Charlie. It's perfect." He turned to her, and put an arm around her waist. "You know me well."

"I should think so," she said back, giving him a little smile.

"Char!"

They turned as one, and he saw a tall man coming toward them. Sam assumed it was the curator, and stuck out his hand, ready to say 'I'll take it' but Charlie had gone a bit rigid.

"Hello Peter."

Sam's hand dropped without thinking how rude it might look. The man drawing up with them was not only tall, but he was built well, with groomed hair and good looks. He was athletic, just like Charlie, and had a genuine smile.

"Hey! Fancy seeing you again." The man was glowing, and Sam realized it was because of the newly discovered pregnancy in his life. He almost wanted to walk away in disgust. Did the man have no feelings for his ex-wife?

"Yes. Peter. This is Sam. My boyfriend."

The word caused a bit of a light to change in Peter's eyes, but he was still jolly and good-natured and took out his hand. Sam reached and shook it automatically, still unable to say anything.

"What are you doing here?" She was still tense, but she gripped Sam's hand the minute it was free from Peter's. He squeezed her fingers.

"There was a series of small watercolors that Erin remembered. I thought it'd be a great gift in light of everything." He looked satisfied, vindicated, happy, and Sam wanted to hit him.

"Of course." Her voice was neutral, uncommitted. Sam glanced at her to realize she looked utterly uncaring. She honestly didn't seem to be affected by Peter's nearness, or his obvious pleasure at having a baby on the way.

Sam's gut jumped a bit. He thought of his boys, how happy and excited he'd been when they were on the way, how much better it was when the baby arrived, and how cool it was now that they were older and involved in his life. Charlie didn't really understand the glow of that, but she could have his boys. He'd readily share them with her.

"Right, right. Well, anyway, Charlie, it sure was good to see you after all this time. I'm glad you're doing well."

"Thank you. Congratulations, Peter. And Erin as well. I wish you the best."

There was a final dismissal in her tone, but her ex-husband didn't pick up on it at all. Peter obviously didn't realize the Charlie had no intentions of ever speaking to him again. He nodded, and walked away, looking around in a semi-interested fashion, a bounce to his step that Sam wondered if it was natural or just because he was so happy to be an expectant father.

He turned to look at Charlie, but she was gazing back up at the painting, a surprisingly serene look on her face.

"Are you okay?"

She glanced at him and gave a little sigh. "Yeah. I am. I saw him and I just didn't care. That felt wonderful. I don't give a damn about his happiness, or whether he gets what he wants out of life. I want to be with you, Sam. The reality of that hit me the hardest just now all over again."

He couldn't help himself. He bent down and kissed her strongly, a palm on her cheek, the taste of her on his tongue.

They found the curator and he paid for the painting. As they took the long, traffic clogged way back up north out of the city, they spoke on their cell phones, rehashing bits of Peter as needed, reconfirming their feelings about the furniture, the painting, what they could do for dinner tonight and other nights. Charlie wanted to go riding this week, and take the boys out when they came next weekend. She wanted to give a party for his friends. He wanted to take her out to the O'Brien winery, and have her attend the meeting with one of the young start-ups that he was investing with. He was filled with happiness talking to her, excited to have her home again, and overwhelmed with the realization that this could be his. She loved him, and there was an extraordinary chance that he could have his peace and his woman both.

ℰhapter 20

Time flew at the ranch. A week went by filled with sun and love, horses and wine. Suddenly Sam was picking up Cole and Conner for the weekend. They barged in and stopped short.

"Hey! There's new stuff!" Cole exclaimed.

"That there is," Sam walked in behind them, carrying duffel bags. Charlie pulled grapes and cheese out of the fridge and Conner immediately sat opposite her, popping the chunks of dairy into his mouth in quick succession. Cole immediately went and slid on the new wood trestle bench, his shiny pants making a swoosh as he glided along the length.

"This is cool!" he declared. Conner concurred, and then they both fell to devouring their snack. Charlie met Sam's eyes over their heads. His eyes were soft, his face peaceful with a contented leftover grin.

"You have Charlie to thank for the new furniture," Sam told them, coming up behind each boy and putting a firm hand around each neck.

"Did we get new stuff in our room too?" Cole asked around a cheekful of grapes.

"No." Sam shook his head. "What makes you think you need new furniture?"

"We're getting bigger?"

"You don't need anything. Ask me again when you're in high school."

"I'm going to be in high school next year," Conner chimed in. Sam shook his head.

"When *both* of you are in high school then," he modified. Charlie smirked at him.

"Maybe some new art for their walls though?" she asked. "When they're in high school," she amended quickly, not wanting to undermine Sam. Now it was his turn to shoot her a twisted grin. It felt good to add the boys to the mix, to have them to fuss over, discipline and...well, raise. Sam generally didn't question anything she did with them, and she wanted to respect his support of her by still remaining united.

It wouldn't do for the boys to see her as someone who would spoil them over their father's head.

The talk turned to plans for the weekend. Conner wanted to have Shelly over for dinner again while he was over, and so Saturday afternoon was spent in a flurry of preparations for a taco bar. He was heavily involved in chopping and putting out all the bowls, and Charlie was glad the boys fell into the rhythm of helping around the house again. It had been a wonderful week with just Sam, but she so enjoyed having the boys in the house.

As they cleaned up, and Conner and Shelly were waiting on the front porch for her parents to come and pick her up, Charlie shot Sam a look.

"Did you have the birds and bees talk with him yet?"

Sam looked sheepish. "Um. No. Not really. I was hoping Amy was going to do that."

"Isn't that supposed to be the dad's job if the children are boys, and vice versa?"

"I thought that rule was just made up," Sam groaned. "I...I just think it will come out all...dumb."

"You know he probably knows more than he should. And you said it was important," she reminded him.

He nodded, bending down to fill the dishwasher with soap. She stood by, handing him the JetDry.

"Do you...you want to do it with me?"

"Why?" she felt her nerves spike. "You're articulate, Sam. You really are."

He gave her a hopeful look. "Yeah, but it's different when it's the kids. Besides...this is your chance to play full-on mom."

He meant it gently, and she waited for the feelings of inadequacy to hit, surprised when all she felt was a single, dull flip of her stomach. It seemed her pain at being barren was tempered by his offer, that he wanted her to have an opportunity to parent at a big, momentous moment with him. Was she up to it? How could she possibly do it right given she had no long history with Conner?

"Won't my presence make him all weirded out?" she whispered as Cole wandered back into the kitchen.

Sam shook his head, reaching out to tousle Cole's hair.

"Where's Conner?"

"Waiting for Shelly's parents in front," Charlie told him, and he looked thoughtful.

"Do you think Conner likes her? Like, *really* likes her?"

Sam and Charlie's eyebrows shot up in unison.

"Probably," she found her voice first. "That's normal."

Cole's nose twitched. "It's kinda gross to have a friend that's a girl."

Sam's relief at Cole's innocence was palpable. He slung an arm around his younger son's shoulders and squeezed. "Oh, it happens. Look at me and Charlie."

"Yeah, but that's different. You guys are old," he explained.

Shaking his head, Sam steered his son over to the back patio. "Want to help me check the horses tonight?"

Cole shrugged, but Sam still had him firmly in tow, so they disappeared over the ridge of the stairs together. Just as their voices dissipated, the front door slammed and Conner strolled back in.

"Shelly's off?" she asked him, taking him in warily. Was Sam right? Would she truly be helpful in parenting this moody teen?

"Yup," he said, his eye casting over the counter. "You guys cleaned up fast. Thanks."

His gratitude covered more than kitchen duty, and she knew it. How she wanted to touch him, and fold him into a hug, but she knew it would make him back up in embarrassment.

"Of course. We enjoy it too. We're—your father—is so thankful you let us meet her and spend time with us. It means a lot."

Conner looked at her with interest. "Really?"

She nodded. "Yeah. If you were sneaking around behind him, or keeping secrets…even something as small as having a girl you like…it would hurt your dad."

"But I'm not keeping secrets!" Conner's eyes were wide, and Charlie hoped she could take that to mean that his relationship with Shelly was still sweet and simple.

"I know!" she hustled to soothe. "I know, of course. I'm just saying, is all."

330

"Where is Dad anyway?" he glanced around.

"Checking the horses with Cole." As she explained, two heads appeared over the top of the patio. They were back already.

"Bedtime?" Sam yodeled into the cavernous space.

"Awwww." The moan was collective, a combination of youthful and maturing sounds, and Charlie and Sam both laughed at the drooping faces of the two boys.

"It is bedtime," he said, sliding the door closed behind him. "Come on, seriously guys. It's school time, not summertime. I am supposed to keep you on some sort of routine or you mom will be annoyed."

They trudged to the bathroom together, shoulders bumping and arms poking. Sam cocked his head at Charlie.

"Did you consider my offer?"

"To play step-mom?" she said, unable to help the small grin that spread as she said the word.

He sidled up. "Yeah, that." His arm slipped around her hip and pulled her close, their pelvises bumping.

"I…" She couldn't deny she was curious. "I will be there. I'll let you lead and try not to talk over you."

"That's one thing you don't do," he stated, then leaned in for a slow kiss.

Cole was in bed first, and they paused when they stopped outside Conner's room.

"Fuck, this is gonna be hard," Sam whispered, just loud enough that she could hear him. What was so important about this chat? Obviously, Conner would have to know the general physical mechanics of it – didn't they teach that in middle school?

Or was there something more? Charlie felt completely out of her element.

"Conner?" The boy's head came up, and a frown chased itself across his brow. The two of them lining into his room was not the usual.

"I…I need to do the dad thing," Sam sighed, and Conner's eyes turned wary and self-conscious.

He took a seat on the side of the bed, and Charlie tried to melt into the scenery, pressing herself against the wall where the texture scratched at her arms. She rolled down her sleeves in a nervous tick, then interchangeably folded and unfolded her arms.

"You know the whole...the sex thing, right?" Sam asked, his voice pleading. Conner's cheeks blazed with pink, the bright spots splotchy next to his wide eyes.

"Yeah, Dad, they teach us all about it in school."

"I know, I know..." Sam paused, as if gathering his thoughts. Charlie tried to send good energy. He had always been so articulate, so good with words for her. He could get to the bottom of a problem, see clearly. Was so much riding on this?

"I...do they teach you about STD's? And um...not being stupid?"

"I don't plan to get a girl pregnant, Dad," Conner said, looking down at his knobby knees, covered in a thin blue sheet. He ran his hands down his calves and gripped his ankles, as if trying to make himself shrink. "I don't want to deal with a baby."

"That's good," Sam seemed encouraged. "It's just...everything has...consequences."

"Like what?" Did Charlie detect a note of defiance in his voice?

"Well. You know sex can lead to a baby. Or an STD. I'm guessing you don't want either of those."

"Well, no. But they say it's possible to be careful so you don't get them." Suddenly Conner seemed to crack open. "And that birth control and condoms together work. And if you know someone's past partners you will know what you're getting into. And that...everyone eventually does it." The last part was mumbled.

Sam sat silently, and Charlie heard herself asking, quietly, from her dim corner of the room. "Do you want to do it?"

Conner's head shot up. Had he forgotten she was there, or was it so natural to have her in the room? He shrugged. "Not too much, really. I mean. They scare you with all the bad stuff."

"Does Shelly?"

Conner started to shake his head no, then paused. "Well. I don't think so. We haven't talked about it."

"OK." Sam seemed to relax. "We just...Charlie and I have seen all the things that can happen with sex.

Girls can get crazy, demanding you do it with them to prove that you care for them. They will stop taking their birth control to get pregnant on purpose. They'll—."

"Shelly's not like that," Conner interrupted, his earnest insistence endearing him more to Charlie. "Really, Dad, Charlie," he turned to her. "You've met her."

"Of course." Charlie hoped that Sam wouldn't delve now into the ways that girls could be two-faced; showing a sweet side to parents, but getting frisky and demanding behind closed doors. Thankfully, Sam seemed to think the same, because he sighed and patted Conner's knee.

"I just…I wanted to make sure you were aware. It's just fine you're dating Shelly. She does seem really great. I like her. Charlie does too," he glanced at her and she nodded, holding Conner's glance.

"And we…your father especially…if you ever have questions in the future. With Shelly or other girls. If they're making demands you're not comfortable with. Or if you don't know what they're doing…we—he—we're here. OK?"

Conner nodded and pressed his lips together.

"Yeah," Sam stood, putting his hands on his hips. "I guess that's the big thing. Girls...dating can be a bit crazy and we just want to always talk about it. Just...we're here to help."

Charlie laughed a little, trying to lighten the mood with levity. "I remember one time my father answered the door when a boy came over. He had wanted to kiss me, and I didn't want to, and he sent the boy home. It was kinda embarrassing, but also a huge relief to have backup."

Conner cracked a grin. "Oh yeah? Did your dad have a shotgun too?"

Now everyone laughed. "No, no," she said. "But the threat, and the protection, was still the same."

The three of them looked at each other in unison, bonded by the chuckles and the shared intimacy of an uncomfortable discussion delivered and successful. Charlie hoped that it was all Sam had hoped.

She ducked out as Sam tucked Conner in, giving them some father-son privacy, feeling as though she'd witnessed enough frank and earthy moments for the night. Sam crept out, shutting the door behind him.

"It never stops, does it?" she asked. "The worry over your children."

He shook his head. "Nope. I don't think so."

They walked back to the great room together. She was eager and anxious to hear his thoughts. "So...did it go well, do you think?"

Sam shrugged. "I hope it did. One never knows the fruit of one's labors until later, usually. At least, that's how it seems. I just...I don't want him to do something stupid, and I don't want him to feel like he has to shut us out...or that sex is, overall, bad...just not smart right now."

"You're not going to push for abstinence?" she wondered.

He sighed. "That's one I'll talk about if he ever actually asks me. I just want him to tell me things and know I won't judge...and I hope I can catch red flags ahead of time."

Chapter 21

The next few weeks became a rhythm. She and Sam sometimes popped into the city, or took day trips to wineries. When the boys visited, they all got terribly busy with activities, and the Playstation rarely made it on. Sam told her that these were golden times for him. He said things that made her felt necessary, integral and important. And she believed him.

At night, she and Sam would sleep together, and he told her in the quiet dark how much he loved her, how happy he was to be active, and doing things with his sons, and how lucky they were to have her here. She couldn't stop herself from wanting him, and she desperately clung to him as they made love. She wasn't as free with her words as Sam was, but she did tell him how she felt when she could muster her courage. And whenever she told him she loved him, he looked at her like he was the most fortunate man in the world. Could this really all be hers again?

She rarely thought of Peter - by confirming his awfulness to her, he'd finally closed the door on anything she ever dreamed would happen. The notion that she had been at fault seeped and filtered out of her slowly but with a constant flow, much like the grapes that Sam was experimenting with. Perhaps she would come out as something new and different, just like his vintage. It could happen. Charlie honestly did not want to be anywhere else but in the moment, and with Sam. It was a delightful feeling.

They spent time just existing together with the boys coming and going again, and then Charlie looked at him one night. He was so handsome, and dear, and a great father. She wanted to do something special with him, and she slid over on the couch. His arm came around her shoulders automatically, but he continued to read his article. She waited until he sighed and looked at her, and kissed her forehead.

"How're you, my dear?"

"I'm wonderful. But I'm wondering if you want to have a party, like you've always said?"

His eyes lit up. "I'd get to show you off to all my friends!"

She brushed off his flirt. "And I'd get to make friends of your friends," she said, knowing they needed to have shared friendships to make things fuller.

"Absolutely. When?"

"In two or three weeks...probably not while the boys are here - they'd be bored stiff. Gives enough time for people to plan, maybe?"

Sam nodded and smiled at her, and she warmed to the idea. "If it's not too cold, we could do something outside on your patio. I'm not sure how many people you'd want to invite? And then do a sit-down dinner on your new big table."

"*Our* new big table," he corrected her. "You found it."

"Yes, well..." she blushed. He was always reconfirming how solidly and easily they shared life, things and memories. It made her feel young and newly in love all over again, every time. It would get old, eventually, and he would cease to remind her how much they shared, and she would stop flushing when he got romantic, and they'd settle in. They'd both been married, and they knew what time did. But that didn't mean it had to go bad and stale and end. Charlie felt she knew enough about relationships now to make sure she and Sam always stayed on the same page.

"How about three couples? A total of eight? That's just enough chairs. I'll make the calls tomorrow morning."

"You will?" She was amazed at how he would always dive into new ideas with her and share the load of it to boot.

"Sure. And then we can spend some time figuring out the menus and music...and whatnot."

"I'll try to stay off Pinterest in the sake of our sanity," she vowed and he chuckled.

"Ah, we'll have to do a few things fancy, since I've been going on about this for years and never do it."

"If it goes well, we should do something for Halloween."

He started to nod, and then stilled. Charlie wondered what had drawn him up, and then did the math quickly in her head. That was still a month away. She'd be gone by then, her weeks on the ranch up. She wondered if he was worried, if he had been waiting for her to leave to get his life back, albeit with a girlfriend attached. She shouldn't have assumed he would want to do things after she went back to LA - the idea had come out so naturally, so quickly.

"I'm sorry. That was forward of me," she backtracked hesitantly. "I'll be gone, of course. You might not want to do anything for Halloween."

He sat forward, rubbing his eyes and throwing the magazine on the coffee table. It reminded her she was still trying to find a good solid wooden piece to replace the glass and iron one.

"Sam, I'm sorry I assumed." She put her hand on his back, rubbing up to his shoulder.

His fingers pinched his eyes, but then he sat up straight. "Jesus. No. It made me count and I realized you'll be gone in three weeks or so. That dinner party will be towards the end of your stay. Damnit Charlie."

She wasn't sure why he was so upset. "We don't have to do the dinner party, then."

He shook his head, looking at her. "It's not that. Let's do the party - I want to. It's that you'll be gone."

"We'll visit. The drive isn't that bad."

Sam sighed and took her hand. "I don't want to visit. I want you to stay."

She felt herself get wrapped with his words. To stay? To move to the ranch? The idea was warm and wobbly at the same time. "But...I...what would I do with Clear Studios?"

He turned to her, suddenly anxious, eager. She was taken aback with his energy. He had it bad for her, she realized. And how long had he been wanting to ask her such a question? She hadn't even done much to encourage him - but he really *really* wanted to be with her. She didn't think she'd ever been with someone who felt so fully, nor knew what he wanted in the blink of an eye. Was he impulsive? She didn't think so. He just always seemed to *know*.

"Start working from here. We could clear out one of the rooms downstairs for your office, or you could rent one in town. There's a lot of work around here, and people have the money to spend on it. And then you could drive in, like I do, as needed to see your staff and take care of specific things, or find pieces. It could work, Charlie."

She stared at him. She was, honestly, fascinated with the idea. At this point, it didn't spook her, nor frighten her. It was a rational, calm decision. She wondered if it was because out here she could just *be*...she didn't have to work hard, could enjoy her days, and forget about everything - from her divorce to schmoozing with clients. Or was it because she was with him, and he made everything fall into place? She had to believe that at some point, the questions would stop. That their comfort with one another would deepen and develop to an innate knowledge of one another.

He was right, too. If they wanted, they could make it work. She could move to the ranch, make it her base, work from home. So many people did the remote thing, and it would be possible to get new clients out in a large radius of wine country. Still...it would be a leap, to move in with him. Should she tell any of her current clients about it? What would her staff think? Was it all moving too fast?

"You're thinking about it." His voice, hopeful, broke into her litany and the myriad questions queuing. She smiled at him, liking his direct honesty.

"I am," she admitted, squeezing his fingers. "I can't deny it would be really great to stay here with you."

"Let's talk it through then."

"Should I keep my apartment or get rid of it? It seems...awful *permanent* to just move my whole life out here."

"That's the point," he said. "I do want you to move out here for good."

He was really asking her to move in with him. Charlie felt winded. It seemed so sudden, and yet it would be so easy. She knew why people did it, and it was apparent she was up against that choice now herself. Could she make the plunge? Living separately from him, after spending a few months together, would feel like a self imposed divorce all over again. Her heart and head seemed joined in this one.

"Thank you, Sam," she said slowly. "I *will* think about it seriously."

"You need to mull on it, I know," he fell back against the couch and pulled her with him. "I'll wait."

"You always do," she said softly, feeling grateful she'd found someone so understanding of her nature. She'd always thought Peter was the only one in the world who could put up with her, but she had been proven wrong, and she was glad.

They eventually got up from the couch and went to bed. She'd moved all her clothes into Sam's room and closet, and as she stared at their things, co-mingled and squeezed together, her heart started to pound. They'd already nearly done it, just never made it official. They *were* living together, playing house, acting as if they were married. And she found she loved it, craved it. To leave this would be incredibly desolating.

As her eyes wandered over their combined closet, she noticed her suitcase still sitting on the floor, unzipped and haphazardly splintered, she spied the box of tampons. They were still unopened.

"Holy shit." She dropped like a stone to the floor. "You've got to be kidding me."

Wild hope and horrible fear rose in her stomach all at once. She couldn't be pregnant. It was impossible. She had no way to make it feasible - her body had betrayed her so much that she had accepted her barrenness so fully. It was as if she had been slapped. Sweat and coldness ran up and down her body as she stared at the sealed tampons and counted the weeks.

No. It'd been over six weeks. She knew it. How could it be?

Sam came around the corner to get out his pajamas and stopped in mid movement.

"What is it?"

She held up the box of tampons wordlessly. He stared at them, and then shrugged.

"Alright, so no sex tonight. I can wait a few nights, but then be prepared, woman!" he joked lightly, moving around her to grab his clothes. As always, he was unflappable, but Charlie knew this would throw even him.

She slowly got to her feet, still holding the box. Her breathing felt tight, and she felt like she might be sick. This was not happening. She was not pregnant - it would make everything so...it was inconceivable.

"Sam. I don't have my period."

He swung around, still buttoning the pajama shirt. She was struck with how handsome he was, and how much she loved him. He might not want this, after all, and in turn, would not want her.

How ironic that she'd lost her first love to the absence of children, and now she might lose her second to the roll of emotion with – once again – her reproductive health.

No. No. She stopped herself. It couldn't be a baby. It had to be something else. Something else was wrong with her.

"You what?"

"I don't have my period. I haven't gotten it. Not at all."

"What are you saying?" He had frozen.

"I don't know. I just...I haven't...I'm two weeks late, Sam."

His hands dropped and he stared at her. "I thought you said you couldn't conceive."

"I can't."

"You're sure?" His voice was incredulous, disbelieving, alarmed. He looked blank, his face a white slack of shock.

She nodded. "Countless doctors have said so, and so have all the tests. I can't make babies, Sam."

"But you're late."

She nodded miserably. There was a yawning silence between them. She'd never thought it would be like this: discovering something about her fertility in the closet of a lover. It was supposed to be special, or lazily romantic – or at least, happen after years of togetherness.

She shook her head mentally. There was no baby, of that she was sure. It was not possible.

"Do you..." He trailed off, and she thought he was going to ask if she had a way to check, like a pregnancy test, and knew the question to be futile. He asked it anyway. "Should we take a pregnancy test?"

"I'm not pregnant, Sam."

"We don't know that. We've had ample time, and no protection—."

"That's not it!" Her voice, low at first, had risen to a hoarse shout, and Sam froze. She closed her eyes against it all. "It's not possible. We can't – I can't – go there. It has to be something else."

He inhaled long and loud, and then to her absolute surprise a grin started to work its way across his face. "Well, I guess you'll be moving in, then. If it's a baby, or even if it's some bizarre issue, you should probably be here with me instead of dealing with it all alone."

His attempt to be lighthearted, and to do so genuinely and with true kindness made Charlie lose it. She started to cry, and Sam crossed the distance between them in seconds. He had her in his arms tightly, holding her, kissing her hair and silently rubbing her back.

She couldn't think. She was almost forty and she was divorced and she had to go through something else with her broken body? It would almost be easier if there *were* a love child on the way. It was obvious Sam still held onto the vestiges of hope, but she knew it was not a pregnancy. How could it be? It was medically impossible, scientifically unsound. She hadn't had any symptoms other than this late, missed period, and she was devastated by what this meant for her, for Sam, for what they had started to build.

He pulled her to the bed, and laid with her, letting her sob into his shoulder until she could finally get her breath. Her thoughts were reeling, unable to condense into a single coherent idea. What would she do? What was wrong? The questions poured and tumbled and stumbled across her mind.

They were quiet together, Sam slowly rubbing her shoulder blades. God only knew what was running through his mind. Health issues changed everything. Finally she raised her head and found his face. He was looking no worse for wear. How could he be so calm?

"Are you angry at all?" she whispered.

He shook his head firmly, running a finger up and down her arm. "No. Nervous. We should get that pregnancy test tomorrow."

"That's all? It's a pointless test, Sam."

"But we should check, just in case," he mandated, and gripped her tightly on the bed. In the light of the single lamp, the shadows were deep and soft. "Charlie...I have to say, having a baby again wouldn't be easy, but I really...don't mind."

"*What?*" She couldn't believe him. "Sam, that's very kind of you to say, but you have to understand – it's not possible. It's something else."

He kissed the top of her head, still holding her near. "I'm just saying...if it is a baby, I'm here for you. I like being a dad, a lot, Charlie. There's never a perfect time for a new little one...or health issues, if that's what this is."

"But..." she sputtered. "But we're not married." It was the only argument she could say for the moment, and it was a weak one. She knew it was not the first time a baby had been created and born out of wedlock, she just never ever thought it would be her.

"Who cares?" Sam half shrugged. "If it ends up mattering, I'll marry you. I was thinking that would be our end game, someday, anyway."

His blasé mention of forever shook her almost as much as the one second she had thought she could be pregnant. She knew he wasn't proposing, but the realization that he viewed their future in terms of marriage brought an uplifting calmness to her soul. Maybe he just said that to calm her anyway, but it worked deep inside her core. "You're not mad? I just...I didn't think...it's my fault to create all this drama in your life. I'm so sorry."

He pulled away from her at that, his arms tightening with emotion. "Charlie. Charlotte. My love. It is most definitely no one's fault."

She started to cry again. She couldn't help it and couldn't think of anything else to do with the feelings she had bubbling and gurgling in her stomach. "We'll go get a pregnancy test, but I don't believe it. It's not possible."

"Whatever it is, it'll be fine."

She was skeptical, but kept it to herself. He was trying to comfort her, and he was doing a good of job of it. Maybe he even meant some of what he said, and she hoped to God he did. *Too many uncertainties, too many worries. It could be anything. It could be cancer. It could be a tumor. It could be...*

He didn't even try to get in her pants; they shut off the light and curled together, and she clung to him as if he was the only solid thing in her life. And really, this night, he was.

When she woke up in the morning, it was as if they hadn't shifted an inch. Sam was still sleeping, but his arms were a tight iron band around her. She tried not to wake him, but as she shifted slightly to change her position, he stirred and pulled her closer.

"Was it a dream?"

His mutter was quiet, and she barely made out what he said. And she knew exactly what he meant.

"I don't think so."

He nuzzled into her neck, pressing himself into her back. She felt his arousal, surprised he still found her sexy after such a tumultuous night. And while it was true that she was overwhelmed, it didn't cover her desire for him either.

They made love slowly, languidly, carefully, and his hands were gentle and soft. She was able to get through it without crying - from fear, relief, happiness

- all of it. She just thought of him, allowing herself to get swept into his body, his scent, his flesh. When they'd finished, he shifted to her side, and put a hand lightly on her lower abdomen.

"We should go get that test. Just in case."

He was wonderful. She felt undeserving, as if she had somehow deceived him, that he had no reason to be so content when she herself didn't know how to feel. At least he obviously was glad with all the arrangements that came with it.

To have a man's hand on her belly, loving and caressing where a baby was supposed to grow was what undid her again, and she wept silently in the deep dusky morning light. Sam didn't even know until he bent to blindly kiss her, and instead came up with a wet temple instead of her lips.

"Charlie honey." He pulled her tight, their nakedness touching everywhere again, her head tucked under his chin. "Are you still so sad?"

She shook her head. "No! Not at all. Scared, yes. Nervous, of course. But happy, Sam. I'm so happy I'm with you." As she said it, she knew it was true.

$\mathscr{C}$hapter 22

Sam gazed at Charlie from across the table. They were going into the doctor today, and then their dinner party was in another three days.

There was no baby – at least, the pregnancy stick said negative, but there was a small part of him that held on to some strange, oddly conceived hope that it was something else, that perhaps the test was wrong.

Oh, he knew he wasn't as young as he once was. The late night feeds and wakes, the sleep training, the days of toddler chasing – a lot of that would likely kick his ass. It was probably best for him if Charlie wasn't pregnant.

Her generally stoic response had confirmed what he'd long thought – that her temperament was a good match. She cried a little, here at there, but it was mostly nerves. She wanted to know what was wrong, what was happening to her, and the unknown was what burdened her. But it didn't phase him. He wanted her to move in – baby or no. He'd told her that, and had started to clear out the room in the basement with the big window overlooking the backyard for her office. She had brought over most of her clothing, small items, and little things from her apartment. They had to figure out what to do with her furniture. Charlie would be staying with him - forever, maybe, hopefully.

She was handling it all rather well, he thought, considering. Her silences stretched now, and she looked pensive, the usual glow of her personality dampened by her chewing, gnawing worry that hit her at times. He made it a habit of asking direct questions to get personal, emotional conversation going and that helped to keep things aired between them, he hoped. Her response to lock her heart and her feelings away seemed to be a reflex, or a habit, and Sam was determined not to let her do it.

He still couldn't believe that she had felt like a horrible person at first. It'd taken a few hours of digging into her psyche to uncover that particular notion. She had felt like she'd lied to him, that she should have somehow guessed that a pregnancy could happen, even after being told over and over that medically it was impossible. She hated taking him on yet another journey into her reproductive health. She worried it was something bigger, unbeatable. *Cancer...* She would gravitate between wondering whether she could – somehow – be pregnant and then other days fretting that it was something else, something sinister and that would tear her from her health and her life.

They were getting into the doctor's office as soon as they could for a blood test and initial ultrasound. As Charlie's fertility history raised a lot of red flags, the nurses were keen to get her in as soon as they could. The urgency did nothing to calm Charlie's nerves, nor Sam's for that matter.

"Sam - how long do you think the whole doctor visit takes?" She was checking her phone. "I think the painting is coming today and one of us should be here when it's delivered."

"Can't we just leave a key for the driver? I want to be with you." He didn't really give a damn about the painting now. This visit was one he would *not* miss.

"I'll call and find out the delivery window, see if they can get it later in the day." She flicked off her screen and flashed him a smile. Sam knew now was not the time, and probably wouldn't be for several months – until she...they...figured out what was wrong with her - but he was going to marry her. He had to think about the best time to broach the subject. The last thing he wanted was her thinking he was popping the question just because he felt obligated. He wasn't asking her to move into his house as a frivolous gesture. He loved her, he was following what he knew to be true in the fibers of his gut and the peace that accompanied it. He wanted to be with her.

They hadn't said anything to anyone yet – she was waiting for the ultrasound and a diagnosis of something – anything. Charlie would repeat over and over some nights that she just couldn't – wouldn't – believe that it was anything but bad new. She was convinced it was cancer at the very least. Sam, on the other hand, felt like he was hiding a kernel of happiness. He couldn't wait to tell the boys, if it was a baby. He worried a little about Conner, but he knew Cole would be over the moon. A part of him hoped for a tiny daughter, one to spoil and cuddle. And nine years wasn't so far a gap between children. Whenever he went there, though, he had to remind himself that it was very likely not a pregnancy. He was surprised at how hopeful he was – was it that he wanted to be a father again? Or that he simply wanted a reason to be tied to Charlie?

"OK, set. They'll deliver on the night shift. We'll surely be back." She turned from her phone again and sipped her water. "I'll be glad when this is all over and we know what's going on."

"I can help with any kind of sex therapy they give you!" he jumped in, giving her a suggestive, devilish grin. She smiled watery at him, and took his hand.

"You're sure you want this whole ride? You can back out any time - I can do it." She sounded anything but certain about it, but he knew she meant what she said.

"We've been over this. You were thinking you might move in; well, the decision's been made. You aren't going through anything alone. And yes. Hell yes, Charlie. I want it all."

He never tired of telling her this, and she seemed to need to hear it often.

They got up and did the morning chores, Sam keeping a protective eye on Charlie. He had stopped letting her lift much, and generally pampered her, *just in case*. She had at first been hesitant about the chivalry, but eventually seemed to like it, though it was never expected. And oh, he loved to make love to her even more, if such a thing was possible.

"We'll have to convert the guest room," he said to her casually, as they brushed down the horses. He glanced at the dark corner where the spider'd gotten him. "If there is a baby, that is."

Her hands stilled, but only for an instant. "I didn't realize. Oh my God, Sam. I'm disrupting your entire world. So much for your peace. But...really. There's no baby."

"You're probably right, but a guy can wonder. Or at least, offer that he's not repulsed by the idea, right?"

She sighed. "No matter what, I feel as though I've upended your peace."

He thought about it, briefly. True. She certainly had changed his thoroughly designed life on the ranch. He thought of it abstractly. He'd manage.

Putting down the brush, he went around to her, touching the horse carefully as he went, feeling the bunched, hard muscles under the coarse hair. "Charlotte. You have never been a disruption to my little world. If anything, you've made it better. I've been through this. If I'm not worried, you shouldn't be either."

She sighed, and moved into his arms. They stood in the barn for a moment quietly. All that could be heard was the munch and shift of the horses, the occasional bird outside. "I love you." Her words were soft as usual, and yet he knew she meant it. "I feel a bit overtaken by all of this."

"You feel that way for a while. Until they're about five...aw, hell, pretty much always." He couldn't help himself – he liked alluding to the fact that they could be parents together.

She laughed a little, but the sound was forced, and they went back to their chores.

At lunch, at his prodding, she started to admit that she had always wanted a neutral nursery in creams and greys and bits of black, and he watched her get soft-eyed and almost shy before hardening back into her protective response.

"It's not a pregnancy, but it's fun to pretend." Settling back in the seat by her computer, she rubbed the back of her neck and sighed.

"I never expected to look at this furniture – especially not for myself."

"You never designed nurseries for your clients?" he was surprised. She shook her head.

"No, not really. I usually gave that room to one of the staff. It was too difficult for me to do. It's like playing house – all of this. It's not real, but it's nearly so."

He understood, and reached the inches between them to replace her hand at the base of her skull, his blunt fingers rubbing and massaging the bumps of her neck bones and shoulders.

"Do you think Conner will freak out if I move in? What if, by some strange miracle, I'm not full of tumors or cancer and there's really a baby in there?"

Her words mirrored his occasional worry and wonder. "I have been thinking that myself," he mused, his fingers pressing lazily at her skin. "It certainly is going to be tricky. Here we were talking about how he shouldn't do anything stupid that might get a girl knocked up and now we went ahead and...got knocked up."

Charlie shot him a sly glance. "That we did *not* do, but you're doing a good job with the pretending."

Sam laughed. "To be honest, I have no idea how to tell him about making safe choices so that it dovetails into our little lesson."

They were silent for a minute as she absently scrolled past the furniture on the computer screen. Sam kept his hand on her neck, moving down to her upper back. It was delicious to touch her.

They were still talking about Conner as they got into the car after lunch. Then Sam mentioned having a baby shower, and she became embarrassed and angry.

"No. That's too far. It's fun to speculate, Sam, really, but that's too serious."

"Bull. We have to keep this silly or you'll start to panic. I can see it in your face." God, he couldn't tell her how he really felt right now. He couldn't wait to see the tiny heartbeat flash on the ultrasound monitor, the little limbs swimming like a gummy bear. She would warm even more to the whole idea when she saw that - a dream fulfilled. He felt as though her infertility was not impossible to overcome, that somehow, this time they'd gotten lucky. That she had one egg sitting there waiting, and he'd claimed it.

"This is so ridiculous," she repeated. "I just want answers."

"I know, hon," he said, taking her hand as they pulled into the hospital parking lot. "This will make it better. Let's go."

*C*hapter 23

Charlie sat gingerly on the edge of the examining table as the nurse busied herself with preparations. They had to take a lot of medical history as this wasn't her usual doctor. Sam sat in the chair at hand, looking comfortable, excited and relaxed all at the same time. She still couldn't understand how calm he could be, how he continued to remain perfectly serene. Her heart and head felt disconnected and frizzled, and her body did not feel as if it was hers. It took gigantic amounts of control to keep from constantly weeping, and sometimes she couldn't keep it together anyway.

"So you're thirty-nine, no prior pregnancies, correct?" The nurse checked off boxes briskly.

"Correct," Charlie felt nervous, as if this was more than routine, that this was all fake, that she wasn't really here, getting a check-up for a possible pregnancy or God knew what else.

"Any symptoms?"

"Like…what?"

"Fatigue, nausea, sore breasts, any random bleeding?"

"Um…" She didn't think anything had been out of the ordinary. "No. As my intake said – I can't get pregnant."

"Mmhmm." The nurse was scribbling constantly. "And was that diagnosed by…?"

"Doctor Fillimore out east." She knew the name of the well-respected OBGYN would get attention, and it did – the nurse's head popped up quickly, speculatively.

"And when was the first day of your last menstrual cycle?"

"I guess…let me look." She flicked on her phone and counted. "Seven weeks ago, I guess."

"Alright. And you had a negative pregnancy test?"

Charlie paused mid-pick of the paper under her. "Yes. It was negative. Of course it was. It's got to be something else."

"Generally that's the first step to making sure your missed period is a pregnancy, but we know that's very likely not the issue. We'll take a look."

She was propped up in the compromising position as the doctor came in, and she couldn't bear to look at Sam. This was incredibly intimate, but it wasn't as if it was sharing anything he hadn't already seen. Still, she was slightly mortified as well as shaken, filled with excruciating fear. Please God everything was alright in there.

"Alright, here we go." The doctor was kind, brisk, and smiley. She brought over the equipment, and Sam suddenly stood and went to Charlie's shoulder. His hand was heavy but warm, and he took her fingers. She looked up at him, and his face was so full of happiness, anxious excitement, and absolute devotion she was choked up. He so loved her. He so loved the idea of a baby already too. She wanted to reach up and bring down his head and kiss him, but her position made that highly awkward. *What happens next, though, when the doctor confirms that there is nothing there? He will have to manage that smashing, terrifying crush of discovering there is no baby.*

It would be like facing Peter all over again.

The doctor inserted the ultrasound wand and everything on the screen came to life. Charlie looked at the monitor, not knowing what to look for, and conscious of the probing and moving of the stiff plastic in her most sensitive area. Sam was staring hard, waiting, watching.

The search went on for what seemed like a long time. Finally the doctor made a "hm" sound and pulled out the wand. She looked at Charlie thoughtfully.

"You say you had a negative pregnancy test?"

She nodded her head, mute, and felt something cold slide down her stomach and spine. It was a cyst. A tumor? Cancer... She'd even been foolish enough to play along with Sam's game of the possibility of a baby, knowing full well it was a futile idea. *Oh dear God.* Dear God. What would Sam think? What if...? How stupid was she? The perception that she was not pregnant hit her like a wave of water, swaying her senses, creating a tilting unbalance to her equilibrium and made her afraid to sit up. Before the doctor said it, she knew already. It was déjà vu. It was a repeat of her previous life.

"Well, we can't find a baby, or even an embryo sac with the ultrasound, so we'd have to agree that your over-the-counter test was correct. We'll do a blood test, of course, so I'll send you to lab next as this isn't a pregnancy, which it sounds like you knew. If anything, we'll have to talk about a missed period, or a skipped ovulation."

"A what?"

"Well, you may not have ovulated, so there wouldn't be a build up of lining, or a period. It can happen, sometimes by just a fluke of nature."

The doctor peeled off her gloves and patted Charlie's knee, so she could sit up, reeling, feeling light headed and dizzy. What the hell? What. The. Hell. Sam was still standing there next to the table, his face flat and his eyes watching the doctor acutely. He jumped in.

"What could it be, otherwise? What are we facing?"

Dear Sam. He already was looking at this as a problem they shared. She gave him a raw look, and he clasped her hand harder, gripping it tight and sound. He would have to deal with this too - the loss of the idea of a child, the crash of expectations. Everything that had sent Peter running from her. No man wanted damaged goods.

This was going to be worse. Charlie remembered all too well the range of emotions they would both have to endure on top of the euphoria of losing a dream. Her marriage to Peter had been longer, less uncertain, and even he had left her. Sam's time was fleeting. He had no need to stay with her now that he knew the trauma and dealing with the whole ordeal that was her broken body. As if adrenaline was pumping through her, she felt her fingers tremble and twitch. Unable to look up at Sam, she clenched his hand with both of hers, pressing her lips together. She could not talk.

The doctor was typing fast, and paused to look at them collectively. "Well, like I said, it could just be a fluke. I'm not familiar with you, personally, Charlotte, but looking at the history you've given us today, we could even be looking at ovarian failure, or peri or full menopause. It's definitely a likely option in your case."

So it was even worse. To know she was not only *not* pregnant, but any semblance of hope she'd held onto, that perhaps the doctors were really wrong, that one good egg might find its way down someday, and by some miracle become a baby...all of that gone.

She was losing everything. Now she knew how her one friend who had had a hysterectomy at thirty felt. It was the stripping of possibilities. Now she was not only damaged goods, but she was less a woman, a dead husk of a body that could never – would never – give life. The potential diagnosis was a flattening echo of everything she'd ever heard from doctors.

Charlie's next horrified realization was that she could very easily lose Sam over this. That he might still want a wife to give him children. God knows he had been so excited about this - he might have realized he still wanted babies, and that followed that she was not a candidate at all for him to fill that dream and desire. And he probably didn't want this type of roller coaster disrupting his peace and quiet on the ranch.

After the doctor left, leaving instructions to go and give blood at the lab for a final test, Charlie sat without moving. Depressing thoughts swirled in her, and she finally gave in and buried her face in her hands, giving in and sobbing hard and silently. She cried for the loss of the baby that never was, for the hopes she and Sam had built already, for her loss of femininity and for how much this would probably change how he felt about her. It was too collapsing, too much to ask.

"Honey." His arms were around her, but he didn't ask for anything, thankfully. He held her, and she gave herself into the tears, hoping they would stop at some point. That she could go back to who she was only a few weeks ago - confident, accepting of her divorce, looking at another brilliant man who wanted to be with her and content with that vision. How could she go back to that?

"Charlie. Let's get you to lab."

She shook her head, finally lifting her eyes to his. She almost dreaded what he would look like. He was a bit deflated, but he wasn't teary, and he looked as patient and calm as usual. How could he bear it?

"I don't want to go. I'm so stupid, Sam. I let you build dreams, and I know I should be happy there aren't growths or cancer but... I'm so sorry. *I'm so sorry!*" She dissolved into tears again, and willed herself to get over it. Stop crying. It does nothing – she knew this. *Shut off the tears.*

He came to stand in front of her, waiting patiently, not touching her now. Her thoughts felt scattered, her feelings a river running through her without being able to dam and break.

After another minute she took a deep breath and drew up her shoulders. This was nothing new, really. Not for her. Not the journey she continued where her fertility was concerned. She could be strong again, at least for a little while. When Sam decided she wasn't right for him, when he realized he still wanted babies, then...then she'd allow herself to truly break.

"I'm sorry," she repeated, and stood to draw on her clothes. He waited silently as she dressed, and then as she turned to head to the lab, he caught her arm.

"Charlie. Do not be sorry. Please don't."

She spread her free hand. "How can I not be? I'm an idiot. I got us - you - all excited about something that was a lie. And now you find out I'm not even able to have children ever. I'm sure I'm full onto menopause and I haven't even hit forty yet."

"We don't know that." His optimism was born of being early in the game. He did not have the years of being beaten down by tests, doctors, and negative results. She sighed and pulled away from him.

"Oh, it's me, Sam. I'm sure it's the worst case scenario."

She went to the lab, him trailing behind, and tiredly gave over her arm for the familiar prick of the needle.

They didn't speak as they got into the jeep and headed back to the ranch. She wondered how they would be able to split now, if he wanted. They'd jumped into living together even faster once there was talk of a baby, however speculative. Maybe now he'd want to take a step back. How would he tell her?

Should she offer it? But the truth of it was, Charlie wasn't sure she wanted to leave Sam. In fact, she absolutely did not want to go. Now that there was even the slightest chance he would want to move on without her, she realized she couldn't do it. Not willingly, at least. She needed him, his kindness, his optimism, his calmness. He was connected to her, or at least, she was connected to him. Could she manage being alone again? Could she hear from yet another lover that she was just not enough? To be told that he did want babies, that she could not give him what he needed to feel fulfilled? How could she do it?

Her chest felt as though it would fly out of her body, tight and unyielding, capturing her airway, and pulsating in waves of overriding ache.

The wind zipping and zinging through the jeep kept them from talking until they reached the ranch. The late afternoon light was bending around the corners of the house, and she glanced at her watch. The painting would be arriving in an hour. They'd made decent time, at least.

As she started to get out, Sam took her hand. He looked down at their fingers, and then at her.

"I want you to know that I really wanted that baby."

"I know." She was miserable. And yet...his words did not surprise her. It was the beginning of the end. She'd let him down. Another man, another love, that she had disappointed by her inability to have a child. "I'm sorry, Sam."

He shook his head. "Stop apologizing, damn it. It's not your fault. What I mean to say is, I would have been thrilled to have a little one around and raise it together. Ah, shit, I'm not saying this right. What I mean is—."

She couldn't believe how torturous it was to hear this, and she knew he had to stop. His words cut her, bled her, made her feel as though she was peeling off the last strips of her heart. "I can't talk about this right now, Sam. Please." She pulled away before he could continue talking, and got out, leaving him no other option but to follow her and unlock the front door.

"Supper? Wine, I guess," she gave him a half-rueful smile. He barely returned it, looking pained. He liked to talk, and hash things out, she knew, but she just couldn't now. She needed normalcy, where conversation did not involve babies. And if they did not talk, he could not tell her how disappointed he was.

"I'll fire up the grill for the fish," he intoned, and walked out. The quiet between them was a gaping hole, but she was too upset to try and mend it. Perhaps if this had never happened, if it was a regular tiff or fight, she would be able to bridge it and share Sam's pain and sadness. But she couldn't.

They ate outside, still hardly speaking, and she wondered how they would finish planning the dinner party in a few days when they could barely choke down food together, let alone prepare a full multi-course meal. How could she play hostess now, in a place where she might need to leave?

"How are you doing?" he tried again as they readied for bed. She assumed he still wanted to sleep next to her, or at least he was too kind to ask her to go back to the guest room.

"I don't know," she said, a rueful cough to the end of her words. "I don't know, Sam. I can't put it into words. Don't ask me to."

When they climbed in, Sam held her so tightly she could hardly breathe at first. They didn't make love, it was understood that that was too much now. But he seemed to be trying to talk to her even though she wouldn't listen to his words. He curled next to her, and kissed her neck and hair, and she heard the silence in the house and the breeze outside, and closed her eyes against it all.

Chapter 24

"Did you want to go get the groceries? I'll go with you." Sam's voice broke into her blank stare across the patio. It made her start, and he came behind her and bent to cradle her shoulders. His rough cheek touched hers, and she inhaled his nearness. It had been many days since they'd left the doctor's office, and he still hadn't asked her to leave. Why was he waiting? Why introduce her to all his friends at this stage?

"I suppose we should if we want to get it all ready in time." She caressed the cool ceramic of her coffee. The shallow slip of cold liquid rolled around the bottom. How long had she been sitting out in the chill morning? He usually left her be lately, as if allowing her space for wide and untamed thoughts and worries. Their silences often grew. They were not uncomfortable, just heavy.

"Let's. All we have left are the perishables," he reminded. They'd somehow pre-made everything that could be, and Charlie smiled a little at the memories from the past two days. They'd at least been able to pretend all was well as they made food together, the act of creating nourishment a strange balm for the awkward aura she sometimes had now.

"Alright." She stood and his arms slid off, but as she walked by, he put his hand on her waist.

"It's going to be fun tonight," he told her earnestly. "It really will be. I know it."

She wanted to believe him. "I'm looking forward to meeting your friends, Sam."

He smiled at her, his eyes warm against the burnt brown of his flannel shirt. Affection seemed to radiate from him, and she set down her mug on the counter before spinning toward him, cupping his face with both of her hands and kissing him hard.

"Oh really?" he whispered against her mouth. "I've been missing this."

"Truly?" She wanted to believe him.

"Desperately." He dove in for another, bending her over his forearms and pressing her hips to his.

It was hard to feel inadequate after such a hungry kiss, so she felt oddly uplifted as they broke apart and moved out toward the garage. She wore one of his work flannels, a worn red one with holes in the elbows that she rolled up to her own. Swinging into the passenger seat, she checked her pocket for her credit card.

"Do you have the list?" he asked, as he hit the engine and it rumbled to life.

"Yes." She felt the crinkle in her pocket and inhaled. It had to get better. He was kissing her like he still loved her, still wanted her, kept desiring her. There was, perhaps, a good reason to hope.

The grocery store was quiet, and they gathered the fresh vegetables and fruit, stopping by the florist for an arrangement she'd had the presence of mind to pre-order. Stashing the backseat full, they went back toward the ranch, ticking off reminders to one another about how to set the table.

He reached for her hand as they drove. His consistent and constant grasping for interaction with her was overwhelmingly wonderful. Glancing at him, she took in his profile, with all its imperfections, and recognized a pure, unhindered capacity for words.

Was this what he was trying to do this whole time? Find words? Get her to use them?

"Sam...you really don't care about there being...no baby?"

He didn't say anything, and she wondered if she'd misjudged her reasoning. His hand tightened, and he slowed the jeep. Glancing out of the windows, she realized they were near the pastures.

"Get out," he said softly. "I want to be able to look at you."

Her throat caught and blocked air, stopped her voice. Was this it? On the night of their planned party, he was going to get serious with her? Vowing not to get weepy and sad, she released his hand and climbed out without another word.

He pushed down on the rough-hewn fence, testing its soundness and then shifted to look at her, a hand in a pocket and another draped across the wood.

"You asked if I cared," he repeated. She stood opposite him, her arms loose at her side. She felt as though she should just run away – anything to keep from hearing the truth. But she stayed. She had no other option, and besides, this was what he wanted. He wanted to talk.

"Yes."

"You want to talk about this?" he asked softly. "You're ready?"

"I am," she spoke, but her voice caught and pulled. Clearing her throat, she nodded. "The baby was...mythical. How can you go from being happy about being a father again to...not caring?"

He sighed and reached for her, then paused and dropped his arm. "I do care. But...I would have been happy with or without a child in the house. I was...*I am*...happy, Charlie. Are you? Because that is important to me. Are you happy?"

"You have been asking me that," she reminded.

"And you don't really answer." His eyes went from calm to strained. "I am so worried you're unhappy, and you won't talk to me. You've been holding me at arm's length since we returned from the hospital."

"I..." Charlie inhaled. "It's been stupid of me."

She watched him carefully. He was hurting too, on a lot of levels. The realization flashed in her mind suddenly, like quicksilver. Had her behavior been creating the same questions in his mind? Was he worried she would leave *him*?

Maybe that was one reason she and Peter couldn't keep it together. They'd put their feelings away from one another, in separate boxes. They had never leaned on shoulders to cry it out, or talk about their frustrations. It'd just been a slew of more treatments or doctors instead of facing their emotions. She'd gotten used to the routine, and had immediately shut out any conversation with Sam, assuming that by keeping quiet she could ignore any possible ugly outcome. Perhaps it was the other way – perhaps she should have let her full despair rush out of her. But would that have scared him?

Her eyes fell away and drifted over the grass. They were quiet for a long moment, listening to the wind whisper and shake the long stems of the weeds along the fence line. Next to her, Sam exhaled. "We need to get back and put things in the fridge."

They pulled themselves back into the jeep with reluctance, and Charlie felt the unspoken discussion drag with them – a heavy bag of unhealed unhappiness.

After they set the table, and placed stemware out, she pulled on a sweater as the doors were all open and the weather had turned chilly. Sam had changed already and looked delicious with his dark jeans, loafers and knit sweater, and as he brushed by, she stopped him midway to the counter for more glasses.

"Sam..." He sensed innately that she was giving up the fight, and he turned to her, catching her up.

She didn't need to cry again. She'd done enough of that, and instead she just inhaled his scent, and buried her face in his neck. His hands spanned her waist, and then crushed her close. They rocked together, pressed tightly, and he sighed finally, speaking into her hair.

"Don't pull away from me like that again."

Her arms constricted, and guilt riddled her. "I won't."

"I mean mentally. We always need to talk it out, Charlie. If we're going to make this work."

"You still want this? Us? Me?" She was incredulous, shocked that he might feel strongly about her yet. "I can't be a woman for you, Sam." She was glad he couldn't see her face; she had no idea what she looked like as she admitted this. "I can't give you a baby. And I know you wanted it once we started to play with the impossible."

Now he pulled them apart, bending down a bit so he could get a good look at her directly. His gaze was intense, pinning her. "That's what I mean. You don't realize how I feel – hell, you've probably been beating yourself up, not knowing you don't need to. Charlie...if I can't have a baby with *you*, ever...then I don't want one at all. That's what I've been trying to explain. I wanted a baby with *you*. If you can't, then we won't. So be it."

"Just like that?" She disbelieved his sincerity. It was all very easy to say. Look at Peter. Look at how much a child had meant to him.

"Christ, Charlie. Think about it. I have two children already. I don't feel like I'm missing out anywhere. We don't have to worry about that. We have two boys to raise and watch grow up. We have it all already. A baby would have just added another dimension, but it's not essential to our happiness in life. Together."

She shook her head. "That's beautiful of you to say." But could she really think he felt that way, truthfully?

He sighed again. She had the distinct feeling he felt like he had more to say, but didn't know quite how to say it. That he wasn't convinced she believed him, and he was right. But there was too much to do before their guests arrived, and everything else was left unsaid again. Besides, she didn't think she could articulate it.

She went about in a bit of a daze, half concentrating on a marinade and sauce, and preparing the salads, prepping the dessert. And the other part of her mind was insanely active. If he meant it all - then her life was set. She had no other expectations then, other than the hope he wanted to be with her for always.

And - hadn't he said he loved her when he thought she was already barren? The remembrance of this hit her as she was wiping down the guest bathroom and she had to stop moving to take it in.

Didn't that speak to his character at all? She felt herself get drawn into the enormity of what it meant. *He really didn't need a baby to love her.* That he didn't mind that she had a silly body that betrayed her - that he meant what he'd just told her. Charlie was overwhelmed with the idea, and clung to hope she'd get to talk to him more, somehow, before the guests rang the doorbell.

They dressed companionably, their earlier silences forgotten and now the quiet between them was filled with sweetness. Sam told her a bit about the personalities that were coming to the party. Tom was bringing a girlfriend whom they hadn't met yet, and the other two couples were long married with half grown children, but they ran wineries or vineyards around the area that Sam frequented. As she pulled on the jersey dress, letting the cool fabric slide down her sides and settle around her collarbone, Sam came up behind her. She saw his face in the mirror; his eyes were closed with happiness, and he still looked serene and peaceful, just like she always thought of him. His arms were around her waist, and his chin on her shoulder.

"I do love you, you know," she told him, saying it more boldly than she ever had before. His eyes opened and met hers in the mirror and he smiled widely.

"I know, but I like to hear it anyway."

She gave a light chuckle. "I'll try to remember that."

"Do. I want us to always talk, Charlie. It's why my marriage failed. Amy and I never kept up with each other."

She gave a half smile. "I'm sure that's a big part of why Peter and I had difficulties dealing with everything too."

"So tell me again..." he teased, and she laughed fully.

"That I love you." She turned in his arms and kissed him, and he kissed her back hard, pushing into her. They hadn't much touched in the past three days, and now her desire for him pummeled through her. He paused the kiss and gave her a crooked look.

"Do we have time?" His question was full of hope. She knew what he meant and she fell into his chest, pressing her hips against his and delighting in the erection already building for her.

"I think so. I can do my hair and make-up rather quickly, and we have a good half hour before the first guest would dream of making an appearance...I hope." She tossed her head, and he captured her lips again, lifting her up onto the vanity to take her quickly, naughtily. Her mind was just filled with Sam, then, and only Sam.

She could taste him still as their first guests arrived. Tom, and his girlfriend Mari. And then the O'Briens and the Stevensens. Everyone was jovial, excited to really meet Charlie, and all the guests got to chatting and sipping wine outside, breaking and reforming groups easily. Entertaining was so wonderful when everyone knew each other and got along so well. Charlie was glad to get to know Sam's friends, eager to fit in. The O'Brien pair - Julia and Adam - lived and breathed wine, and had brought several bottles to enjoy and discuss.

"So, Charlie, you've moved in?" Annie Stevensen asked conversationally. "Or are these Sam's new pieces?" She was looking around the house, taking in the new light fixtures and the softer wood elements.

"They're Sam's," Charlie said firmly, but Sam overheard as he was walking past with a bowl of chips for the guacamole.

"Charlie found them."

Annie gave a nod of appreciation. "They all are starting to flow nicely together." She had the air of someone who understood art and room flow, and Charlie filed away the information - perhaps, if all worked out and she stayed here for good, she might have a client in Annie, though the woman gave the impression of being particular about details.

"You are an interior decorator, aren't you?" Tom asked, joining the conversation with a refreshed glass of wine that Adam O'Brien was pouring and explaining animatedly to Sam outside on the patio.

"Yes."

"Mari's in art," he said, obviously trying to insert his new flame into the circle, but she had already joined a conversation effortlessly across the room. He waved at her, and she rolled her eyes teasingly before excusing herself from the wine lovers to come over.

"I'm not *in* art, Tom," she said playfully, clinking her glass to his. She was dwarfed by him - a petite, dark haired little beauty. "I just sell it. I'm a curator at a local gallery."

"You are?" Charlie was interested. She needed to know where the cultural highlights were here. Maybe she could take Conner and Cole one of these weekends, especially once winter arrived. The realization that they'd be the closest she'd ever have to children was setting in, and she wanted to do so much with them, show them the world and bits of culture that she liked. And now that she was warming to the notion that Sam still wanted to keep her around, she felt even more interested and invested in the raising of the two boys.

Mari nodded, finishing her glass of white. "You'll have to pop in. Just got a bunch of really great landscapes."

She wandered back over to Julia O'Brien for a refill, and Charlie drew Tom into her conversation with Annie by discussing the latest crop at the local farmer's market.

Sam came into the kitchen to start up dinner, and as Charlie began to gather out the things for the courses, Mari came in again.

Charlie really enjoyed Tom's girlfriend. Mari was vivacious, bright, and yet had a wonderful way of being genuine. She flitted easily from the O'Briens and Stevensens, who knew each other well and had much to talk about. But she and Charlie really hit it off as the two newest arrivals, and Charlie was glad to have someone to chat with. Mari helped her with getting the salads out, and was the first to jump up and clear with her. They had a very good laugh over Sam's jostle with the steaks and the marinade. Charlie felt like she'd found a kindred spirit, and was thrilled.

Dessert was once again on the patio, and by then, everyone had had several glasses of wine and the laughter, political jokes and chitchat had turned into a bit of a party. It was exactly what Charlie had hoped for.

"Hey - can I borrow a sweater?" Mari was at her elbow. Annie and Julia had thought to bring light jackets, but Mari was still bare armed.

"Of course!" Charlie moved into the dimness of the hallway, not realizing Mari was following her until she registered the click of heels behind her. They walked into Sam's bedroom - their bedroom - and she flicked on a lamp to dig in the drawer.

Mari took up the sweater cardigan. She folded it over her arms, looking at the softness of the material.

"Have you known Sam long?"

Charlie paused, then closed the drawer. "A couple of months, I guess."

"That's all?" She slung the sweater around her dark shoulders. "I would have thought longer, though I wouldn't know. I've only been dating Tom for a couple of weeks."

"It seems like he likes you a lot," Charlie encouraged.

"Well, he doesn't romance me the way Sam does you. Do you know how he introduced you to me, when I walked in?"

Charlie looked at her strangely. What was Mari getting at? She thought back a few hours, now muddled a bit by wine. Tom had come in forthright, knowing the place, holding two platters of appetizers in his meaty hands. Mari had been straggling behind, and Sam had been giving her a lowdown of who was already at the party.

"How did he?" she asked, wondering why it mattered.

"He introduced you as the woman he hopes to marry."

Her world spun. He'd said that? Before wine? Charlie sat on the edge of the bed, her own jacket in her limp hands. Mari looked down at her in concern.

"I take it that's a surprise."

Charlie looked up at this woman she had just met a few hours ago, someone who she felt close to already, who she found herself hoping Tom would keep around. She shook her head, then paused and nodded.

"Yes, a surprise. Sam is usually surprising me with his notions."

"You think he...he meant it, then?" Mari asked kindly.

"Sam is always quite sure of what he wants."

"Well, he wants you."

She nodded again, letting it sink in. The first thing she felt was absolute joy. She'd be able to stay with him, should he ask her. He loved her and wanted her. Thank God. Thank you, God.

They got up and left the room, leaving on the lamp. Charlie tugged on the jean jacket and went to check on how her guests were getting on with chocolate, and if they needed coffee to help sober up.

As she brought in plates from the patio with leftover dessert, Sam followed her with stacks from the rest, and she glanced at him, giving him a happy grin. She felt like she had a golden secret, that she knew how he felt about her. She wondered why he had not even hinted at his hopes for their future today, when things had been so raw and tough between them.

"What are you thinking about?" he asked playfully, dumping the cutlery in the sink.

"You. And this food. The dessert would go over well with the kids, or some night when Conner wants Shelly over again."

He sidled over, and his eyes were bright with laughter and wine. "You're so good to my boys."

She couldn't help but give him a kiss, even with their guests still milling about outside. "I'm glad you approve of it all."

"I think I need to get you liquored up a bit more, Charlotte Paggo. I like all this PDA," he said, kissing her again briefly, giving her hip a pat, and moving away. She watched him go, and wondered how long she'd have to wait to get him alone, to tell him again she loved him once more.

*C*hapter 25

"We need to get you a salad spinner and a whisk," Charlie reminded him, as they crawled into bed on a whippy and whistling cold late December night.

"What?" he was still reading his magazine as he moved around the room, putting it on the side table only at the last minute next to his glasses. She was wearing her winter flannels, a cozy mix of warm fabric and a silken camisole underneath. He loved to run his hands up her shirt and touch it all.

"Now that you've had a woman in the house for the past five or so months, you should have all those things."

"Has it been less than six months? It feels like eons," he kidded her. "A good eon or two, though." He squeezed her tight, and then reached back around to shut off the light.

"Well, we'll have to go get you some."

"*Us* some," he corrected her. She still gave him and his things respect, not actually seeing the place as hers. He knew she felt that way - he innately understood that she still did not feel truly at home even though sometimes she called the ranch so. He knew it would take time, maybe even years, for them to be comfortable together fully - hell, any combination would take time for that, and they were both older and a bit set in their ways.

Charlie had successfully set up shop in her new office space downstairs, and would go into LA every several days. He would usually schedule any meetings around then, so they could take one car and make a day or two of it. They'd found lots of new restaurants, and things were actually transitioning smoothly.

He was hopeful, eager for their future to really take off, but he still worried that she wasn't emotionally ready for the next step. He'd even had a ring made, not that he was going to present it any time soon, he thought. Oh, New Years was right around the corner, and in Sam's perfect world, he would get a diamond on Charlie's finger and a wedding in short order all around the holidays. He'd waited long enough for her to come into his life, but until she gave him any sign of readiness, he told himself that was content to simply have her around, and in his bed.

"Us," she reaffirmed drowsily. "I guess most things in this house are ours."

"Damn right," he said.

"Oh Sam," Charlie sighed. "I hope we can be like this for always."

"We can," he promised.

"Really? You still want to keep me around? I have to ask, you know. Make sure you're staying honest." She was light in her words, but under them was the same unbelieving worry.

He could not understand what made that so hard to believe. He wasn't Peter, and they'd been through a bit of a roller coaster over the past months to prove their loyalty for each other. There was nothing to keep them apart, other than they weren't legal...his thoughts trailed off and again went to the ring in the dresser drawer.

Maybe...maybe if he asked her the right way, so she wouldn't get scared...maybe offering her that ring would make her believe him. That he *did* want her for always. She said she wanted it, too. Well...

Sam rolled away from her and flicked on the lamp. In the shuffle and swish of the sheets, he heard her sit up.

"Sam?" There was worry in her tone; he realized he hadn't actually answered her question.

"One second." He opened the drawer and stared at the little box. So much was wrapped up in such a little thing, such promise and expectation and demand. To dive back in was something neither of them would take lightly. But he knew he wanted it, and her. It fit together too nicely not to try it again. Taking a deep breath, he turned around and held up the box, fixing on her face in the dim light. Her eyes widened as she registered what he was doing.

"You say you want this for always? That you don't believe I want you?" he questioned back at her. "Charlotte honey, trust me, I do."

He went back to the bed and pulled her up to stand next to him. He wouldn't get down on a knee or profess his undying devotion. Such a show was for the first time, and for younger love. This was something they would do on equal footing, together.

"I had this made for you, in the hopes that someday you might feel ready enough to say yes to me, should

I ask you to stay always, in all seriousness. You don't even need to answer now. Take a day, a week, five months, a year, five years. I don't care how long - as long as you realize that I'll be here waiting with this ring for you."

"What if I don't want to take all that time?" Her response threw him. He was expecting emotion, maybe, and definitely expected her to want to think. She took the box out of his hand and opened it. It was a simple, low set diamond - practical, clean, athletic - just like her. She smiled softly as she looked, and Sam felt hope leap up. He suddenly knew her answer before she even gave it. "I want to say yes now, Sam. Let's not wait."

"You're saying yes. You'll get married." He said it like a fact, challenging his mind and ears to hear it correctly. Now it was his to turn to be disbelieving that it should be so quick and easy; Charlie was agreeing to his non-traditional, casual proposal. He watched her pull the ring up, pause, and then slide it onto her finger. She barely looked at it again before she had his face in her hands and was kissing him, and it took a moment for the shock to wear off so he could kiss her back and fold her into his arms.

She stopped for a moment to breathe and answer him fully. "I'll marry you, Sam. Whenever you like."

Here was the next challenge - he was going to be honest with her. He was almost more nervous about this request than actually getting her to accept him. "To be frank, I'd like to do it when the kids are here for a bit. Like before or right after New Years."

"In a week?" She paused again, thinking hard. "Maybe a weekday so we can get up two witnesses in the evening? I'd want Amanda up from LA at least."

Sam stared again. He had to ask. "You're not remotely shaken by this. Why?"

Charlie laughed a little and blushed. "I had an inkling you might want to ask me someday and I had time to think it all through."

"*What?* You found the ring?" Sam was flabbergasted and also wholly pleased by her reaction to everything he was bringing up. It was so smooth! He was waiting for the hitch. When he'd proposed to Amy, it had been romantic and lovely, and then the frenzy and painful stress of planning the wedding itself had been awful. This way would be so perfect to his personality he was afraid if he blinked he might mess it all up.

She shook her head. "No - you spilled the beans a bit to Mari, and she told me."

"No I didn't! When?"

"At the first dinner party." There had been several since that fall night, and Sam had to think back a few months. Charlie prompted him. "You told her I was the woman you hoped to marry."

"Oh God." Now he remembered. Well, that explained a lot! He'd have to thank Mari somehow. Maybe by prompting Tom to the altar when the time came. He owed her.

"Well, it was a good thing, because it made me realize how much I craved marriage too. So I just waited for you to ask, and made sure I told you how much I loved you, so you wouldn't doubt my answer."

"I have been," he admitted. "I thought you weren't ready yet, and wouldn't be for a while."

"Sam," she said softly. "I'm glad you didn't wait several months or years to find out. I'm ready - just - can I run into town to find something nice in the next few days?"

"Oh yes," he said, getting practical. "We'll file for the license tomorrow so we're set when the boys arrive. You're okay with something at the courthouse?"

"Whatever," she nodded. "We've both done the big wedding thing. I just want to be married."

He stared at her, gauging her sincerity, and saw she meant it all, that there were no glances away, no tremors of remorse. Charlie really wanted want he did - a quick, simple wedding - to make it all official. Dear Lord, he was getting himself a wife.

Sam let out a breath, and stared at her hand, where the new gold and fresh diamond winked. "Well, that was a lot less painful than I thought."

"Now, will you make love to me and cement the deal?" she kidded, only half joking. He knew she meant the sex part. He was so elated he nearly pounced her, and they spent the next hour or two confirming their affection and the clockwork of physical attraction that heightened their relationship.

As they drifted to sleep, he felt another happy pang. He could tell his boys some good news where he and Charlie were concerned. They'd be thrilled.

When they woke up in the morning, he felt more refreshed than he had in years. Turning over in the early light, he saw her still sleeping soundly. It was her day off from running and she slept hard those mornings. He saw the diamond wink and smiled to himself. Yes, it would all work out.

He got up carefully and went to start breakfast. Eggs, toast, coffee and some fruit. It felt a bit of a feast, but he had a big appetite this morning, and as he poured grounds into the coffee machine, he thought about what paperwork they'd need for the courthouse. He pulled a notepad up and started to make a list. Charlie had got him making so many lists now, but he found he enjoyed the cleansing exercise.

"Morning, love." She was walking toward him from the dark shadow of the hallway, and he felt a little happy jump in his stomach when he saw her detach from the bedroom.

"Good morning." He smiled at her and started the eggs, realizing that they could go get that whisk this morning. "Hungry?"

"Definitely." She slid next to him and poured a cup of coffee. She was the same, strangely. Still the same Charlie he'd had in his kitchen for months.

It would continue to be a work in progress. They would have fights, and they would disagree how to manage Conner and Cole as they got older. But she'd be there for their high school and college graduations and dance with him at their weddings. He would grow old with her, and ride the ranch horses with her and have a lot of wine with her. Funny, how after all the work he put into making his existence so perfect out here that it still hadn't been complete without someone to share it all with. There was truth to that old adage, and he was living proof of it.